Dutton Cook

Hours with the Players

Volume 2

Dutton Cook

Hours with the Players
Volume 2

ISBN/EAN: 9783337847975

Printed in Europe, USA, Canada, Australia, Japan

Cover: Foto ©Andreas Hilbeck / pixelio.de

More available books at **www.hansebooks.com**

HOURS WITH THE PLAYERS

By DUTTON COOK

AUTHOR OF

"A BOOK OF THE PLAY," "ART IN ENGLAND," "PAUL FOSTER'S DAUGHTER,"
"LEO," "HOBSON'S CHOICE," ETC., ETC.

IN TWO VOLUMES

VOL. II.

London

CHATTO AND WINDUS, PICCADILLY

1881

CONTENTS.

HOURS WITH THE PLAYERS.

CHAPTER I.

MR. AND MRS. BADDELEY.

THE late Mr. Robert Baddeley, comedian, gave directions in his will that the interest accruing from a sum of one hundred pounds Three per Cent. Consolidated Bank Annuities should be expended in the purchase of a Twelfth-cake, wine, and punch; and he requested the ladies and gentlemen who should form the Drury Lane company for the time being to partake of those creature comforts in the great green-room of the theatre every recurring Twelfth Night. In the earlier part of his life Mr. Baddeley had followed the calling of a cook and confectioner; the Drury Lane Twelfth-cake may be supposed, therefore, to symbolize his connection both with plays and pastry. But a higher claim to fame on Mr. Baddeley's part arises from the fact that he was concerned in the first representation of "The School for Scandal;" he was indeed the original performer of *Moses*, and his name consequently is so registered in every publication of Sheridan's immortal comedy. It did not occur to the actor, perhaps, that the play would so long endure, that *Moses* would keep his place upon the stage so persistently. In any case, he preferred to be remembered by means of his cake. Nor did Mr. Baddeley ever chance to think that in the years to come Drury Lane might possess no regular company of comedians, that its stage might be occupied wholly by pantomimists and posturers, and that Johnson's famous prologue might be prophetically considered, and its fulfilment seen to be almost literal :

> " Perhaps where Lear has raved and Hamlet died,
> On flying cars new sorcerers may ride ;
> Perhaps (for who can guess the effects of chance ?)
> Here Hunt may box or Mahomet may dance."

Even more deplorable events, still more beyond the prospect of Mr. Baddeley's belief, were to happen. He could not possibly have dreamt that his Twelfth-cake would ever fall a prey to foreign invaders, to a troop of French performers. Yet the Twelfth Night of 1849 saw Drury Lane Theatre converted into a circus, and in the possession of Franconi's equestrian company from the Paris Cirque. On that occasion the Twelfth-cake, wine, and punch of poor *Moses* must have been forthcoming for the benefit of a troop of riders, gymnasts, and clowns whom the fame of "The School for Scandal" had not reached, and to whom the name of Robert Baddeley was altogether unknown.

Robèrt Baddeley was born about 1733. Little enough is known of his parentage and early history; but he was bred a cook, it seems. Possibly, like Betterton, he was the son of a cook. For some time he officiated in the kitchen of Lord North; he afterwards entered the service of Samuel Foote. It may be that he acquired in the household of Foote an inclination towards the stage. He quitted the kitchen, however, to fill the situation of *valet de chambre* to a gentleman proceeding upon what used to be called "the grand tour." Baddeley remained absent from England about three years, acquiring some knowledge of foreign languages, and, as a biographer describes it, "sprinkling his mind with a number of bagatelle accomplishments." He reappeared as a fine gentleman with a taste for the pleasures of the town, his master's generosity enabling him to figure at the theatres and other public places of resort. In this manner he met with a Miss Sophia Snow, the daughter of the king's serjeant trumpeter, and presently confessed himself deeply enamoured of her. The lady, born in the parish of St. Margaret, Westminster, in the year 1745, had received a very genteel education, and was possessed, moreover, as her biographer states, of "an uncommon degree of softness and delicacy in her features and person, with every necessary external accomplishment of her sex." At this time she attracted the attention and esteem of all who knew her, and "the tenour of her conduct being regulated by the strictest decorum, ensured her general respect."

Miss Snow received musical instruction from her father, who proved himself a somewhat severe master; but he was anxious that she should become a thorough mistress of the harpsichord. She often complained to a neighbour of the tyranny of the serjeant-trumpeter, of the hardships she was compelled to endure as his pupil. Now, it so chanced that close by lodged Mr. Robert Baddeley, who, hearing of Miss Snow's distresses, quickly proposed to her a means of escaping from them. He threw himself at her feet, and avowed his love. After an obstinate siege of three weeks Sophia Snow surrendered, and, eloping from home, became the wife of Robert Baddeley. This was in the year 1764.

Meanwhile Baddeley had become an actor, making his first appearance in October, 1761, at the Smoke Alley Theatre, Dublin, under Mossop's management, as *Gomez* in the comedy of "The Spanish Friar." He also undertook, during the same season, such characters as *Dr. Caius, Sir Francis Gripe, Touchstone,* the *Frenchman* in "Lethe," and *Honeycombe* in the farce of "Polly Honeycombe." He seems to have been the first actor who specially studied what are known as " broken English parts," and may be said to have invented for himself a special "line of business." An early historian of the Irish stage notes of Baddeley that he imparted a peculiar manner and originality to " Frenchmen, Jews, and parts of dry cynical humour." His success in Dublin soon secured him an engagement at Drury Lane. He made his first appearance there on the 20th September, 1763, as *Polonius* to the *Hamlet* of Holland, for Garrick had started upon his long-projected visit to the Continent. The other characters assumed by Baddeley at this time were the *Old Captain* in " Philaster;" *Alderman Smuggler* in " The Constant Couple ;" *Lockworth* in the farce of " Love at First Sight," written by King, the actor ; *Flute* in " A Midsummer Night's Dream ;" *Sir Philip Modelove* in " A Bold Stroke for a Wife ;" *Dr. Caius ;* *Aristander* in " The Rival Queens," etc. Baddeley soon introduced his wife to the Drury Lane management. She had displayed some histrionic ability, and without doubt her beauty was very remarkable. She was forthwith engaged at "a decent salary." She is believed to have been the anonymous actress described in the playbills as "a young gentlewoman," who appeared as *Ophelia* on the 27th September, 1764. There is a story, however, that in consequence of the sudden illness of Mrs. Cibber, Mrs. Baddeley made her first essay upon the stage as *Cordelia* to the *Lear* of Powell, when she was so alarmed at the aspect of the *Edgar* of the night as *Mad Tom* that she screamed and fainted away. At the close of the season "The Beggar's Opera" was presented, for the joint benefit of Mr. and Mrs. Baddeley, the husband personating *Filch*, and the wife *Polly.* Among other characters assumed by Baddeley at this time were the *Lord Mayor* in "Richard III.;" *Razor* in "The Provoked Wife;" *Don Lopez* in "The Wonder;" and *Petulant* in "The Way of the World." During the summer Mrs. Baddeley sang songs at Vauxhall and Ranelagh, at a salary of twelve guineas per week, and was received with great applause.

The season of 1765–6 saw the production of the famous comedy of "The Clandestine Marriage," Baddeley's Swiss valet Canton supporting admirably the *Lord Ogleby* of King. In later years Mrs. Baddeley used now and then to assume the character of the heroine, *Fanny Sterling,* when the audience were much amused to hear Baddeley, as *Canton,* commending Miss Fanny's charms to his master, and professing to find that great sympathy existed between the young lady and his lordship. "The youngest is delectable," observes the old beau, as he takes snuff. "Oh, oui, my lor, very delect, inteed," says the valet; "she made doux yeux at you, my lor." In a later scene *Lord Ogleby* exclaims : "Ah, la petite Fanchon. She is the thing, isn't she, Canton ?" "Dere is very good sympatie entre vous and dat young lady, mi lor," replies *Canton.* For it was within public knowledge that Mr. and Mrs. Baddeley had quarrelled desperately and lived apart ; that although they continued to be members of the Drury Lane company, they exchanged no word with each other save upon the stage, when so required by their histrionic duties. King George III. and his consort are said to have been highly diverted with the passages in the comedy that seemed to reflect upon the private disagreements of the Baddeleys. " This effect of character upon the feelings of the audience caused a universal laugh, in which their majesties heartily joined," writes a biographer of the players. Presently the actress was honoured by a message from the king, brought by the royal page, Mr. Ramus, desiring her to give sittings to Mr. Zoffany, the artist, that her portrait might be included in the scene from " The Clandestine Marriage" he was about to paint by command of his Majesty. This incident greatly extended the fame of her beauty and of her theatrical merit. "She became caressed, adored, and followed by the first persons in the nation." A corrupt society constituted her its special toast and supreme idol. She lived, as it were, in a poisoned atmosphere of fulsome adulation and dishonest compliment ; the pretended homage of the rakes and profligates of the town, and the devotion they professed for her, were but insults in the slightest disguise.

For some seasons, however. scandal seems not to have busied itself concerning Mr. and Mrs. Baddeley; there was, at any rate, no apparent discord between them. In the year 1767, upon the occasion of their joint benefit, "Othello" was presented, when Mr. Baddeley appeared as *Roderigo*, and his wife as *Desdemona*. In 1768 the benefit was for Mrs. Baddeley only; but her husband was not absent from the stage. He represented *Papillon* in "The Liar," to the *Young Wilding* of Palmer. But both husband and wife were presently dismissed the theatre. It was said that the indiscreet conduct of Mrs. Baddeley had offended the green-room, and that the company had unanimously required her departure. Moreover, a dissension had arisen because Baddeley, being liable for her debts, had insisted upon receiving his wife's salary. Mr. George Garrick having advocated the lady's cause with injudicious warmth, was challenged by her husband to fight a duel in Hyde Park. But although swords were drawn and crossed, the combat terminated comfortably in an appropriately theatrical manner, and without bloodshed. A general adjustment of difficulties forthwith ensued, and Mr. and Mrs. Baddeley were formally reinstated members of the Drury Lane company.

From this time, however, the lady's appearance upon the scene became somewhat intermittent, and for about two years she wholly withdrew herself from the theatre;

but she presently resumed her professional duties, and continued upon the London stage until 1781. She undertook a great variety of characters, and, without doubt, proved herself an actress of distinction. She played *Ophelia* to Garrick's *Hamlet*, Baddeley appearing as *Polonius*. She was *Dame Kiteley* in 1767, when Garrick personated *Kiteley*, and Baddeley *Brainworm*. She was *Hero* to Garrick's *Benedick*, and *Jessica* to King's *Shylock*. Among her other Shakespearian characters were *Miranda*, *Portia* in "Julius Cæsar," *Olivia* in "Twelfth Night," and *Celia* in "As You Like It." In tragedy she undertook such characters as *Mrs. Beverley* in "The Gamester," *Leonora* in "The Revenge," *Statira* in "Alexander the Great," and *Lady Elizabeth Gray* in "The Earl of Warwick." When, in 1777, Sheridan's "Rivals" was transferred from Covent Garden to Drury Lane, she assumed the part of *Julia*, while Baddeley performed *Fag*. Sentimental comedy coming into fashion, she was applauded as the original representative of *Harriet* in Mrs. Griffith's "School for Rakes," and of *Miss Marchmont* and *Miss Willoughby* in Hugh Kelly's Comedies, "False Delicacy" and "A Word to the Wise." The unpopularity of Kelly at this time for political reasons, and because of his scurrilous poem of "Thespis," led to a riot that threatened the destruction of the theatre, and lasted two evenings; even the actresses who appeared in "A Word to the Wise" were grossly in-

sulted, while Mrs. Baddeley, we read, " narrowly escaped
being greatly hurt with an orange." Mrs. Baddeley also
appeared as the *Lady* in "Comus;" as *Maria* in Bur-
goyne's "Maid of the Oaks;" as *Rosetta* and *Clarissa*
in the operas of " Love in a Village " and " Lionel and
Clarissa;" as *Patty* in "The Maid of the Mill;" *Philadel*
in "King Arthur;" and as the heroine in very many
after-pieces and farces. She was further of service to
Garrick when he transferred his Shakesperian Jubilee
from Stratford-upon-Avon to the stage of Drury Lane.
Her theatrical engagement not being renewed after 1781,
she appeared as a singer at the Eidophusicon, a dioramic
exhibition contrived by De Loutherbourg the scene-
painter, and presented now in Exeter 'Change, at the
Patagonian Theatre, and now in Panton Square. After
this, she was seen no more in London, but proceeded to
Ireland to fulfil a promising engagement.

The remarkable beauty of Mrs. Baddeley had obtained the early recognition of the public, and was long
held to be almost a matter of general interest. When
in 1771 Foote produced his comedy of "The Maid of
Bath," at the Haymarket, Mrs. Baddeley, by desire of
the manager, occupied a prominent position in a box
near the stage. About the middle of the play, Foote,
in the character of *Flint*, descanting upon the charms
the heroine, who had her prototype, by-the-bye, in the
lovely Miss Linley of Bath, afterwards known as Mrs.

Sheridan, advanced to the footlights and exclaimed :
" Not even the beauty of the nine Muses, nor even of
the divine Baddeley herself, who is sitting here "
(and he pointed to her box), " could exceed that of the
Maid of Bath !" This extravagance is said to have
drawn extraordinary applause from all parts of the house.
The actor was encored, and even called upon to repeat
the words three times. Mrs. Baddeley was greatly confused ; she felt that every eye was upon her. She rose
from her seat and curtsied to the audience, "and it
was near a quarter of an hour before she could dis-
continue her obedience, the plaudits lasting so long."
Her face was suffused with blushes, which remained
apparent the whole evening ; for Mrs. Baddeley was not,
we are assured, "according to the fashion of modern
beauties, made up by art, for she never used any rouge
but on the stage." She was accustomed to be present
at "every public place of resort frequented by the
nobility and people of fashion," where her charms of
presence, the splendour and costliness of her dresses,
the brilliance of her jewels, excited the liveliest attention. However, upon the opening of the Pantheon for
concerts, etc., in 1772, Mrs. Baddeley was refused admission by the proprietors, who desired to be without
the patronage of "any of the players," and preferred to
depend exclusively upon the support of persons of quality
and good repute. The lady's friends declared they

would secure her entrance by force if necessary. Extra
bodies of constables were in attendance to preserve
order, but some fifty noblemen and gentlemen surrounded Mrs. Baddeley's sedan-chair as she approached
the portico of the building. The constables, exhibiting .
their staves, and lifting their hats, stated with the utmost
civility that they were strictly enjoined to admit no
players to the Pantheon. The noblemen and gentlemen
thereupon drew their swords, and declared they would
run through the body all who opposed the entrance of
Mrs. Baddeley. The constables could but yield to
superior numbers; thereupon, with their swords still
unsheathed, the lady's partisans, having secured her
admission, declared that they would not suffer the
entertainments to proceed until the managers had
humbly apologized for their insulting conduct. They
were constrained to beg the pardon, not only of Mrs.
Baddeley, but of all her champions individually, and to
rescind their order as to the exclusion of the players.
Thereupon Mrs. Abington (to be afterwards famous as
Lady Teazle), who had been quietly waiting to learn the
issue of the contest, presented herself at the door of the
Pantheon, and was admitted without further question
as to character or calling.

But soon debt and difficulties of various kinds beset
the beautiful Mrs. Baddeley. Her recklessness and
improvidence, the viciousness of her life, knew no

bounds. She fled hither and thither to escape the bailiffs; she was arrested and her goods seized by the sheriffs again and again; she was carried from spunging-house to spunging-house. No longer secure of her liberty in England, she sought refuge now in France, now in Ireland, now in Scotland. Her beauty waned; her health gave way; she suffered at times from extreme poverty. The degradation and misery of her later years can scarcely be described. She reappeared upon the stage at York in 1783, having become a member of Yate Wilkinson's company, and personated *Clarissa, Polly, Rosetta, Imogen,* and other of her more admired characters. But she now made excessive demands upon the indulgence of her audiences. As Wilkinson writes of the performance for her benefit at York: "She was very lame, and to make that worse was so stupidly intoxicated with laudanum that it was with great difficulty she finished the performance." She went with the company to Leeds, "but what with illness, laziness, and inebriety, I was never certain of Mrs. Baddeley's performance from one night to another, so she sank into neglect and contempt." In reference to her poverty, Wilkinson relates that, although she received "very genteel payment" from him, "she was in truth reduced to beggary —not worth a single shilling." He adds: "Her friend and companion, a Mrs. Stell, was with her, who, I fancy, had always occasion for such sums as the unfortunate woman received." She was a member of the Edinburgh company during the seasons of 1783–4–5; but her health failed more and more, and whatever the terms of her engagement may have been, she probably appeared upon the stage but seldom. She seems, indeed, at this time to have subsisted mainly upon the charity of her playfellows. "The kind hearts of the Edinburgh company, to their great credit, exhausted their own little stock to prevent her absolutely starving, and provided something like an interment, with a poor coffin, which, but for their laudable humanity, she must have wanted." She died in July, 1786.

The Mrs. Stell of whom Wilkinson makes mention was, of course, the Mrs. Elizabeth Steele who in 1787 published the scandalous Memoirs, in six volumes, of the unfortunate Mrs. Sophia Baddeley, of Drury Lane Theatre. In the last century books of this class were only too numerous, and it has been suggested that the Life of Mrs. Baddeley was published by way of rivalling the shameless Autobiography of Mrs. George Anne Bellamy, of Covent Garden Theatre. Mrs. Steele had acted in the capacity of confidant and abigail, or what used to be called "convenient woman," to Mrs. Baddeley, and did not long survive the appearance of her book. The newspapers recorded on the 14th November, 1787, the death, at the Dolphin Inn, Bishopsgate, "in the most extreme agonies and distress," of Mrs. Elizabeth

Steele, "lately advertised for a forgery committed on a respectable house in the city," but better known from her having published the Memoirs of Mrs. Baddeley. It appears that the woman, absconding from the officers of justice, had taken refuge at the Dolphin, her real name and condition being unknown to the landlord and his servants. She had arrived at the inn about a fortnight before in a shabby old chariot, when she asked to be provided with a lodging and a nurse, because of the infirm state of her health. She was buried in Bishopsgate churchyard, "in a manner little better than a common pauper."

Meanwhile Baddeley continued to serve faithfully the Drury Lane management, usually fulfilling an engagement during the summer months at the little theatre in the Haymarket. His repertory of characters was somewhat confined; the public did not encourage him to enterprise in his impersonations, or to depart much from the special "line of business" he had marked out for himself. In "The Theatres, a Poetical Dissection," published in 1771, the actor is briefly mentioned :

> "We think that Baddeley can never miss
> A crouching Frenchman or a flattering Swiss,
> Yet for all else his talents are but small," etc.

Hugh Kelly, in his "Thespis," while referring to the wife as

> ". . . the gentle Baddeley, whose form
> Sweet as her voice can never fail to charm,

> Whose melting strain no Arne's eccentric skill
> As yet has tortured into modern thrill," etc.,

thus described the husband :

> "In foreign footmen Baddeley alone
> Preserves the native nasalness of tone,
> And in his manner strongly shows allied
> Their genuine turn of abjectness and pride.
> If proofs are wanting on Canton I call,
> And ask the general sentiments of all.
> Here then, secure of competence and name,
> He ought to rest his fortune and his fame," etc.

A later and more malicious satirist, Anthony Pasquin, in his "Children of Thespis," 1792, writes of Baddeley's "crab-apple phiz," his grim front, and dissonant voice, and charges him with being "turgid and rough," careless and slovenly :

> " He snarls through his parts, be they easy or hard,
> Like a mastiff that's chained to bay thieves from a yard.
> Though none the misanthrope can copy so well,
> As an actor he's slovenly—candour must tell," etc.

The writer concludes, however :

> " His enacting coarse Brainworm's a noble exertion,
> And Polonius and Trinculo feed our diversion."

Nothing being said of his skill in personating foreigners.

Michael Kelly relates of Baddeley that he was "a worthy man," although he was often called "Old Vinegar;" but this was after a character he sustained with much applause in the farce of "The Son-in-Law," produced at the Haymarket in 1779. He had a habit

of smacking his lips when speaking, justifying Charles
Bannister's jocular remark : " My dear Baddeley, everybody must know that you have been a cook, for you
always seem to be tasting your words." Kelly adds :
"An excellent cook, to my knowledge, he was, and,
moreover, extremely proud of his skill in the culinary
art. He had been cook to Foote, and once when he
was acting at the Haymarket, of which Foote was the
proprietor, they had a quarrel, and Baddeley challenged
him to fight with swords. 'What! fight!' cried Foote.
'Oh, the dog! So I have taken the spit from my
kitchen fire, and stuck it by his side, and now the fellow
wants to stick me with it!'"

Baddeley, the first performer of *Moses* in "The
School for Scandal," was also the original representative
of *Lory* in "A Trip to Scarborough," in Sheridan's
adaptation of " The Relapse." He served the theatre
by undertaking such characters as *Lord Sands* in
Henry VIII.," *Menenius* in "Coriolanus," and one of
the witches in "Macbeth." He personated Shakespeare's Welshman *Fluellen,* and the Welsh *Dr. Druid*
in Cumberland's "Fashionable Lover." Other of his parts
were Foote's *Vamp* and *Puff,* Steele's *Sir Harry Gubbin,*
Hardy in "The Belle's Stratagem," *Major Oakley* in
"The Jealous Wife," *Medium* in "Inkle and Yarico,"
M. Le Médécin in "The Anatomist," *Captain Trapan*
in "The Lord of the Manor," and *Catch-penny* in "The

Suicide." In Genest's "History of the Stage" is contained a list of upwards of eighty-five characters supported by Baddeley during his professiohal career of six and thirty years. He died quite suddenly on January 20, 1794. On the preceding evening he had been seized with a fit while assuming the dress of his old character of *Moses.* He was carried to his house in Store Street, but his state was hopeless; the medical efforts made to save him were all in vain. " His Swiss and his Jews, his Germans and his Frenchmen," notes Boaden, " were admirably characteristic ; they were finely generalized and played from actual knowledge of the people, not from a casual snatch at individual peculiarities."

His will bore date April 23, 1792. It is clear that he desired to stand well with posterity, and that he felt he had been slandered in his lifetime, notably in the Memoirs of his wife. He desired his executors to republish every year a letter he had printed in the *General Advertiser*, April 20, 1790, "representing his disagreement with his unhappy wife, to prevent the world from looking on his memory in the villainous point of view as set forth in certain books, pamphlets," etc. He desired to be buried in the churchyard of St. Paul's, Covent Garden. He left rings to his fellow-players Charles and John Bannister, Wroughton, and Dodd. His salary could never have been large, yet he had saved money enough to purchase a small free-hold house and garden at Upper Moulsey, Surrey. This little property he bequeathed in remainder to the Society established for the relief of indigent persons belonging to Drury Lane Theatre, as an asylum for decayed actors and actresses, to whom small pensions were to be allowed, " to constitute them respectable in the eyes of their neighbours ; " the pensioners, who were to wear "a regalia," being further required to spend twenty shillings on the 20th of April in every year, in honour of the birth of the founder, and especial care being taken to have the words "Baddeley's Asylum" inscribed on the front of the house. The famous be-quest of Twelfth-cake and wine followed.

Adolphus, in his " Life of John Bannister," suggests that the devise of the freehold at Moulsey was void in law by the Statute of Mortmain, and that the property for want of heirs escheated to the crown. Michael Kelly, however, is distinct in his statement that the trustees of Drury Lane Theatrical Fund became duly possessed of the estate, and thought proper to sell it. Kelly writes in 1826 : "It has been purchased by, and is now in the possession of, my friend Mr. Savory of Bond Street, at whose hospitable table I have many times been a welcome guest. In his parlour is an ex-cellent likeness of Baddeley in the character of *Moses* in 'The School for Scandal,' painted by Zoffany; and

on a part of the premises are the boards of the old
Drury Lane stage, on which the immortal Garrick displayed his unrivalled powers.   It seems no unnatural
coincidence that the *ci-devant* cook's property should
have found a *savoury* purchaser."   Kelly's Memoirs, it
may be added, were edited, if not absolutely written, by
Theodore Hook.

CHAPTER II.

" MARRIED BENEATH HER."

In the novel of "The Virginians" is contained a particular account of the loves and the marriage of Lady Maria Esmond, daughter of the Earl of Castlewood, and Mr. Geoghegan, or Hagan as he was called on the stage, the handsome young actor from Dublin who greatly distinguished himself, it may be remembered, as the *King of Bohemia* in Mr. George Warrington's famous tragedy of " Carpezan." " The grace and elegance of the young actor Hagan won general applause," we are told : her ladyship gaily giving "The King of Bohemia !" as her toast at the jolly supper given by the successful dramatist after the curtain had fallen at Covent Garden. A foundation of fact for the fiction of Lady Maria's adventures may be found in the clandestine union of Lady Susannah Sarah Louisa Fox Strangeways, the eldest daughter of the Earl of Ilchester, with Mr. William O'Brien, comedian of the Drury Lane company, which occurred in the year 1764, and apparently much dis-

turbed polite society. Horace Walpole writes to Sir
Horace Mann, on the 9th of April : " A melancholy
affair has happened to Lord Ilchester : his eldest
daughter, Lady Susan, a very pleasing girl, though not
handsome, married herself two days ago at Covent
Garden Church to O'Brien, a handsome young actor.
Lord Ilchester doated on her, and was the most indulgent of fathers. 'Tis a cruel blow." A few days later
Walpole writes to the Earl of Hertford of Lord Ilchester's " sad misfortune," supplying further particulars.

The affair had been in train some eighteen months,
it seems. The lover had learned to counterfeit the
handwriting of Lady Sarah Bunbury, and thus addressed
his lady securely enough in a disguised and feminine-
looking hand. The unsuspecting father had himself
delivered several of the actor's letters to Lady Susan.
The family learned of the existence of the intrigue only
a week before the catastrophe occurred. The lovers
were wont to meet at the house of Miss Catherine Read,
a clever artist, now chiefly remembered by her charming
portrait, in a frilled cap, of the beautiful Duchess of
Hamilton, formerly Miss Gunning. Lord Cathcart had
called upon Miss Read. She said softly to him : " My
lord, there is a couple in the next room that I am sure
ought not to be together ; I wish your lordship would
look in." He looked in, closed the door again, and
went straightway and informed Lord Ilchester. Lady

Susan, questioned by her father, flung herself at his feet and confessed all. She promised, however, at once to terminate her engagement with her lover and dismiss him, if one last interview only were permitted to her, that she might bid adieu to him for ever. "You will be amazed," writes Walpole to Lord Hertford; "even this was granted. The parting scene happened the beginning of the week. On Friday she came of age, and on Saturday morning, instead of being under lock and key in the country, walked downstairs, took her footman, said she was going to breakfast with Lady Sarah, but would call at Miss Read's; in the street pretended to recollect a particular cap in which she was to be drawn, sent the footman back for it, whipped into a hackney coach, was married at Covent Garden Church, and set out for Mr. O'Brien's villa at Dunstable. . . . Poor Lord Ilchester is almost distracted; indeed, it is the completion of disgrace—even a footman were preferable. The publicity of the hero's profession perpetuates the mortification. . . . I could not have believed Lady Susan would have stooped so low. She may, however, still keep good company, and say 'nos numeri sumus'— Lady Mary Duncan, Lady Caroline Adair, Lady Betty Gallini—the shopkeepers of next age will be mighty well born!" Mr. Walpole had been already scandalized by the condescension of these ladies in their marriages. Lady Maria, daughter of the seventh Earl of Thanet,

had become the wife of Doctor Duncan, M.D., afterwards created a baronet. Lady Caroline, daughter of
the second Earl of Albemarle, had married Mr. Adair,
a surgeon. Lady Betty, or Elizabeth, daughter of the
third Earl of Abingdon, had bestowed her hand upon
her dancing-master, Gallini, afterwards the proprietor of
the Hanover Square Rooms, calling himself Sir John
Gallini, the foreign order of the Golden Spur having
been conferred upon him. And now Lady Susan had
married an actor! "Even a footman were preferable,"
held Walpole, the players being but lightly esteemed in
the eighteenth century. So Foote's *Papillon*, in "The
Liar," narrating his experiences, observes: "As to
player—whatever happened to me I was determined not
to bring disgrace upon my family; and so I resolved to
turn footman." A preference for a footman over all
mankind was presently manifested by Lady Henrietta
Alicia Wentworth, the youngest sister of the Marquis of
Rockingham. In 1764 the lady became the wife of her
own footman, John William Sturgeon. She was twenty-
seven, and possessed little beauty. She had, however,
as Walpole relates, "mixed a wonderful degree of prudence with her potion," settling "a single hundred
pounds" a year upon her husband for his life, entailing
her whole fortune upon such children as might be born
of the marriage, with reversion to her own family, and
providing that in case of the separation of man and wife

his annuity should still be paid to him. This deed of settlement, drawn by her own hand, she sent to Lord Mansfield, her uncle by marriage, and constituted him her trustee. His lordship pronounced the deed to be " as binding as any lawyer could make it." Walpole wrote to Lord Hertford, informing him of the matter, and demanding : " Did one ever hear of more reflection in a delirium ? Well, but hear more. She has given away all her clothes, nay, and her ' ladyship' says linen gowns are properest for a footman's wife, and is gone to his family in Ireland, plain Mrs. Henrietta Sturgeon ! "

Why were they proud, these fine gentlemen of George III.'s period ? We may ask with Keats : " Why in the name of glory were they proud ? " The Walpoles were. Norfolk squires of old descent, worthy and well-to-do, but not otherwise very distinguished until Robert Walpole entered Parliament as member for Castle Rising, to become in time First Lord of the Treasury, Knight of the Garter, and, on his retirement from office, Earl of Oxford, with a pension of four thousand pounds per annum. A spurious parentage has been assigned to the superfine Horace. In any case his mother was Catharine Shorter, the daughter of John Shorter, Lord Mayor of London, arbitrarily appointed by the king in 1688, and timber merchant, as his father had been before him.

" Why were they proud ?   Because red-lined accounts
    Were richer than the songs of Grecian years."

The founder of the Fox family was Stephen Fox, of
obscure origin, who as a youth in Charles I.'s time had
sung in the choir of Salisbury Cathedral, and won the
approval of good Bishop Duppa. The boy afterwards
entered the service of Lord Percy, retiring with him
to the Continent when the cause of royalty in England seemed hopelessly lost. The Restoration brought
Stephen Fox home again. He was knighted in 1665,
appointed head of the Board of Green Cloth, and lived
to sit in Parliament, member for the city which had
first known him as a choir-boy. At the age of seventy-
six he took for his second wife Margaret Hope, the
daughter of a Lincolnshire clergyman. Of this marriage
was born, among other children, Stephen, who in 1736,
on his union with Elizabeth, daughter of Thomas
Strangeways Horner, of Mells Park, in the county of
Somerset, added the name of Strangeways to his own
surname of Fox. He was created Baron Ilchester in
1741, and Earl of Ilchester in 1756. After all, Mr.
William O'Brien, who eloped with this nobleman's
daughter Susan in 1764, could probably boast as pure
and ancient descent as either his lordship or his lordship's compassionate friend, Horace Walpole. Mr.
O'Brien had chiefly sinned in that he was an actor.
" Even a footman were preferable. The publicity of

the hero's profession perpetuates the mortification." In the peerages recording Lady Susan's marriage with O'Brien he is described not as of Drury Lane Theatre, comedian, but as of Stinsford, Dorsetshire, esquire. There prevailed a disposition, indeed, to suppress as much as possible Mr. O'Brien's connection with the stage, or to represent his histrionic career as a sort of adventurous episode in the life of a young gentleman of birth and fortune. In the "Biographia Dramatica" he is described as of an ancient Catholic family : certain of his kindred, in their loyalty to James II., after the capitulation of Limerick following the royal fortunes into France, and serving as officers in the Irish Brigade under the head of the house of O'Brien, Lord Viscount Clare. It is believed, however, that O'Brien's father had gained his living as a fencing-master, and that the young man for some time followed the paternal calling.

William O'Brien made his first appearance at Drury Lane in 1758 as *Brazen* in "The Recruiting Officer" of Farquhar. Woodward, an admired actor of eccentric characters, had deserted London for Dublin. Garrick was thought to be fortunate in at once securing O'Brien as Woodward's substitute. Tate Wilkinson and Tom Davies in their separate accounts of the stage in Garrick's time are each careful to suppress all mention of O'Brien by name. Deference was paid to the prejudices of the Ilchester family and others by treating the actor as an anonymous person. Davies, describing Garrick as "never without resources," proceeds to relate how after the favourite Woodward's departure "an accomplished young gentleman, whose family connections have long since, to the great regret of the public, occasioned his total separation from the stage, for some years acted with great and merited applause a variety of characters in genteel life, some of which had a mixture of gaiety and levity and a peculiar and pleasing vivacity. In elegance of deportment and variety of graceful action he excelled all the players of his time." Tate Wilkinson writes of O'Brien as "an intimate friend," and relates how Garrick, meeting with him by accident during the summer vacation, took "infinite pains" with the young man, and "formed a great partiality and friendship for him." There is some hint of his former occupation in the mention of the "swiftness, ease, grace, and superior elegance" of his manner of drawing his sword: his action in this respect, it was said, "threw all other performers at a wonderful distance." " He had more ease," says Wilkinson, "than any old or young actor I ever remember," and he proceeds to mention that Mr. Garrick was afterwards much indebted for the applause he received in *Hamlet* in the fencing scene with *Laertes* to the instructions or the example of O'Brien : "there 'twas visible Mr. Garrick's pupil was the master."

The second character essayed by O'Brien was *Poly-*

dore in Otway's tragedy, "The Orphan." "Oh, my lord, my Polydore!" Lady Maria Esmond is said to have "bleated," and forthwith declaimed certain lines from *Polydore's* speech to *Monimia:*

> "Oh ! I could talk to thee for ever, for ever thus
> Eternally admiring—fix and gaze
> On those dear eyes ; for every glance they send
> Darts through my soul and fills my heart with rapture."

Carpezan, by-the-bye, is supposed to have been presented in 1759 at Covent Garden, Mr. Hagan being described as a member of Mr. Rich's company.

During his six years' stay upon the stage O'Brien sustained a long list of characters in light and eccentric comedy and in farce, occasionally undertaking severer duties in tragedy. He represented Farquhar's *Sir Harry Wildair*, Congreve's *Tattle*, and Cibber's *Lord Foppington; Marplot* in "The Busybody," and *Don Felix* in "The Wonder;" *Squire Richard* in "The Provoked Husband," and *Master Johnny* in "The Schoolboy." In Shakesperian plays he appeared as *Laertes*, as *Lucio* in "Measure for Measure," as *Slender*, *Guiderius* in "Cymbeline," *Valentine* in "The Two Gentlemen of Verona," *Sir Andrew Aguecheek*, the *Prince of Wales* in "King Henry IV., Part I.," and *Mercutio.* The "Dramatic Censor" of 1770 pronounces O'Brien's *Mercutio* as inferior only to Woodward's. Among the characters of which O'Brien was the original representative may be mentioned *Lovel* in "High Life Below Stairs," *Young Clackit* in "The Guardian," and *Lord Trinket* in "The Jealous Wife;" *Beverley* in "All in the Wrong," *Clerimont* in "The Old Maid," *Belmour* in "The School for Lovers," and *Sir Henry Flutter* in "The Discovery." "Cibber and O'Brien," wrote Walpole, "were what Garrick could never reach—coxcombs and men of fashion." In the "Rosciad," however, O'Brien, while said to be "by nature formed to please," is condemned as a mere imitator of Woodward; his performance of *Master Stephen* in Ben Jonson's comedy is mentioned as showing "which way genius grows;" otherwise it is charged against him that he

> "Self quite put off, affects, with too much art,
> To put on Woodward in each mangled part ;
> Adopts his shrug, his wink, his stare, nay, more—
> His voice, and croaks ; for Woodward croaked before.
> When a dull copier simple grace neglects,
> And rests his imitation in defects,
> We readily forgive ; but such vile arts
> Are double guilt in men of real parts."

In the satirical pamphlet of the time, called "A Dialogue in the Shades," Mrs. Cibber is supposed to inform the deceased Mrs. Woffington : "The only performers of any eminence that have made their appearance since your departure are O'Brien and Powell; the first was a very promising comedian in Woodward's walk, and was much caressed by the nobility; but this

apparent good fortune was his ruin, for having married
a young lady of family without her relations' knowledge,
he was obliged to transport himself to America, where
he is now doing penance for his redemption."

O'Brien did not appear upon the stage after the fact
of his marriage had been published. In the case of
Lady Maria Esmond's union with Mr. Hagan it may
be remembered that "a fine gentleman's riot" was
threatened in the theatre. Mr. George Warrington
found the manager Rich "in great dudgeon." The
Macaronis were furious, and vowed they would pelt Mr.
Hagan and have him cudgelled afterwards. Will Esmond,
at Arthur's, had taken his oath that he would have the
actor's ears. Mr. Rich was afraid to let Hagan appear
again, and, meanwhile, was careful to stop his salary.
In the end, Hagan left the stage, led an exemplary life,
and became renowned for his elegance and his eloquence
in the pulpit. He had, it seems, kept almost all his
terms at Dublin College; so he returned there to enter
holy orders, Lord Castlewood subsequently obtaining
for him an ecclesiastical appointment in Virginia. Lady
Maria meekly resigned her rank, and was known in the
colony as Mrs. Hagan. "As we could get him no
employment in England," says Mr. Warrington, "we
were glad to ship him to Virginia, and give him a
colonial pulpit-cushion to thump." He preached sermons
on the "then gloomy state of affairs," and he read plays

to Madame Esmond, among them Mr. Warrington's unsuccessful tragedy of " Pocahontas," "which our parson
delivered with uncommon energy and fire."

Mr. O'Brien was provided for with greater difficulty.
He had not Hagan's opportunity of taking orders and
entering a Protestant pulpit. As Walpole wrote to
Lord Hertford of the newly-married couple: " Poor
Lady Susan O'Brien is in the most deplorable situation,
for her Adonis (O'Brien) is a Roman Catholic, and
cannot be provided for out of his calling. Sir Francis
Delaval, being touched by her calamity, has made her
a present—of what do you think?—of a rich gold stuff!
The delightful charity! O'Brien comforts himself, and
says it will make a shining passage in his little history."
As the actor was not allowed to earn money by acting,
however, and as Lord Ilchester declined to assist his
son-in-law, the prospects of the young couple seemed
rather hopeless. Eventually it was decided that the
expense of maintaining Lady Susan and Mr. O'Brien
should devolve upon the public. A government grant
of lands was obtained for them, and they were despatched
to America. In this way it was thought the young
couple would be fairly disposed of, and the disgrace
which had befallen the noble family of the Foxes be so
effectually hidden that in time it might really be forgotten. "O'Brien and Lady Susan are to be transported
to the Ohio, and have a grant of forty thousand acres,"

writes Walpole to Lord Hertford in August, 1764. Even in this matter of the grant some juggling and jobbing occurred apparently; for Walpole continues: "The Duchess of Grafton says sixty thousand were bestowed; but a friend of yours, and a relation of Lady Susan, nibbled away twenty thousand for a Mr. Upton."

On Christmas Day, 1764, Charles Fox is able to furnish news of his cousin Lady Susan and her husband to Sir George Macartney. "We have heard from Lady Susan since her arrival at New York. I do not think they will make much of their lands, and I fear it will be impossible to get O'Brien a place." Some account of the emigrants is also contained in a book published at Harrisburg, America, in 1811, and entitled " Memoirs of a Life chiefly passed in Pennsylvania within the last Sixty Years," etc. Lady Susan and her husband are described as the inmates of a lodging-house in Philadelphia. Mr. O'Brien is recognized as "a man of parts," and mention is made of his fame as a performer of fine gentlemen, his easy manner of treading the stage, his swift and graceful manner of drawing his sword, "which Garrick imitated, but could not equal," etc. The writer proceeds : "Mr. O'Brien is presented to my recollection as a man of the middle height, with a symmetrical form rather light than athletic. His wife, as I have seen it mentioned, obtained for him, through the interest of her family, a post in America. But what this post was or where it located him I never heard." The appointment secured by O'Brien was in the gift of the Board of Ordnance.

Boswell records certain of Dr. Johnson's observations, made in 1775, upon "a young lady who had married a man much her inferior in rank," and Croker supposes that the union of Lady Susan and Mr. O'Brien was in question; but Croker errs in assigning the marriage to the year 1773: it occurred, as we have seen, in 1764. "Madam," said Johnson to Mrs. Thrale," we must distinguish. Were I a man of rank, I would not let a daughter starve who had made a mean marriage; but, having voluntarily degraded herself from the station which she was originally entitled to hold, I would support her only in that which she herself had chosen, and would not put her on a level with my other daughters. You are to consider, madam, that it is our duty to maintain the subordination of civilized society, and when there is a gross and shameful deviation from rank, it should be punished so as to deter others from the same perversion."

The actor and his wife were absent from England some seven or eight years. They returned home without the permission of the authorities. Ordered to resume his post, O'Brien refused to obey. The matter is referred to in the "Last Journals" of Horace Walpole. "O'Brien received orders, among the rest, to return, but he refused. Conway declared they would dismiss him. Lord and Lady Holland interposed, but Conway was firm, and he turned out O'Brien."

Actors can but rarely have influenced political affairs. The newspapers in 1772, however, attributed Fox's resignation of his post, as one of the Lords of the Admiralty, to Lord North's refusal to bestow upon Mr. O'Brien "a kind of sinecure," afterwards given to one Maclean, and worth £1000 a year. Fox, it was alleged, demanded this place for O'Brien in exchange for two lucrative offices, worth about £800 a year, enjoyed by the actor abroad, and requiring his constant absence from England. Lord North proposed that, with the consent of Maclean, O'Brien should be appointed his deputy; "but this Fox received with contempt." To Lord Ossory Fox wrote: "It is impossible to tell you the real reason of my resigning: it is very complicated." For some years Fox continued in violent opposition to Lord North.

The player now became a playwright, the managers receiving his efforts with unusual cordiality. The night of December 8, 1772, saw the production of his comedy of "The Duel" at Drury Lane, and of his two-act farce of "Cross Purposes" at Covent Garden. A dramatist has rarely enjoyed such a double chance of distinguishing himself. "The Duel," an adaptation of "Le Philosophe sans le Savoir," by Sedaine, failed to please, however, although supported by the excellent acting of Barry and

Miss Younge. The failure was ascribed to the super-senti-mental scenes which the adapter had introduced at the instance of certain of his noble connections, who, having spoiled his play, made him pecuniary compensation for its ill-success. In January, 1773, Walpole wrote of the play to the Rev. William Mason: "O'Brien's 'Duel' was damned the first night. I saw the original at Paris when it was first acted, and though excessively touched with it, wondered how the audience came to have sense enough to taste it. I thought then it would not have succeeded here; the touches are so simple, and delicate, and natural. Accordingly it did not. I have been reading the transla-tion, and cried over it heartily." Mr. O'Brien printed his play to shame the playgoers who condemned it. "Cross Purposes," adapted from "Les Trois Frères Rivaux," by Lafont, was received with cordial applause, the actors Shuter and Quick greatly pleasing the audience. O'Brien seems to have made no further contributions to dramatic literature.

He survived until 1815. In the "Biographia Dra-matica," 1812, he is described as "still living in advanced age in Dorsetshire, of which county he is the receiver-general." The Rev. Mr. Genest recounts that he was told in 1803, when living in O'Brien's neighbour-hood, that he desired as much as possible to "sink the player," and to "bury in oblivion those years of his life which were the most worth being remembered—ashamed, perhaps, of a profession which is no disgrace to any one who conducts himself respectably in it, and in which to succeed is, generally speaking, a proof of good natural abilities and a diligent application of them." Lady Susan survived her husband some twelve years.

CHAPTER III.

"A GENTLEMAN OF THE NAME OF BOOTH."

EARLY in the year 1817, Covent Garden Theatre was the scene of great confusion and uproar—almost of riot, indeed. "A gentleman of the name of Booth"—so Hazlitt describes the performer—had essayed the part of *Richard III.,* seeking the good opinion of a London audience, after having won considerable applause in the provinces. According to subsequent announcements in the playbills, Mr. Booth's *Richard* "met with a success unprecedented in the annals of histrionic fame." Nevertheless the managers of the theatre carefully avoided backing this strongly expressed opinion. They declined to pay their actor more than two pounds per week for his services—certainly a very small salary, even fifty years ago, for a player of any pretence. It was generally agreed that they were wrong, "either," as Hazlitt stated the case, "in puffing the new actor so unmercifully, or in haggling with him so pitifully." Forthwith Mr. Edmund Kean intervened. In times past he had played with

Mr. Booth in the country; he was now the most prominent member of the Drury Lane company. He took
his fellow-actor by the hand, and obtained for him an
engagement at Drury Lane, upon a salary of ten pounds
per week.

Booth had played *Richard* at Covent Garden on the
12th and 13th of February: on the 20th he appeared at
Drury Lane as *Iago* to the *Othello* of Kean. Two nights
afterwards, however, he was back again at Covent
Garden, playing *Richard III.* to an angry house, that
hissed and hooted him persistently and vehemently.
Scarcely a syllable of Shakespeare, or perhaps we
should rather say of Cibber, could be heard. There
was, indeed, a great tumult. The enraged public would
neither listen to the play nor to the apologies attempted
both by Booth and by Fawcett, the stage-manager of the
theatre. It must be observed that a spirit of partisan-
ship, of a kind scarcely intelligible nowadays, characterized the playgoers of that period. Men espoused the
interests of Drury Lane or Covent Garden with the heat
and acrimonious zeal they displayed in political contests.
It could, in truth, matter little upon which stage Mr.
Booth chose to strut and fret; his appearance and his
disappearance were not really events of vital importance.
But "the play" was indeed "the thing" just then; and
Mr. Booth's conduct was considered as a due incentive
to excitement. If it was absolutely necessary to ad-

minister rebuke, the managers who had influenced his proceedings might justly have shared the odium devolving upon the actor. The public, however, held Mr. Booth solely accountable. Upon him alone they poured forth their indignation.

Of course the considerations moving "the poor player" were obvious enough. He was tempted from Covent Garden by the promise of an improved salary. Then misgivings troubled him touching his professional prospects. It was clear to him that there was danger of his being shelved at Drury Lane. Had Kean's kindness been of a cruel sort — his friendship but disguised enmity? Was he aiding a comrade, or ridding himself of a rival? If Mr. Booth was permitted to play at all at Drury Lane, it must needs be as second to Mr. Kean. At Covent Garden there was less fear of competition, at any rate. Kemble was retiring from the stage; Macready was but a novice. Booth might be recognized as the legitimate rival of Kean—might, perhaps, surpass him and reign supreme, the leading actor of his time. So when the Covent Garden managers upbraided him for leaving them, threatened him with legal proceedings, and then solicited his return to them upon a larger salary even than that promised him at Drury Lane, he hastened back to the stage from which he had made his first bow to a London audience.

For some nights he encountered bitter hostility. He

published an appeal to the public, entreating their for-
giveness for what he was willing to admit had been grave
misconduct upon his part. His first friends were slow to
pardon him, but their opposition gradually diminished.
At length he was enabled to express in the playbills his
heartfelt gratitude to his patrons for the complete pardon
they had extended to him, and there was an end of the
Junius Brutus Booth controversy.

There seems, indeed, to have been a general amnesty.
The actions at law, that had been commenced by the
Drury Lane committee against the actor, and against
Harris, the manager of Covent Garden, were abandoned.
In the course of the season, Booth undertook a variety
of characters: *Sir Giles Overreach; Rinaldo*, in Di-
mond's "Conquest of Taranto;" *Fitzharding*, in
Tobin's "Curfew;" *Sir Edward Mortimer*, in "The Iron
Chest;" *Jerry Sneak*, on the occasion of his benefit;
and *Iago* to the *Othello* of Young. His engagement
was prolonged over the three following seasons. His
appearances, however, were not frequent. He played
Gloster in "Jane Shore," and *Lear* in Nahum Tate's
adaptation of Shakespeare's tragedy, to the *Edmund* of
Macready and the *Edgar* of Charles Kemble. His
services were afterwards transferred to Drury Lane, at
which theatre, in the season of 1820–21, he appeared as
Lear and *Iago ;* as *Cassius*, to the *Brutus* of Wallack ;
as *Dumont*, in "Jane Shore;" and as *Opechancanough*

(tributary to the Powhatan) in the American drama of "Pocahontas; or, The Indian Princess." He was not re-engaged until October, 1825, when he played for three nights only, personating *Othello, Richard III.,* and *Brutus*, in Howard Payne's tragedy. These performances brought to a close the career in England of " the gentleman of the name of Booth." He quitted the country hastily, to avoid, it was alleged, the consequences of an assault committed upon a noted rope-dancer of that day, styling himself Il Diavolo Antonio. Mr. Booth betook himself to the West Indies, whence, after a brief sojourn, he removed to the United States. There he found a home, and passed the rest of his life acquiring fame as an actor of extraordinary ability—even of rare genius. He was born in London, May 1, 1796. He died at New Orleans, in December, 1852. He was the father of Edwin Booth, an actor of distinction, and of John Wilkes Booth, the murderer of President Lincoln.

Was this Mr. Junius Brutus Booth undervalued in England? Regret did not attend his departure hence ; he was not missed. He occupies but a very subordinate position in the list of British actors. His name, indeed, is scarcely remembered amongst us. Opportunity did not fail him, although allowance may have to be made for the untoward incident of his first engagement in London. He was entrusted with many of the most important characters of the tragic repertory, and several new characters were allotted to him. The position assigned to him in the theatre was above that enjoyed by his fellow-actors Macready and Charles Kemble. There is no evidence of hostility in the criticisms upon his histrionic efforts. Hazlitt writes calmly about him, without enthusiasm in his favour, still with every desire to encourage the actor. But to Hazlitt, and the public he wrote for, Booth was from first to last little more than the mere imitator of Kean. " Almost the whole of his performance was an exact copy or parody of Mr. Kean's manner of doing the same part [*Richard*] ; it was a complete, but, at the same time, a successful piece of plagiarism. We do not think this kind of second-hand reputation can last upon the London boards for more than a character or two." And then it is pointed out that the best passages in Mr. Booth's acting were those " in which he now and then took leave of Mr. Kean's decided and extreme manner, and became more mild and tractable, . . . seemed to yield to the impulse of his own feelings, and to follow the natural tones and cadence of his voice." A second criticism, by Hazlitt, deals with Booth's *Iago*. He is still described as an imitator ; his performance " a very close and spirited repetition of Mr. Kean's manner of doing the part." And the critic concludes : " We suspect that Mr. Booth is not only a professed and deliberate imitator of Mr. Kean, but that he has the chameleon quality (we do not mean that of living upon air, as the Covent Garden managers supposed, but) of reflecting all objects that come in contact with him. We occasionally caught the mellow tones of Mr. Macready rising out of the thorough-bass of Mr. Kean's guttural emphasis, and the flaunting *dégagé* robe of Mr. Young's oriental manner flying off from the tight vest and tunic of the 'bony prizer' of the Drury Lane company." Hazlitt, it would seem, was the spokesman of the playgoers of his time. Booth was almost unanimously rated then as an actor of the second class, of limited capacity—an imitator of Edmund Kean.

Macready, in his memoirs, makes occasional mention of Booth, but avoids all recognition of his merits as an actor. Macready, however, was slow to praise his playfellows, and even judged severely his own performances. He noted that "Booth, in figure, voice, and manner, so closely resembled Kean, that he might have been taken for his twin-brother;" and then follows a statement that Booth, in the last scene of his *Sir Giles Overreach*, had resorted to a manœuvre which was severely commented upon. "One of the attendants, who held him, was furnished with a sponge filled with blood [rose-pink] which he, unseen by the audience, squeezed into his mouth, to convey the idea of his having burst a bloodvessel!" But in regard to these early accounts of Booth, one fact should be borne steadily in mind—his extreme youth. He was little more than twenty when he first set foot upon the stage of Covent Garden. It was natural enough that at that age he should be an imitator. There prevailed among the young actors of the time a sort of rage for imitating Kean, all hoping that such theatrical triumphs as he had obtained might also be in store for them. In Booth's case, the inclination to imitate was stimulated by the circumstance of physical resemblance, which, if less close than Macready imagined, was yet remarkable enough. "His face is adapted to tragic characters," wrote Hazlitt, "and his voice wants neither strength nor musical expression. . . . He has two voices: one his own, and the other Mr. Kean's. The worst parts of his performance were those where he imitated or caricatured Mr. Kean's hoarseness of delivery and violence of action, and affected an energy without seeming to feel it." His voice was, no doubt, superior to Kean's in clearness and music, and probably in power also. He was of Kean's low stature, but with nothing of his gipsy look. He was of pallid complexion, blue-eyed, dark-haired, with features of the antique Roman pattern, until an accident grievously marred his facial symmetry, and brought about, it was observed, "a singular resemblance to the portraits of Michael Angelo." His figure was like Kean's in its spareness and muscularity; his neck and chest were "of ample but symmetrical mould; his step and movements elastic, assured, kingly."

This description of Booth is gathered from a work entitled "The Tragedian," published in New York in 1868—less a biography of the actor than a collection of essays upon his histrionic method—written "in grateful testimony to the rare delights his personations have afforded, and in the hope of giving body to the vision and language to the common sentiment of his appreciators." The author is Mr. Thomas R. Gould, a statuary by profession, it would seem, who prefixes to his volume a photograph of a marble bust he had sculptured of Mr. Booth. This portrait, while it represents a very noble head, encourages a high estimate of Mr. Gould's artistic skill. And it may here be added that Mr. Gould writes with great originality and force, if sometimes, in his desire to impress, he allows himself to be carried beyond the bounds of good taste, and by a certain extravagance of expression dissuades when he would attract, and prompts the doubts he is most anxious to dispel. It is, indeed, hardly possible for an English reader to accept Mr. Gould's valuation of Booth. Mr. Gould speaks as an eye-witness, and his acquaintance with his subject is not for a moment to be questioned. Few, however, can ever admit, implicitly, other evidence than their own in regard to the qualities of actors and acting. To be judged, the performer must be seen ; the best description can but furnish forth the most shadowy idea of his achievements ; and Mr. Gould, at times, so deals with his case as to shock credibility. Not content with affirming Booth to be a great actor, he would have him regarded as "the greatest of all actors." He continues: "Two names alone, in the history of the stage, may dispute his supremacy—David Garrick and Edmund Kean." Garrick is dismissed from consideration as "a tradition." The record of his histrionic power is meagre. He was hampered by conventionalism; he played in a tie-wig and knee-breeches. No satisfactory analysis of his method has reached us. He was best in comedy; his comic parts far outnumber his tragic. Altogether it must be concluded that his tragic acting, although a rare entertainment, did not touch the deepest springs of feeling; it was rather a skill than an inspiration. With regard to Kean, "nothing could be farther from the truth" than to suppose that it was upon his acting Booth formed his style. It is admitted that the two actors were alike in height and figure. "In temperament, also, there was a partial similarity—both being distinguished by passionate energy and by daring to displace the prescriptive habits of the stage by the action and the tones of nature." But Kean "lacked imagination." Mr. Gould does not write from knowledge of Kean at first hand, and founds his view of him upon Hazlitt's "English Stage." Now Booth, it is asserted, possessed imagination "of a subtle kind, and in magnificent measure. It lent a weird expressiveness to his voice. It atmosphered his most terrific performances with beauty. Booth took up Kean at his best, and carried him farther. Booth was Kean, plus the higher imagination." The impression left by Kean on the minds of his reviewers and biographers records his "mighty grasp and overwhelming energy in partial scenes;" while Booth is remembered "for his sustained and all-related conception of character." Kean took just those words and lines and points and passages in the character he was to represent which he found suited to his genius, and delivered them with electric force. "His method was limitary. It was analytic and passionate, not in the highest sense intellectual and imaginative." To see Booth in his best mood was not like reading Shakespeare by flashes of lightning, "in which a blinding glare alternates with the fearful suspense of darkness ; but rather like reading him by the sunlight of a summer's day, a light which casts deep shadows, gives play to glorious harmonies of colour, and shows all objects in vivid light and true relation."

While thus according to Booth the gift of supreme histrionic power, however, Mr. Gould would not imply that his performances were faultless. He may have been matched by others, and haply surpassed in all secondary histrionic qualities, with the exception of voice ; "he holding, beyond rivalry, the single, controlling quality of a penetrating, kindling, shaping imagination." He was, perhaps, "the most unequal of all great actors." To casual observers, therefore, he often seemed to fall short of his great reputation. "During the forty years, save one, which bounded his dramatic career, Mr. Booth's habit of life, both on the farm and on the stage, was exemplarily temperate." His reverence for the sacredness of all life amounted to a superstition. He abstained for many years, on principle, from the use of animal food. But he was subject to an extravagant and erring spirit allied to madness, which sometimes induced him to depart from the theatre at the very time fixed for his performance; whereupon the disappointed audience not unnaturally explained his conduct by ascribing it to intoxication. It is confessed, indeed, with grief and pity, that the baser charge was often true, and that the actor sometimes relieved, "by means questionable, pitiful, pardonable," the exhaustion attendant upon his great exertions. Something by way of further apology for the actor might have been urged touching the habits of intemperance which prevailed generally a generation ago—it was not only the actors who drank deep in the days of Edmund Kean.

Famous and prosperous as Mr. Booth became in America, it is admitted that he was never "the literary fashion." He arrived in the States unheralded, unknown, unprovided with letters; he was obliged to introduce himself to the manager of the Richmond Theatre, to

secure a first appearance upon the American stage. He
proceeded to Boston, and there played *Octavian*, in
"The Mountaineers," to a very poor house. "But the
fire took; and the next day the town was ablaze with
interest in the new tragedian—an interest that scarcely
flagged during the following thirty years." It was his
wont to avoid listless and fashionable audiences, "with
the blue blood sleeping in their veins," and to play at
second-rate theatres, assured of that fulness and heartiness of popular appreciation which he found infinitely
preferable to the "cool approval of scholars." Certain
eccentricities he has been credited with, although of
these Mr. Gould says no word. It is understood that he
was accustomed to play *Oroonoko* with bare feet, insisting
upon the absurdity of putting shoes upon a slave. At
Philadelphia he appeared as *Richard*, mounted on a real
White Surrey, thus reducing the tragedy to the level of an
"equestrian drama." Some minor notes of his histrionic
method are worth recording. His articulation was distinct to excess; he was accustomed to pronounce
"ocean" (in Richard's first soliloquy) as a word of three
syllables. His "hand play," or "manual eloquence," is
described as singularly beautiful. Mr. Gould, referring
to his performance of *Sir Edward Mortimer* ("The Iron
Chest")—the last part in which the actor ever appeared
—speaks admiringly of the motion of his hands "towards those heart-wounds—

' Too tender e'en for tenderness to touch ; '

the creeping, trembling play of his pale, thin fingers over his maddening brain ; and his action when describing the assassination." "No actor we have ever seen," writes Mr. Gould, "seemed to have such control over the vital and involuntary functions. He would tremble from head to foot, or tremble in one outstretched arm to the finger-tips, while holding it in the firm grasp of the other hand. . . . The veins of his corded and magnificent neck would swell, and the whole throat and face become suffused with crimson in a moment in the crisis of passion, to be succeeded on the ebb of feeling by an ashy paleness. To throw the blood into the face is a comparatively easy feat for a sanguine man by simply holding the breath ; but for a man of pale complexion to speak passionate and thrilling words pending the suffusion, is quite another thing. On the other hand, it must be observed that no amount of merely physical exertion or exercise of voice could bring colour into that pale, proud, intellectual face. This was abundantly shown in *Shylock*, in *Lear*, in *Hamlet*, where the passion was intense, but where the face continued clear and pale. . . . In a word, he commanded his own pulses, as well as the pulses of his auditors, with despotic ease."

Mr. Gould devotes a distinct essay to each of Booth's impersonations, but we may not closely follow the author throughout his critical labours. He describes the

feats and accomplishments of his favourite actor with
much minuteness, finding reason for applause in almost
every particular.   Yet he writes so vivaciously, so intelli-
gently, and withal seems to be so thoroughly in earnest,
that his book rarely ceases to be interesting, and, indeed,
instructive.   *Hamlet*, we learn, was Booth's favourite
part, and special mention is made of a performance at
the Howard Athenæum, Boston, towards the close of the
actor's career.   The nobility of his profile had been
destroyed by the accidental injuries he had received ;
but the beauty of his voice, at one time gravely affected
by this mischance, was now completely restored.   He
wore no wig, and his hair had turned to an iron-grey
hue ; he had no special help from costume or scenery, or
from his fellow-players.   The audience was fit though
few ; but "it was a noteworthy fact, however it might be
accounted for, that Mr. Booth invariably seemed to play
better to a thin house."   And never did the soul of
Hamlet shine forth more clearly "with its own peculiar,
fitful, far-reaching, saddened, and supernatural life," than
on this particular occasion.   We do not find, however, that
Mr. Booth's *Hamlet* was very unlike other *Hamlets*,
except in so far as the physical ‸qualities of the actor
differed from those of other representatives of the part.
Mr. Gould speaks with surprise of the applause awarded
to the *Hamlet* of " that sensible but unimaginative actor
Macready," who, in one scene of the play, "seemed to

change natures with Osric, the waterfly, and to dance before the footlights, flirting a white handkerchief over his head." Mr. Rufus Choate, comparing Kean and Booth in *Hamlet*, said, "This man (Booth) has finer touches." A strange reading may be noted. Mr. Booth read the line, "With a bare bodkin who would fardels fear," as we have printed it, after an unpunctuated fashion, affirming that "bodkin" was a local term in some parts of England for a padded yoke to support burdens on either side ; and that a "bare bodkin" was a yoke without the pad, and therefore galling. Mr. Gould observes simply, "The meaning assigned has, we believe, escaped the notice of all lexicographers." It is mentioned that in the year 1831 Booth, being the temporary manager of a theatre in Baltimore, supported the *Hamlet* of Mr. Charles Kean by assuming the part of *Lucianus*, or "the second actor," whose function in the play is to deliver the brief speech beginning, "Thoughts black, hands apt, drugs fit," etc. Says Mr. Gould : "In Booth's delivery of these fearful lines, each word dropped poison. The weird music of his voice, and the stealthy yet decisive action, made this brief scene the memorable event of the night"—which is not saying much for the *Hamlet* of Mr. Charles Kean.

Booth's conception of the character of *Shylock* was, it seems, influenced by "the Hebrew blood which, from some remote ancestor, mingled in the current of his life, was evidently traceable in his features, and, haply, determined the family name—Booth, from Beth, Hebrew for house or nest of birds." Booth's mind was deeply exercised by religious problems, by obstinate questionings of futurity and human destiny. "He passed into all religions with a certain humility and humanity, and with a certain Shakesperian impartiality. Among Jews he was counted a Jew. He was as familiar with the Koran as with the Hebrew Scriptures, and named a child of his after a wife of Mahomet. At other times, and in sympathy with his favourite poet, Shelley, he delighted to lose himself in the mysticism of the faiths of India." It was Kean's fancy, the reader will remember, to join a tribe of Hurons, to wear the strange dress, including war-paint, of a Red Indian chief, and to assume the striking name of " Alantenaida."

The last scene of Booth's *Othello* is described as "full of fate." He entered with an Eastern lamp, lighted, in one hand, and a drawn scimitar in the other. "The oriental subjective mood had obtained full possession of him. The supposed 'proofs' had sunk into his mind, and resolved themselves into a fearful unity of thought and purpose. . . . The expression of constrained energy in his movements—the large, low-toned, vibrant rumination of his voice, sounding like thought overhead—filled the scene with an atmosphere at once oppressive and fascinating." When he spoke of "the very error of the moon," his gesture seemed to figure the faith of the Chaldean, and to bring the moon "more near the earth than she was wont." " 'Roderigo killed !' (with wonder), 'and Cassio killed !' (glutting the words in his throat)." The lines that follow he delivered with burning intensity. His speech over his dead wife seemed the ultimate reach of blended grief and love and wild, remorseful passion of which the human voice is capable. At the summons, "Bring him away!" and as he was beginning his final speech, he took a silken robe, and carelessly threw it over his shoulder ; then reached for his turban, possessing himself of a dagger he had concealed therein. He uttered the word "pearl," as though it were indeed "the immediate jewel of his soul," his wife, with a lingering fulness and tenderness of emphasis, and with a gesture as if in the act of throwing it away he cast his own life from him.

Booth's *Iago* was not as Kean's, "a gay, light-hearted monster—a careless, cordial, comfortable villain ; " so Hazlitt wrote of it. Booth gave quite another version. His conception was saturnine ; the expression of it strangely swift and brilliant. "He showed the dense force, the stealth, the velvet-footed grace of the panther ; the subtlety, the fascination, the rapid stroke of the fanged serpent. His performances of this part did not vary much. Whatever difference might be discovered arose from the greater or less intensity of the representation." He came on the stage as though "possessed by his most splendid devil." The voice he used was his "most sweet and audible, deep-revolving bass." His delivery of the text was a masterpiece of colloquial style. It [had all the abrupt turns, the tones of nature, the un-expectedness, and the occasional persuasive force which belong to the best conversation. His address to Othello had "a fearful symmetry of falsehood." "He lied so like truth, that had we been in Othello's place we felt he would have deceived us too. . . . Yet was the odious-ness of Iago's nature lightened and carried off by the grace and force of Booth's representation."

Kean's *Macbeth*, according to Hazlitt, "was deficient in the poetry of the character—he did not look like a man who had encountered the weird sisters." Booth's performance, on the contrary, was "constituted by ima-gination, kindled and swayed by supernatural agencies." The dagger-speech was given "in volumed whispers—it was filled with fearful shadows." After the murder, when Lady Macbeth was gone to gild the faces of the grooms with Duncan's blood, and Macbeth, left alone, hears a knocking at the door, and delivers the lines beginning "Whence is that knocking?" Booth looked at his hands with starting eyes and a knotted horror in his features, the while he wiped one hand with the other from him with intensest loathing. "The words came like the weary dash on reef rocks, and as over sunken

wrecks and drowned men, of the despairing sea. . . .
He launched the mysterious power of his voice, like the
sudden rising of a mighty wind from some unknown
source, over those 'multitudinous seas,' and they swelled
and congregated dim and vast before the eye of the
mind. Then came the amazing word 'incarnadine,' each
syllable ringing like the stroke of a sword. The whole
passage was of unparalleled grandeur ; and in tone, look,
action, conveyed the impression of an infinite and unavailing remorse."

The success of Booth's *Lear*, as Mr. Gould is enabled
to show, dated so far back as his first assumption of the
part at Drury Lane in 1820. " We have seen Mr. Booth's
Lear, with great pleasure," writes Hazlitt, whom Mr.
Gould cites as an unwilling witness, for he went on to
say, " Mr. Kean's is a greater pleasure to come, as we
anticipate." Yet when Kean did play the part he disappointed his admirer, who even ventured to describe
the performance as a failure. Mr. Gould is entitled to
infer that Hazlitt preferred the *Lear* of Booth, and, seeing
that Booth's performance came first in order of time, the
question as to his imitating Kean, " a question first put
by prejudice, and since repeated by dulness," could not
be raised in regard to *King Lear*, at any rate. It is
suggested, indeed, that danger arose lest Kean should
be charged with imitating Booth, and was thus induced
to adopt a certain perverse reading, which Hazlitt has

duly noted.   It was as *Lear*, at the National Theatre, Boston, in 1835, that Mr. Gould saw Booth for the first time.   "The blue eye, the white beard, the nose in profile, keen as the curve of a falchion, the ringing utterances of the names ' Regan,' ' Goneril,' the close pent-up passion striving for expression, the kingly energy, the affecting recognition of Cordelia in the last act—made a deep impression on our boyish mind."   Mr. Gould admits that he witnessed with a certain pleasure Mr. Macready's scholastic performance of *Lear*—but it did not move him much.   "It was marred by the cold premeditation which marked all the efforts of that educated gentleman.   Marvellous as was the imitation of the signs of passion, we felt the absence of the pulse of life.   He was the intellectual showman of the character, not the character itself.   He never got inside.   Conception is a blessing not vouchsafed to actors of his school.   With Booth, the case was different"—then follows a high-flown account of the achievement of Mr. Gould's favourite actor in the part, concluding with—"in a word, the interior life of *Lear* came forth, and shone in the focal light of Mr. Booth's representation."

Booth's voice was a "most miraculous organ;" "it transcended music;" it was guided by a method which defied the set rules of elocution; it brought "airs from heaven and blasts from hell;" but it was marked by one significant limitation—it had no mirth—there were tones of light, but none of levity. Yet, now and then, on such occasions as his benefit, Mr. Booth appeared in farce, as *Jerry Sneak* and *Geoffrey Muffincap*. But his farce was simply the negation of his tragedy. "The sunny blue eye, the genial smile, the pleasantry we found so winning in social intercourse, never appeared upon the stage." He could not be comic. "His genius, and the voice it swayed, were solely dedicated to tragedy." Garrick danced; Kean danced and sang exquisitely; Booth could neither dance nor sing. A certain comic song he did attempt at times, by way of enlivening his perform- ance in farce ; but it was simply "a grotesque jingle, scorning melody, and depending for its success on odd turns of expression, verbal and vocal." He was, in truth, to Mr. Gould's thinking, always the Tragedian. Yet was his art "unremovably coupled to nature." The term "theatrical" could never be justly applied to him. "Nature was the deep source of his power, and she imparted her own perpetual freshness to his personations. We could not tire of him any more than we tire of her. His art was, in a high sense, as natural as the bend of Niagara, as the poise and drift of summer clouds, the play of lightning, the play of children, or as the sea, storm-tossed, sunlit, moonlit, or brooded in mysterious calm—and his art awakened in the observer correspond- ing emotions."

Mr. Gould's book is altogether a curious and interesting memorial of the actor, but it necessarily is an incomplete reply to the question touching Booth's histrionic merits. To Mr. Gould he was very great indeed; but how far is that conclusive? The honesty of Mr. Gould's convictions is not to be impugned; his book abounds in force and ingenuity; but is his judgment to be trusted? It is possible that Booth, an imitator in his youth, developed originality in his maturity, and really deserved to rank at last among the great actors of his time, as indeed he was ranked generally in America. But, on the other hand, conventionality and plagiarism in dramatic matters were less likely to be recognized in America than in this country. Actors of note had visited the States from time to time before the arrival of Booth; but the American playgoers were scarcely familiar with acting of the highest class—were, perhaps, likely to be content with inferior histrionic displays. In any case, Mr. Gould has done good service to the memory of Booth. He has placed upon record the high estimation in which the actor was held by the American public; for, without doubt, the essayist speaks on behalf of a large majority of his countrymen. And we may deduce from the matter the rather commonplace moral, that unanimity of opinion is a rare thing, in regard to the transactions of the theatre not less than in relation to other subjects. Even when jurymen agree upon their verdict, it must be understood that oftentimes there has been real sacrifice of preference or conviction—some yielding to coercion for the sake of concord, quiet, and escape from the box. When Kean said, "The pit rose at me," he did not mean, absolutely, that none of the audience kept their seats. Be sure there were dissentients, who did not join in the chorus of enthusiastic applause—who sat unmoved, perhaps unsatisfied, preferring acting of another kind and school to that exhibited by the new performer. There is always a minority—an opposition. As the proverb tells us, the meat of one is the poison of another. So a man may be at once idolized and scorned—to these a tragedian, to those a buffoon or a blockhead. And there can be no distinct right or wrong in such matters.

CHAPTER IV.

MISS SMITHSON.

SOME fifty years ago, when there raged in Paris furious war between Romanticists and Classicists, the arrival of an English troop of actors engaged to represent Shakesperian plays at the Odéon Theatre occasioned very great excitement. The new-comers were received with enthusiasm by one of the contending factions, at any rate. Shakespeare, of whom, until then, the Parisian public knew very little indeed, was warmly welcomed; not so much because he was Shakespeare, however, but in that he was accounted a Romanticist—a departed leader of the school of which Victor Hugo, Alexandre Dumas, and Alfred de Vigny were recognized as the living representatives and champions. The success of Shakespeare was unquestionable; it was only surpassed by the curious triumph enjoyed by one of his interpreters. This was not Edmund Kean, nor Macready, nor Charles Kemble; but a young lady of rather small fame as an actress, whose appearances upon the

London stage had been ineffective enough, and whose
merits generally had been held but cheaply in her own
country. For a time "la belle Smidson," as they called
her, was the absolute idol of the Parisians. Mr. Abbott,
actor and manager, who had brought the company across
the Channel, confessed with some amazement that his
" walking lady " had proved the " best card in his pack."
" Jamais en France aucun artiste dramatique n'émut, ne
ravit, n'exalta le public autant qu'elle ; jamais dithy-
rambes de la presse n'égalèrent ceux que les journaux
français publièrent en son honneur." So wrote concerning the lady Hector Berlioz, destined at a later period to
become her husband.

Harriet—she was known in France as Henriette—
Constance Smithson was born in 1800, at Ennis, County
Clare. Her parents were English, William Joseph
Smithson, her father, claiming to be of a Gloucestershire
family. He had been for many years a travelling
manager in Ireland, however, the theatres on the Waterford and Kilkenny circuit coming in turn under his
direction. His health failing him, he urged his daughter,
in her own interest, to adopt the profession of the stage.
She had been disinclined to take this step. Strictly
brought up under the eye of the Rev. Dr. Barrett, of
Ennis, and afterwards at Mrs. Tounier's school at Waterford, she had imbibed no theatrical tastes ; had, indeed,
it is said, expressed herself " averse even to witnessing

dramatic exhibitions." She duly overcame her scruples, however, and Lord and Lady Castle-Coote appearing as her friends and patrons, she readily obtained an engagement from Jones, the patentee of the Dublin Theatre Royal, to whom John Wilson Croker in 1806 had addressed his acrimonious " Familiar Epistles." She made her first appearance " upon any stage " as *Albina Mandeville*, in Reynolds's comedy of " The Will," a character originally represented by Mrs. Jordan. Her success was considerable. She afterwards played *Lady Teazle*, fulfilled engagements at the Belfast, Cork, and Limerick theatres, and returned to Dublin to represent *Cora, Mrs. Haller, Yarico, Lady Contest*, etc. In 1817 she came to England, appearing at the Birmingham Theatre, then under the management of Elliston. In the following year the committee managing Drury Lane Theatre graciously allowed Miss Smithson " to see what she could do;" and accordingly, as *Letitia Hardy*, in " The Belle's Stratagem," she made her first curtsy to a London audience. The theatre was in a most embarrassed state; the exchequer was empty, the managers deeply involved in debt. Nevertheless, it was decided that no orders should be issued; the new actress could not provide even her nearest relatives with free admissions. Poor Mrs. Smithson paid her money at the door in the customary way, although she came to witness the *début* of her daughter.

It cannot be said that Miss Smithson's first efforts in London stirred much enthusiasm. The critics were certainly calm on the subject. It was noticed that the lady was tall, well-formed, handsome of countenance; that her voice was rather distinct than powerful; that her style of singing was more remarkable for humour than sweetness; that she rather overacted the broadly comic scenes, which nevertheless she "conceived and executed with spirit;" and that in the minuet de la cour "her fine figure and graceful movements were displayed to advantage." She played some few other parts in the course of the season: *Lady Racket*, in "Three Weeks after Marriage;" *Eliza*, in the comedy of "The Jew;" and *Diana Vernon*, in Soane's bungling adaptation of "Rob Roy," which represents Helen Macgregor as Rob's mother, not his wife, and destroys her suddenly by a flash of lightning, so that no obstacle may exist to the chieftain's lawful union with his true love Diana Vernon!

Miss Smithson's success had not been great; still, she had not failed. She was engaged for the following season, when the theatre opened at reduced prices under the rather inglorious management of Stephen Kemble. The characters she sustained, however, were of an inferior kind: *Julia*, in "The Way to get Married;" *Mary*, in "The Innkeeper's Daughter;" *Eugenia*, in a melodrama called "Sigesmar the Switzer;" *Lilian*, in the farce of "Wanted a Wife;" and *Jella*, in the drama of "The Jew of Lubeck." The season closed prematurely, and Miss Smithson returned to Dublin, to reappear in the winter at the newly opened Coburg Theatre, known in later times as the Victoria. During Elliston's first season at Drury Lane Miss Smithson had no engagement, but she rejoined the company in 1820, appearing as *Rosalie Somers* in the comedy of "Town and Country." Among other characters, she also represented *Maria* in "The Wild-goose Chase," *Rhoda* in "Mother and Son," *Lavinia* in "The Spectre Bridegroom," *Adolphine* in "Monsieur Tonson," and for her benefit *Lydia Languish* in "The Rivals," and *Ellen* in the Scottish melodrama of "The Falls of Clyde." As *Ellen* she seems indeed for the first time to have impressed her audience. The critic of the *Morning Herald* assured the public that Miss Smithson's performance of this character left the imagination nothing to desire. Her voice was described as "exquisitely susceptible of those tremulous and thrilling tones which give to the expression of grief and tenderness an irresistible charm." The critic continued : "Every scene, every situation, and indeed every point, told upon the audience with unerring force and effect. The talents of this young lady are not even yet fully appreciated, for they are not fully developed. We should wish to see her in some of those characters in what is called youthful tragedy, where the graces of youth are no less essential than talent for complete illusion and identity with the part." In the following season Miss Smithson was entrusted with more ambitious duties. She appeared as *Lady Anne, Desdemona,* and *Constantia* to Edmund Kean's *Richard, Othello,* and *Sir Pertinax,* undertaking also the less important characters of *Georgiana* in " Folly as it Flies," and *Lady Rakewell* in " Maid or Wife." Her further advance was no doubt rendered difficult because of the positions occupied in the theatre by Miss Foote, Miss Kelly, Mrs. West, Mrs. Bunn, and others. The company was strong; for every prominent character there seemed several candidates. In the season of 1823–4, Miss Smithson appeared as *Lady Hotspur*, with Wallack as *Hotspur*, Dowton as *Falstaff*, and Elliston as the *Prince of Wales.* She played also the parts of *Louisa* in " The Dramatist," *Isabella* in " The Wonder," *Margaret* to the *Sir Giles* of Kean, *Miss Wooburn* in " Every One has his Fault," and *Anne Bullen* in a revival of " Henry VIII.," with Macready as *Wolsey*, and Mrs. Bunn as *Queen Katherine.* She continued a member of the company during the three following years. But she seemed to be subsiding into the condition of a useful and respectable actress, from whom distinguished achievements were not to be expected. A critic of the time, while extolling the lady's beauty, alleged that " her excellence did not travel far beyond that point." He complained that her acting had not improved, and that " the cold precision of her utter-

ance and demeanour was entirely at variance with
nature." She was assigned characters in the melodramas
of " Thérèse," " Valentine and Orson," " Oberon," " The
Blind Boy," " Turkish Lovers," and " Henri Quatre."
She played *Blanche* in " King John," and " The Fatal
Dowry," with Macready as the *King* and *Romont.* She
appeared also in Colley Grattan's tragedy of " Ben
Nazir," upon which Kean's broken health and ignorance
of his part brought complete ruin. She was probably
seen for the last time upon the English stage in June,
1827, when, on the occasion of her benefit, she personated *Helen* in " The Iron Chest," with Kean as *Sir
Edward Mortimer.*

If London was apathetic or critical, Paris was abundantly enthusiastic about Miss Smithson. At Drury
Lane she had been reproached because of her Irish
accent: this was not observed at the Odéon. Indeed,
the distinct articulateness of Irish speech may have been
of advantage to her histrionic efforts in Paris, or was at
any rate a matter of indifference to auditors who probably for the most part knew little of the English
language, and were content to admire simply the actress's
beauty of face and grace of movement. A lady writes
of her : " Her personal appearance had been so much
improved by the judicious selection of a first-rate *modiste*
and a fashionable *corsetière*, that she was soon converted
into one of the most splendid women in Paris, with an

air *distingué* that commanded the admiration and the tears of thousands. . . . I had remembered her in Ireland and in England, but, as I now looked at her, it struck me that not one of Ovid's fabled metamorphoses exceeded Miss Smithson's real Parisian one." Before appearing in Paris she had played for some nights at the little theatre of Boulogne-sur-Mer, under the management of her brother. The "Honeymoon" had been produced, and the favourite melodrama of "The Falls of Clyde." She had sustained the character of *Juliana*, with James Wallack as the *Duke Aranza*.

In Paris she triumphed as *Juliet*, as *Ophelia*, and as *Jane Shore;* she secured, indeed, a run of twenty-five nights for Rowe's dismal tragedy. The distresses of its heroine were clearly intelligible to auditors who but imperfectly understood her language. Macready, in reference to the telling effect upon theatrical spectators of an exhibition of physical suffering, writes in 1856 : " Even in Paris, where Parisian taste was purer in dramatic matters than (as I hear) it now is, I recollect when Miss Smithson, as *Jane Shore*, uttered the line, ' I have not tasted food these three long days,' a deep murmur, perfectly audible, ran through the house—*Oh, mon Dieu !*" In regard to her performance of *Virginia* in Knowles's tragedy of Virginius," a French critic wrote : " On m'a dit que Miss Smithson a été admirable au moment de l'agonie dans la lutte de l'honneur contre

l'amour de la vie : je n'en ai rien vu ; il y avait déjà
quelques instants que je ne pouvais plus regarder." Her
benefit night was the occasion of wonderful excitement.
The house overflowed ; crowds were unable to obtain
admission.   Charles X. presented her with a purse of
gold; from the Duchesse de Berri she received a magnificent vase of Sèvres china.   She was called and recalled
before the curtain ; the stage was quite carpeted with the
bouquets and wreaths thrown to her by the enthusiastic
audience.

Hector Berlioz has recorded in his Memoirs the
extraordinary effect upon him of the Shakespearian
representations at the Odéon, and the appearance of
"la belle Smidson" as *Ophelia* and *Juliet.*   In these
events he found at once revelation and inspiration.
"Shakespeare," he writes, "en tombant ainsi sur moi à
l'improviste me foudroya.   Son éclair, en m'ouvrant le
ciel de l'art avec un fracas sublime, m'en illumina les
plus lointaines profondeurs.   Je reconnus la vraie grandeur, la vraie beauté, la vraie vérité dramatiques. . . .
Je vis, je compris, je sentis que j'étais vivant et qu'il
fallait me lever et marcher."   But the shock apparently
had been too great for him.   A profound melancholy
took possession of him.   He fell into a strangely nervous
condition.   He could not work ; he could not rest; sleep
was denied him.   He could do nothing but wander
aimlessly about Paris and its environs.   He avoided

his home; his old tastes, and studies, and habits of life became hateful to him. When from sheer exhaustion, after long periods of suffering, he was permitted to sleep, it seemed as though he could not waken again; or he rather swooned than slept now in the open fields of Ville-Juif or Sceaux; now in the snow, upon the banks of the frozen Seine, near Neuilly; and now upon one of the marble tables of the Café du Cardinal at the corner of the Boulevards des Italiens and the Rue Richelieu, where he remained motionless for five hours together, greatly to the alarm of the waiters, who dared not approach him lest they should find him a corpse.

All this time, as he confesses, he did not know a word of English. He contemplated Shakespeare only through "les brouillards de la traduction de Letourneur," and was conscious of the severe loss he suffered in this respect. Some satisfaction he found, however "Le jeu des acteurs, celui de l'actrice surtout, la suc cession des scènes, la pantomime et l'accent des voix, signifiaient pour moi davantage et m'imprégnaient des idées et des passions shakespeariennes mille fois plus que les mots de ma pâle et infidèle traduction." It soon became clear, however, that if he loved Shakespeare much, he loved more Miss Smithson, "l'artiste inspirée dont tout Paris délirait." Some months he passed in a kind of "abrutissement désespéré," dreaming always of the poet and the actress, but crushed by the com-

parison of her brilliant fame with his own miserable
obscurity.

Born in 1803, the son of a doctor, Hector Berlioz
had been educated for the medical profession. Greatly
to the annoyance of his parents, however, he deserted
medicine for music. He studied composition under
Lesueur and Reicha, of the Conservatoire. His father
denied him all pecuniary assistance ; he was reduced to
extreme poverty. He dined upon dry bread and prunes,
raisins, or dates ; daily he took his station upon the
Pont Neuf at the foot of Henry IV.'s statue : "là,
sans penser à la poule au pot que le bon roi avait rêvée
pour le dîner du dimanche de ses paysans, je faisais mon
frugal repas en regardant au loin le soleil descendre
derrière le mont Valérien." He applied for a situation
in the orchestra of the Théâtre des Nouveautés : he
could play the flute. But there was no vacancy for
a flute-player, so he entered the chorus 'at a monthly
salary of fifty francs. He gave lessons ; he composed a
mass which was duly executed at the churches of Saint
Roch and Saint Eustache ; he commenced an opera
which he never completed, founded upon the drama of
" Béverley, ou le Joueur," an adaptation of the English
tragedy of " The Gamester." He composed, too, a
cantata, " Orphée déchiré par les Bacchantes," which
a musical committee, consisting of Cherubini, Paër, Lesueur, Berton, Boieldieu, and Catel declared *inexécutable.*

He wrote musical criticisms in " La Quotidienne" and
"La Revue Européenne." Certain of his later compositions obtained for him the first and second prizes of
the Institute.

As yet, however, he was assuredly little known to
fame, and Miss Smithson might well be excused for her
ignorance even of the existence of her passionate adorer.
His love did not diminish; if for a time he emerged
from his state of gloomy inaction and wretched de-
spondency, it was only to plunge into it anew. He was
wholly without hope. He avoided the English theatre ;
he turned away his eyes as he passed the print-shops,
lest he should see a portrait of Miss Smithson—her
portraits abounded in Paris just then. Nevertheless,
he wrote to her letter after letter. No reply came to
him. As he learnt afterwards, the lady had been rather
frightened by the fervour of his expressions, and had
instructed her maid to bring her no more of his letters.
The English performances were drawing to a close ;
Miss Smithson's last nights were announced. He writes :
" Je veux lui montrer, dis-je, que moi aussi je suis
peintre !" For the benefit of the French actor Huet,
two acts of " Romeo and Juliet " were to be represented
at the Opéra Comique. Berlioz applied to the manager
for permission to add to the programme an overture of
his own composition. At last, then, it seemed that the
worshipper and the idol were to be brought together.

He has described the situation : "Au moment où j'entrai,
Roméo éperdu emportait Juliette dans ses bras. Mon
regard tomba involontairement sur le groupe shake-
spearien. Je poussai un cri et m'enfuis en me tordant
les mains. Juliette m'avait aperçu et entendu . . . je
lui fis peur! En me désignant, elle pria les acteurs qui
étaient en scène avec elle de faire attention à ce gentleman *dont les yeux n'annonçaient rien de bon.*" To the
overture, when the time came for its execution, Miss
Smithson paid no heed whatever. It was to her a thing
of the slightest consequence ; she was not in the least
curious concerning it or its composer. In a day or two
she was quitting Paris, with the other members of the
company, to fulfil an engagement at Amsterdam. By
chance, as he states, Berlioz had taken apartments in
the Rue Richelieu. Miss Smithson had been living
opposite, at the corner of the Rue Neuve Saint Marc.
Mechanically he approached his window, after having
been for many hours stretched upon his bed exhausted,
wretched, "brisé, mourant." It was his cruel fate to see
the lady enter her carriage and depart. "Il est bien
difficile," he writes, "de décrire une souffrance pareille
à celle que je ressentis ; cet arrachement de cœur, cet
isolement affreux, ces milles tortures qui circulent dans
les veines avec un sang glacé de dégoût de vivre et
cette impossibilité de mourir," etc. For a time he
ceased to compose ; his intelligence seemed to diminish

as his sensibility increased; he could do nothing but suffer. But soon Ulysses began to console himself for the departure of Calypso. By way of violent distraction he gives way to an extravagant passion for a certain Mdlle. M——. He writes his "Faust" symphony, his "Tempest" fantasia, his "Sardanapalus" cantata. He gives concerts, he travels through France to Italy, he visits Nice, Florence, Rome, Naples. Two years elapse before he is again to see or to hear anything of Miss Smithson.

The English players meanwhile had fulfilled engagements in the chief towns of France. They had performed at Rouen and Havre, reappearing in Paris on their way to Orleans, Blois, and Bordeaux. Miss Smithson had obtained from Mr. Price, the manager of Drury Lane, permission to defer her return to his theatre: her success in France had been so prodigious. But it was now charged against the lady that she had become too conscious of her own merits; that, convinced of her powers of attraction, she demanded of Abbott, the manager, very exorbitant terms for her services, equal, it was said, indeed, to the combined salaries of the whole company. Serious disagreement ensued; in provincial France the English strollers suffered from lack of patronage. It became at last necessary to disband the company. The majority of the actors, in a somewhat necessitous condition, made their way back to

London as best they could. Poor Abbott died some years afterwards under distressing circumstances, neglected and forgotten, in America. Miss Smithson returned to Paris. Confident of the fidelity of her friends and devotees, she hoped to establish there a permanent English theatre. It was the moment also of Berlioz's reappearance in Paris; and, moved by an "impulsion secrète," he had secured lodgings in the house No. 1, Rue Neuve Saint Marc, formerly occupied by Miss Smithson. He found himself under the same roof with her. He had been wholly without tidings of her. He did not know whether she was in France or England, Scotland or America. Was not this curious unforeseen meeting an argument for belief in magnetic influences, secret affinities, "entraînements mystérieux du cœur?" He was now formally presented to the lady. She attended one of his concerts, at which was performed his monodrame of "Lelio," the second part of the "Episode de la Vie d'un Artiste," Bocage delivering, with great animation, the speeches contrived by the composer as expressions of his passion for the actress. She consented to become his wife, notwithstanding the remonstrances both of her own family and of his.

Poor Miss Smithson was completely ruined. Her theatre had failed; she had insufficiently taken into account the fickleness and the frivolity of her Parisian adorers. Shakespeare was no longer a novelty in Paris;

he had helped the Romanticists to triumph ; they needed him no more; indeed, he was rather in their way, his presence provoking inconvenient comparisons. The old idols have to be broken up from time to time to mac-adamize the roads along which new objects of devotion are to pass in triumph. "La belle Smidson" played to empty benches ; the receipts fell more and more ; it became necessary to close the theatre. The actress owed more than she could pay ; her means were exhausted. Then came a sad accident. Descending from a carriage at the door of her house, she slipped suddenly, taking a false step, and broke her leg just above the ankle. Two passers-by saved her from falling heavily upon the pavement, and carried her in a fainting state to her apartments. She was married to Hector Berlioz in the summer of 1833. It was a frugal marriage enough. The lady was still much in debt, and her professional career was for the present closed by reason of her accident. "De mon côté," wrote the gentleman, " j'avais pour tout bien trois cents francs que mon ami Gonnet m'avait prêtés, et j'étais de nouveau brouillé avec mes parents." He gallantly adds : "Mais elle était à moi; je défiais tout !"

To pay the bride's debts, a special representation took place at the Théâtre-Italien. The French players, to do them justice, had shown much kindness to their unfortunate English sister. Mdlle. Mars had generously proffered her purse, but this "la belle Smidson" was too proud to accept. Alexandre Dumas' famous play of "Antony" was presented, with Firmin and Madame Dorval in the chief characters; the fourth act of "Hamlet" was to follow, with a pianoforte solo, Weber's "Concert-Stück," by Liszt, and Berlioz's "Symphonie Fantastique," his "Sardanapalus," and overture to "Les Francs-Juges." The performance produced a sum of 7000 francs, which still left many serious claims upon the actress unsatisfied. And the evening had its disappointments. Madame Dorval had packed the house with her friends to secure herself a triumph : she apprehended a formidable party in favour of the English actress. "Antony" was received with enthusiasm; its heroine was called and recalled before the curtain. Poor Madame Berlioz had been less prudent. She had engaged no *claque.* Her *Ophelia* stirred no great applause; she was not called before the curtain. She had scarcely recovered from the effects of her accident; she had lost something of her old grace and freedom of movement. After kneeling, she rose with some difficulty, "en s'appuyant avec la main sur le plancher du théâtre. . . . Ce fut pour elle aussi une cruelle découverte. . . . Puis, quand, après la chute de la toile, elle vit que le public, ce public dont elle était l'idole autrefois, et qui, de plus, venait de décerner une ovation à Madame Dorval, ne la rappelait pas . . . quel affreux crève-cœur! Toutes les femmes et tous les artistes le comprendront. Pauvre Ophélia ! ton soleil déclinait . . . j'étais désolé." Berlioz was anxious for a second performance, so that his wife should secure "une éclatante revanche;" but English actors to support her could not be found in Paris, and it was felt that the help of amateurs, or her appearance in fragments of scenes, would be unavailing. The actress was seen no more upon the stage.

Little happiness attended her marriage. Berlioz shone as a passionate lover; in the tamer character of husband he was much less admirable. Then they were wretchedly poor; they underwent, indeed, cruel trials and privations. For many years they were weighed down by the load of debt Miss Smithson had incurred in her luckless theatrical speculations. Berlioz had no certain income; he depended upon the returns of his concerts, given sometimes upon so grand a scale that all possibility of profit seemed to be left out of the calculation. He honestly testifies to the moral support he received from his wife on these occasions. She furthered his enterprises in every possible way, although there seemed always likelihood of their involving the household in even deeper distress. He writes: "Mais ma femme elle-même m'y encouragea et se montra dès ce moment ce qu'elle a toujours été, ennemie des demi-mesures et des petits moyens, et dès que la gloire de l'artiste ou l'intérêt de l'art sont en question, brave devant la gêne

et la misère jusqu'à la témérité." Paganini generously
presented him with 20,000 francs. From the Government he received some 3000 francs for a requiem
originally designed for the victims of July, but executed
at the solemn service for General Damrémont and other
soldiers of France who had fallen under the walls of
Constantine. By his visits to Germany and Russia for
the performance of his orchestral compositions, Berlioz
profited considerably.

The merits and qualities of Berlioz as a composer
cannot here be conveniently discussed. In some sort
he was a musical Haydon, engaged in the production of
works of important design and dimensions, which his
countrymen did not prize, but rather derided; and
meantime he struggled hard and valiantly with indigence
and other trying conditions. He had Haydon's acrimony
in debate; he had Haydon's insolent scorn of rivals
and opponents; and he had something more than
Haydon's literary power, considerable as that was. But
Berlioz wrote with great acuteness and brilliancy; he
had all a French critic's wit, fire, fluency, and, it must be
added, recklessness. He founded the symphony-ode, he
was a great conductor, a master of orchestral effects,
inventive and original, if oftentimes vague, uncouth, and
tedious; most ingenious as to new combinations of
sound, finding occupation for more and more instru-
mentalists, for ever increasing the force of his band, and

thus rendering almost impracticable the performance of his works by the means and numbers usually available. He dearly loved a monster orchestra. Perhaps his happiest moment was when, after an Industrial Exposition in Paris, he conducted a musical festival with upwards of a thousand executants. Heine might well find in Berlioz's music something primæval and antediluvian, reminding him of leviathans and mammoths, extinct monsters of land and sea, fabulous beasts and fishes, and recalling Babylonian wonders, the hanging gardens of Semiramis, the sculptures of Nineveh, "et les audacieux édifices de Mizraim tels que nous en voyons sur les tableaux de l'Anglais Martin." In France Berlioz was judged to be deficient as a melodist: in truth, melodies are not absent from his scores, but are so cloaked and entangled in orchestral trappings and vestments that they escape unfelt and unappreciated. In Germany Berlioz was counted among the transcendentalists, arriving a little too soon, however, preceding Wagner, and preparing a harvest of honour and glory for him to reap. "For my part," wrote Schumann in 1838, "I understand Berlioz as clearly as the blue sky above me. . . . I think there is really a new time in music coming. It must come. Fifty years have worked great changes, and carried us on a good deal further." On the other hand, Berlioz himself declined to be associated with the musicians of modern Germany. "Je n'ai jamais songé," he writes, " ainsi qu'on l'a si follement prétendu en France, à faire de la musique *sans mélodie.* Cette école existe maintenant en Allemagne et je l'ai en horreur." He protested that he had always been careful to introduce "un vrai luxe mélodique" in all his compositions. People might contest the worth of his melodies, their distinction, novelty, charm, but to deny their existence was, he maintained, bad faith or ineptitude. Further, he protested that the dominant qualities of his music were "l'expression passionnée, l'ardeur intérieure, l'entraînement rhythmique et l'imprévu."

Some few of Berlioz's works find a place in our orchestral concerts, but the composer himself is little remembered in England. He was here in 1847, conductor of the Drury Lane orchestra, during Jullien's wild attempt to establish English opera upon an extravagant scale, with a fine orchestra, a strong chorus, an admirable company of singers—including Mr. Sims Reeves, Mr. Whitworth, Mr. Weiss, Madame Dorus-Gras, Miss Miran, and Miss Birch—but without a repertory. Berlioz estimated the nightly expenses at 10,000 francs. The receipts never reached this amount. The end, of course, was bankruptcy. And Berlioz was here again in 1853, when an Italian version of his opera " Benvenuto Cellini " was produced under his direction at Covent Garden, to fail ignominiously as it had failed before in Paris, and as his later opera, " Les Troyens," was to fail afterwards at the Lyrique. Against these disasters, however, he could count the successful production of his "Beatrice et Benedict," an operatic edition of "Much Ado about Nothing," at Weimar and Baden, in 1862, and he had at all times to console him the fervent admiration of his friend the Abbé Liszt.

Of the marriage of Hector Berlioz and Miss Smithson one son was born, Louis, who entered the navy, serving in the Anglo-French fleet sent to the Baltic during the war with Russia in 1855, but who pre-deceased his father some years. In 1840 the husband and wife separated by mutual consent, if it can be said that the lady was permitted any choice in the matter, and thenceforward they lived apart. M. Berlioz speaks "quelques mots sur les orages de mon intérieur." His wife, he alleges, was absurdly jealous, and on that account opposed his provincial tours and his foreign travels. He was often obliged in consequence to keep his plans secret, to steal from his house with his clothes and music, and to explain afterwards by letter the object of his departure. In truth, they had a wretched life together, and if originally the poor lady's distrust of her lord was without just cause, this did not continue to be the case. M. Berlioz admits with cynical frankness, " Je ne partis pas seul; j'avais une compagne de voyage qui, depuis lors, m'a suivi dans mes diverses excursions. A force d'avoir été accusé, torturé de mille façons, et toujours injustement, ne trouvant plus de paix ni de repos chez moi, un hasard aidant, je finis par prendre les bénéfices d'une position dont je n'avais que les charges, et ma vie fut complètement changée." At the same time he had the courage to profess that his affection for his wife had in no degree abated. He saw her frequently after their separation : she was even the dearer to him because of the infirm state of her health. For the last four years of her life she suffered severely from a paralytic seizure, which deprived her of all power of motion and of speech. A simple inscription marked her resting-place in the cemetery of Montmartre—" la face tournée vers le nord, vers l'Angleterre qu'elle ne voulut jamais revoir :"

"Henriette Constance Berlioz Smithson, née à Ennis, en Irlande, morte à Montmartre, le 3 Mars, 1854."

Jules Janin wrote of her in the *Journal des Débats*, kindly mindful of what so many had forgotten, the exquisite grace and beauty she had once possessed, the enthusiasm she had roused, her triumphs upon the stage. "Elles passent si vite et si cruellement, ces divinités de la fable ! Ils sont si frêles, ces frêles enfants du vieux Shakespeare et du vieux Corneille ! . . . Juliette est morte . . . Jetez des fleurs ! Jetez des fleurs !" Her husband expressed. his sorrow eloquently, lamenting especially his wife's ruined career, her accident, and the disappointment of her hopes ; her compulsory retirement and eclipsed fame ; the triumph of her imitators and inferiors. Something

he had to say, too, of "nos déchirements intérieurs; son inextinguible jalousie devenue fondée; notre séparation; la mort de tous ses parents: l'éloignement forcé de son fils; mes fréquents et longs voyages; sa douleur fière d'être pour moi la cause de dépenses sous lesquelles j'étais toujours, elle ne l'ignorait pas, prêt à succomber; l'idée fausse qu'elle avait de s'être, par son amour pour la France, aliéné les affections du public anglais; son cœur brisé; sa beauté disparue; sa santé détruite; ses douleurs physiques croissantes; la perte du mouvement et de la parole, son impossibilité de se faire comprendre d'aucune façon; sa longue perspective de la mort et de l'oubli."
. . . Poor Madame Berlioz! This is a long catalogue of sorrows. "Destruction, feux et tonnerres, sang et larmes," cries her husband, "mon cerveau se crispe dans mon crâne en songeant à ces horreurs!" and he calls aloud upon Shakespeare to come to his aid, believing that Shakespeare alone can duly comprehend and pity two unhappy artists: "s'aimant, et déchirés l'un par l'autre." The Abbé Liszt writes to him, proffering consolations, but rather of philosophy than of the Church: "Elle t'inspira, tu l'as aimée, tu l'as chantée: sa tâche était accomplie."

Poor Henriette! there is yet one more glimpse of her. Not even in the grave was tranquillity permitted her. Some two years later Hector Berlioz married again. "Je le devais," he wrote. At the end of eight years his second wife died suddenly of heart disease. He became possessed of a family vault in the larger cemetery of Montmartre, and it was thought necessary to disinter the remains of his first partner, and remove them to the new grave. It was like a scene in " Hamlet ; " but the bones disturbed were those of *Ophelia*, not of *Yorick*. When the widower arrived in the cemetery the gravedigger was already at work. The grave was open; the coffin of poor Henriette, hidden for ten years, was again exposed. It was whole ; but the lid had suffered much from the damp. M. Berlioz must tell the tale after his own fashion. "Alors l'ouvrier, au lieu de la tirer hors de terre, arracha les planches pourries qui se déchirent avec un bruit hideux en laissant voir le contenu du coffre. Le fossoyeur se baissa, prit entre ses deux mains la tête déjà détachée du tronc, la tête sans couronne et sans cheveux, hélas ! et décharnée, de la *poor Ophélia*, et la déposa dans une bière neuve préparée *ad hoc* sur le bord de la fosse. Puis se baissant une seconde fois, il souleva à grand'peine et prit entre ses bras le tronc sans tête et les membres, formant une masse noirâtre sur laquelle le linceul restait appliqué, et ressemblant à un bloc de poix enfermé dans un sac humide . . . avec un son mat . . . et une odeur. . . ." But enough has been quoted.

Berlioz died in 1869. When he was sixty-one he sought a third wife, and addressed a passionate offer of marriage to a lady five or six years his senior, whom he had loved in his boyhood, or even his infancy. She was now a widow, the mother of several children, if not, indeed, a grandmother. He prints in his "Mémoires" her letters rejecting his proposals. M. Weckerlin pronounces these letters of this "dame inconnue" "chefs-d'œuvre de style, de sentiment, de raison et de convenance." She sent her portrait, however, to her inconsolable suitor, to remind him of the realities of the present and to dispel the illusions of the past.

CHAPTER V.

"OLD FARREN."

EARLY in the century, a Quarterly Reviewer described scornfully the technical terms employed upon the French stage to denote distinct classes of impersonation. It seemed to him ridiculous that the players should be known as Pères Nobles, Jeunes Premiers, Financiers, Comiques, Utilités, Mères, Ingénues, Duègnes, or Soubrettes. "Each actor and actress," he wrote, "is obliged to make a selection of a particular *rôle*, from which they are forbidden afterwards to depart : . . . they are not permitted to extravagate into another walk. The *Père Noble* cannot become *Comique*, whatever be his vocation this way ; and the *Ingénuité* must not look to be the *Jeune Première*, whatever ambition she may feel for playing the heroine. . . . In the English theatre all this foolery would be impossible. We represent not *Jeunes Premières*, nor *Ingénuités*, but men and women with all their various and changeable feelings, humours, and passions. . . . The human character is equable

and unmixed on no spot of the globe except the stage
of the Théâtre Français : there man becomes a puppet,
and character is not the growth of nature, but of certain
learned conventions and regulations." In conclusion,
the Reviewer decided "this rigorous destination of parts"
to be "at once a cause, a consequence, and a proof of
the feebleness of the French drama."

There is something in this opinion corresponding
with the prejudice of the English footman in "Zeluco,"
who denounced the blue uniforms of the French infantry,
describing them as of "foolish appearance," and "fit
only for the blue horse or the artillery." And the
Reviewer is at fault as to his facts. Like technical
terms to those he reprobates as "foolery" have long
been employed in the English theatre. Our actors have
their "lines of business" as definitely marked out as
have their French brethren. Not long since Mr. Boucicault, an excellent authority upon such matters, fully
availed himself of professional titles when he adjudged
that a "first-class theatrical company should consist of :
A leading man, leading juvenile man, heavy man, first
old man, first low comedian, walking gentleman, second
old man and utility, second low comedian and character
actor, second walking gentleman and utility, leading
woman, leading juvenile woman, heavy woman, first old
woman, first chambermaid, walking lady, second old
woman and utility, second chambermaid and character

actress, second walking lady and utility walking lady."
What a list for the Quarterly Reviewer! And it is
further to be observed that our players are rarely disposed or permitted to run off their accustomed "lines of
business." One man in his time may, as the poet tells
us, play many parts; but if the man be a player, the
chances are that the parts he plays will closely resemble
each other. There may be promotion and development,
and the rising actor may mount from small to important
characters; but he ascends the same staircase, so to say.
The light comedian of twenty is usually found to be still
a light comedian at seventy: the Orlandos of the stage
rarely become its old Adams. The actresses who have
personated youthful heroines are apt to disregard the
flight of time and the burden of age, and to the last
shrink from the assumption of matronly or mature
characters—Juliets and Ophelias, as a rule, declining to
expand into Nurses or Gertrudes. And the actor who
in his youth has undertaken systematically to portray
senility finds himself eventually the thing he had merely
affected to be: nature overtaking his art, as it were,
and supplying him with real in lieu of painted wrinkles,
and bestowing upon him absolutely those piping tones
he had once but pretended to possess.

This histrionic conservatism is specially illustrated by
the career of the late William Farren, long fondly known
as " Old Farren " to the admiring playgoers of his time.

He is believed to have made his first appearance upon the stage at Plymouth when he was only nineteen years of age : he then played *Lovegold*, the hero of Fielding's comedy of "The Miser." From that time down to his final retirement from his profession in 1855, when he appeared for the last time as *Lord Ogleby* in a scene from "The Clandestine Marriage," the actor was employed in personating the aged, the doting, and the decrepit. From the point of view of his public he had been an old man for half a century.

Born about 1786, the son of a tragedian of rather mediocre ability, William Farren was educated at Dr. Barrow's school in Soho. An actor's children usually incline towards the paternal profession. Percy Farren, the elder brother of William, had made his first essay upon the stage at Weymouth in 1803. He believed himself a light comedian. It was possibly on this account that William, when the time came for his own first histrionic efforts, decided he would play old men, and thus avoid rivalry with his brother, lending him, indeed, useful support instead. Of Percy it is enough to say that he achieved little fame as a player, although as a stage manager, both in London and Dublin, he subsequently proved himself competent enough. William's success upon the stage was from the first quite of a triumphant sort. He appeared at Dublin, and remained for some years a member of Mr. Jones's company in that

capital, his merits attracting the attention of the Lord
Lieutenant, the Duke of Leinster, who strongly recommended the Drury Lane committee to engage the young
actor for their theatre.   Farren, however, had always
a lively sense of his own value; already he had declined
an invitation from the Haymarket management; he now
proposed terms to the Drury Lane committee which
they deemed excessive.   But the actor was in no hurry
to quit his many staunch friends in Dublin; he was wont
to say of himself at a later period that he was the only
" cock-salmon " in the market—the nickname of "cock-
salmon" clung to him through life—and could dictate
his own price.   Presently the directors yielded : they
were glad, indeed, to offer the terms they had before
rejected.   To their great mortification, however, they
found the services of the actor had been meanwhile
secured by Mr. Harris, the manager of the rival theatre.
Accordingly, at Covent Garden, on the 10th September,
1818, in the character of *Sir Peter Teazle*, William Farren
made his first appearance upon the London stage.   He
was assisted by the *Joseph Surface* of Young, the *Charles*
of Charles Kemble, the *Sir Oliver* of Terry, the *Crabtree*
of Blanchard, and the *Sir Benjamin* of Liston.   Miss
Brunton played *Lady Teazle;* Mrs. Gibbs, *Mrs. Candour;*
and Miss Foote, *Maria.*   Farren subsequently appeared
as *Lord Ogleby*, as *Sir Bashful Constant* in " The Way to
Keep Him," as *Sir Anthony Absolute*, as *Don Manuel* in

"She Would and She Would Not," *Sir Adam Contest, Sir Fretful Plagiary, Sir Andrew Aguecheek, Lord Chalkstone, Bayes,* etc. The new actor "drew great houses," says Genest. The playbills were headed, "Paramount Success of Mr. Farren." He remained at Covent Garden some ten seasons, appearing at the Haymarket during the summer months. In 1828 he transferred his services to Drury Lane, but this step involved a breach of contract and a lawsuit. The proprietors of Covent Garden brought an action against the offending actor, and recovered damages to the amount of £750.

Farren personated in turn all the most eminent elderly gentlemen of standard comedy and farce, occasionally undertaking characters of an eccentric kind that stood somewhat removed from that category. Among his Shakesperian parts, in addition to his *Sir Andrew Aguecheek,* were *Stephano, Polonius,* one of the *Witches* in "Macbeth," *Dromio of Ephesus, Shallow, Malvolio, Slender, Casca,* and *Dogberry.* He obtained great applause in the *Marrall* of Massinger, and the *Brainworm* of Ben Jonson; he played *Isaac of York, Nicol Jarvie, Sir Henry Lee,* and *Jonathan Oldbuck* in dramatic editions of the Waverley Novels; on his benefit nights he accomplished the Mathews' feat of personating both *Puff* and *Sir Fretful Plagiary,* or he even presumed to wear a woman's skirts, and appeared now as *Miss Harlow* in the comedy of "The Old Maid," and now as *Meg*

Merrilies in the operatic drama of "Guy Mannering."
He even attempted tragedy upon a special occasion, and
played *Shylock* to a dissatisfied audience at Birmingham.
He portrayed sundry historic characters, such as *Charles
XII. of Sweden, Oxenstiern, Matthew Hopkins, Henry IV.
of France, Pope Sixtus V.*, and *Frederick the Great;* in one
ingeniously constructed little play he "doubled," as the
actors call it, the parts of *Frederick* and *Voltaire;* he was
once in disgrace with the Lord Chamberlain for too
closely depicting the aspect and manner of Prince
Talleyrand; he represented *Izaak Walton* and *Old Parr,*
Goldsmith's *Dr. Primrose* and Addison's *Sir Roger de
Coverley.* He became a member of Madame Vestris's
company at the Olympic, and took part in numberless
dramatic trifles, one-act comedies, and interludes that
are now forgotten : more ambitious performances could
not then be presented upon the stage of a minor theatre.
From his preface to "The Hunchback," it may be
gathered that Sheridan Knowles had particularly designed the part of *Master Walter* for William Farren;
regret is expressed that the character "should have suffered from the loss of his masterly personation of the
part, for masterly it assuredly would have been." It
may be added that Farren was the original performer of
Lord Skindeep and *Old Goldthumb* in Douglas Jerrold's
comedies "Bubbles of the Day" and "Time Works
Wonders;" that Mr. Boucicault contrived for him *Sir*

Harcourt Courtly in "London Assurance," *Jesse Rural* in "Old Heads and Young Hearts," and sundry other characters; that he took part in Mrs. Gore's prize comedy of "Quid pro Quo," in various original plays of pretence by Lovell, Robert Bell, Sullivan, and others, and in many minor productions adapted from the French by Poole, Kenney, Bunn, Dance, and Planché, to name no more. Farren, indeed, pertained alike to the old stage and the new. He triumphed in the classical English comedies of the last century, the works of Sheridan, Congreve, Murphy, Farquhar, Vanbrugh, Goldsmith, Cibber, Centlivre, and Colman; and he achieved curious success in the plays of his own time, vying with the best French actors in his creation of character, his appreciation of detail, the minute finish of his performance, his taste in dress, and his skill in the art of "making up." His stage portraits were executed with English force and breadth, and yet with French subtlety and artistic finesse. He sustained in English adaptations many of the characters first represented by Bouffé, by Samson, and by Regnier upon the French stage; and it may be said that he could well afford comparison with those distinguished artists even in the parts they claimed to have made their own. He was well aware of his merits in this respect. Invited to witness certain of the impersonations of Bouffé, then fulfilling an engagement at the St. James's Theatre, Farren replied out of

the abundance of his self-admiration and confidence :
"No, sir; let him come and see me! Let Bouffé come
and see William Farren!"

Mr. G. H. Lewes, whose "Actors and the Art of
Acting" contains an interesting sketch of Farren, describes him as "a finished actor—whom nobody cared
about." Admitting that "during the memory of living
men no English actor has had the slightest pretension to
rank with this rare and accomplished comedian; " admitting that "everybody applauded him, everybody
admired his excellences, everybody was glad to find his
name on the bill;" Mr. Lewes asserts that "no one
went especially to see him; in theatrical phrase, 'he
never drew a house.'" This statement, however, must
not be accepted unconditionally. It is clear that from
an early period of his career Farren was a most attractive
actor, drawing "great houses," as Genest records ; he
was always able to dictate his own terms to his managers,
and to exact from them most liberal, even somewhat
excessive, rewards for his services. But as a representative of old age, as merely one of the constituents, and
not the most important, of standard comedy, Farren
could not hope to "star" as the tragedians starred who
carried *Hamlet, Romeo,* and *Richard* about with them,
in such wise taking by storm and occupying now this
stage and now that. The "sceptred pall" of Tragedy
needs few bearers ; but Comedy may not be supported

merely by one performer of eminence with the aid of *quatre ou cinq poupées.* Farren's proper place was the one he so long occupied on the London stage as an important member of a strong company. It is true, however, as Mr. Lewes suggests, that the parts represented by Farren "were not those which appeal to general sympathy." The choleric guardians, the testy fathers, the jealous husbands, the superannuated fops of comedy, obtain but a small measure of commiseration from the audience—invite, indeed, rather ridicule than respect. But there is injustice in the charge against Farren that "he had no geniality, he had no gaiety," although it may be true that he was less possessed of these qualities than certain of his contemporaries with whom he was often compared, but who could scarcely be viewed as his rivals. Macready, in his "Reminiscences," noting the engagement of Farren at Covent Garden in 1818—"a powerful addition to its great comic strength"—describes him as "an actor deservedly admired for his studious correctness and the passion of his comedies, though eclipsed by Munden and Dowton in the rich quality of humour." The humour of Farren was genuine enough, but it owned a certain subacid flavour; he could thoroughly amuse his audience by the drollery of his movements, manner, and facial expression, the while he was careful not to deviate from truth and nature; and he had a curious power of depicting passion, of lashing himself into an explosive frenzy that never failed to stir the house deeply, to rouse the heartiest enthusiasm. Of pathos he had less command, though certain of his performances brought tears to the eyes ; but he was pathetic not so much of his own motion as because of the affecting situations contrived by his dramatists, and because of the picturesque senility he had power to assume, his management of his voice, his command of his face. He could bear himself with dignity and even with elegance ; an air of distinction always attended him ; he seemed altogether instinct with the true spirit of high comedy. Looking back five and thirty years, he was, as I remember him at sixty, a very handsome old gentleman, with fine clean-cut features, a fresh complexion, keen clear china-blue eyes, expressive mobile brows, and what Mr. Lewes describes as "a wonderful hanging under lip," of much service to him in his exhibitions of character. His voice was firm and resonant ; he spoke after the *staccato* manner of the old stage ; his laugh was very pleasant. He dressed perfectly, avoiding all unseemly youthfulness of clothing, but ever "point-device" in his elderly accoutrements : he was at home and comfortable alike in the broad skirts, the huge cuffs, and the flowered waistcoats of the times of Anne and the earlier Georges, as in the bright-buttoned, blue swallowtails of the Regency. Heavy perukes or light bobwigs became him as his own white locks ; a pigtail seemed·

an appendage natural to his aspect; coloured watch-ribbons, heavily weighted with keys and seals, swung appropriately from his fob ; he assumed spectacles or plied his double glasses, he took snuff and waved his bandanna with admirable deftness; he was always a gentleman, if "a gentleman of the old school." Polite age had never a more adroit and complete stage representative. Altogether, an actor so gifted and ac-complished as Farren could afford to be less successful than Munden in setting the audience roaring by the extravagance of his drollery. It can be admitted, too, of Farren that he had not Dowton's air of natural cheeriness and benevolence, nor Blanchard's whimsicality, nor Fawcett's rugged fervour of manner, nor Liston's farcical breadth.

Contrasts are always popular ; and the early success of Farren no doubt owed something to the fact that he was really so young while affecting to be so old. People were not soon tired of marvelling at the difference between the true and the fictitious age of the performer. A poetic critic in 1822, after reciting that

> "Each day's experience confirms the truth
>   That old men, ofttimes, love to play the youth,"

proceeds :

> "But rarely do we find the young delight
>   In casting off activity and might,
>   To play the dotard, with his faltering knee
>   And palsied hand and shrill loquacity :

> To bow the head, and bid the manly throat
> Emit a tremulous and small still note,
> And hide the lustre of a fiery eye
> With the pale film of dull senility.
> But Farren has done this, so chastely true,
> That, whilst he lives, Lord Ogleby lives too !
> His would-be youthful gait, his sunken chest,
> His vacant smile, so faithfully exprest,
> His hollow cheek, nay, e'en his fingers, show
> The aged man and antiquated beau."

The actor's versatility is also insisted upon :

> " Yet he to passion's topmost heights can climb,
> Can touch the heart and make e'en farce sublime."

Great praise is awarded to his performance of *Love-gold* the miser, *Sir Peter Teazle, Frederick the Great, Item* in the comedy of "The Steward," and *Sir Andrew Aguecheek.* Of his impersonation of the *Foolish Knight* it is written :

> " In sooth, few men upon the stage can tickle us
> With such a sample of the true ridiculous :
> His antic capers—his affected grace,
> His braggart words and pilchard-looking face,
> Would put old Care and all his imps to flight,
> And call forth laughter from an anchorite."

Leigh Hunt, writing in 1830, confessed that in many characters Farren had "fairly conquered" him ; for "when we first saw him," the critic continues, "we could not endure the assumption of age by a young man, precisely because we relish so heartily the joyousness of youth in one whom we know to be old. . .

What an actor he will be when he grows old in good earnest if we only remain young-hearted enough to be merry with him!" Farren was at this time about forty-three, however.

Farren was assuredly an original actor, although unfriendly critics were wont to aver that he owed much of his histrionic method to the example of an old and obscure performer at one time appearing upon the Irish stage, one Fullam, of whom little is now known. Such a charge, however, is hardly worth serious consideration. Angularity of movement and sharpness of intonation were, it seems, common to both players, and both employed the same kind of grimace, curiously described as "a screwing of the proboscis partially on one side and partially up." Farren impressed his own strong individuality upon all the characters he represented, and owned certain of those personal habits or tricks of manner which are immediately recognizable and always remembered by the spectators, and from which no great actor has ever been free. A critic took the trouble to interlard a speech the actor was required to deliver, as *Sir Christopher Curry* in the play of "Inkle and Yarico," with notes of his peculiarities of manner: "Here stands [*a pause, and a nervous shaking of the head*] old Curry [*a twitch of the nose*], who never spoke [*more shaking of the head*] to a scoundrel [*here an extraordinary elevation of the eyebrows and nostrils*] without telling him [*a pause, accompanied by a kind of dissatisfied snuffle*] what he thought of him!" Mr. George Vandenhoff, in his "Dramatic Reminiscences," relates that Farren had a trick of monopolizing attention by addressing himself exclusively to the audience, fairly fronting them, but exhibiting only his profile to the actors engaged with him upon the scene. Resolved "to pay the old stager in his own coin," Vandenhoff, who in 1840, at Covent Garden, played *Lovewell* to Farren's *Lord Ogleby*, punished him by imitating him, and the two actors were thus to be seen ignoring the existence of each other, and, several yards apart, speaking alternately to the house. The dialogue thus independently given, notwithstanding Farren's animation of manner, fell very flat. Farren, disappointed and perplexed, grew nervous; he began to falter in the words of his part. "As his irritability increased, he turned towards me as if to inquire by a look what was the meaning of the insensibility of the audience." He became aware of the treachery of his young playfellow. "I heard his ominous sniff (a trick he had), I heard his gradually approaching step, I felt his hand upon my arm as he turned me towards him with the words of the text, which seemed peculiarly appropriate: 'What's the matter, Lovewell? thou seemest to have lost thy faculties;' and for the rest of the scene he never turned away from me, but, as a gentleman should do, kept his eyes on the person to whom he was speaking. I did the same, the *vraisemblance* ot the scene was restored, and all went right. . . . He never gave me his side-front after that night, and we always got on very well together." The story is less creditable to Mr. Vandenhoff, however, than he seems to imagine. He overlooks the fact that he had seriously .diminished the entertainment of the audience ; and it is not well for raw recruits to be reading lectures to veteran soldiers.

In a very laudatory review that appeared in the *Times* upon the retirement of Farren in 1855, it is stated : " To many young playgoers our praise of Mr. Farren may possibly seem overcharged ; so we will at once anticipate their objections by declaring that no frequenter of theatres of less than eight years' standing is qualified to utter an opinion on the subject." This refers to 1847 or so, at a time when Farren was still to be seen to advantage. I had opportunities of attending his performances during what may be called his last years of excellence ; and I saw him afterwards when his laurels had become unhappily very sere and yellow. I lay no stress, however, upon my own opinion of Farren's surpassing merits as an actor. I was at the time a very youthful playgoer. But about 1845 I saw him play at the Haymarket, among other parts, *Sir Peter Teazle*, *Sir Anthony Absolute*, *Dr. Cantwell*, *Old Goldthumb*, *Sir Marmaduke Topple* in Robert Bell's comedy of "Temper," *Grandfather Whitehead*, and old *Foozle* in "My

Wife's Mother." I will only say that I thought his acting most consummate and convincing in its fidelity to
nature, its humour, force, and finish.   Looking back
upon it now, after a long lapse of years, I cannot think
my early judgment was at fault.   It was that rare kind
of acting that compelled the spectator absolutely to forget that it was acting.   His *Dr. Cantwell*, I remember,
was not thought to be one of his successful impersonations, and no doubt it lacked the vigour, the breadth,
and the coarse unction of the ordinary *Cantwell* of the
theatre.   But Farren's *Cantwell*, with his venerable white
locks and solemn suit of black, a look almost of the
famous John Wesley, a sleek meekness of demeanour
and an air of superfine piety, was a more likely impostor
to obtain a footing in Sir John Lambert's house than any
Cantwell, or for that matter any *Tartuffe*, that I have
ever seen.   First his terror and then his rage at his final
exposure and dismissal from the scene were supremely
rendered.   Farren was at this time admirably supported :
Keeley was his *Mawworm ;* Mrs. Nisbett his *Charlotte*
and *Lady Teazle ;* Mrs. Seymour was young *Lady Lambert ;* Mrs. Glover played old *Lady Lambert, Mrs. Malaprop, Mrs. Candour,* and the mother-in-law with whom
old *Foozle* combats in "My Wife's Mother." His *Sir
Marmaduke Topple* was an admirable sketch of an old
gentleman whose memory, tenacious of remote events,
is most treacherous as to the present ; he recollects fifty

years much more accurately than five minutes ago. But for this artistic study, the play was poor enough. His *Sir Anthony Absolute* was delightfully irascible, his *Sir Peter* was most humorously uxorious, although I think that, with the majority of *Sir Peters*, he was apt to exaggerate the age of the character—who is only required to be old enough to be her ladyship's father—not her grandfather—still less her great-grandfather. But this is what Leigh Hunt wrote of Farren's *Sir Peter* in 1830, beginning with laudatory mention of Dowton's *Sir Oliver:* "Dowton was the *Sir Oliver*, as of old—excellent. We cannot fancy a better *Sir Oliver*. Farren was the *Sir Peter*—admirable. We cannot fancy a better *Sir Peter*. We saw King once in the character. He was the original, and performed it again on some occasions (we forget what) after having taken leave of the stage. But either he was no longer the old man he was in his youth (which is likely enough), or he was not to be compared with Farren. He was dry and insipid to him. Farren makes the utmost of every passage without seeming to make any effort. His acting in the French Milliner part of that most admirable scene of the screen (one of the most perfect, if not the most so, in all comedy) was wrought up to a climax of humour, the excess of which he contrived, wonderfully well, to refer to the imbecility of age. He twittered and shook, and gaped and giggled, and was bent double with an absolute rapture of incapacity. . . . It is one of the best and richest pieces of comic gusto on the stage, and would alone be worth going to see the play for." The critic concludes with a word in favour of another of the performers : " We do not remember so good a *Joseph Surface* as Mr. Macready."

There seemed a desire on the part of the public that the characters represented by Farren should be not merely aged, but even phenomenally old. In " Grandfather Whitehead," an adaptation from the French, he personated an octogenarian, and greatly affected the audience by his exhibition of patriarchal distress and infirmity. In "The Legion of Honour," an adaptation of " Le Centenaire," he played the part of *Philippe Galliard*, a veteran of 102, whose son, grandson, and great-grandson, represented by Messrs. Dowton, Liston, and Bland respectively, also figured in the drama. " Mr. Farren's old, old man is above praise," wrote Leigh Hunt. " The lumpish inability of his legs, the spareness of the rest of his body, the withered inefficiency of his voice and face, the pardonable self-love and little deciding nods of head retained by extreme old age, and lastly, the almost inaudible but on that account highly real and touching manner in which he sang his songs, are all admirable, perhaps a little too much so for the perfect pleasure of the beholders. . . . In passages at least, if not altogether, his performance was painfully

natural." At the Haymarket in 1843 Farren represented
the prodigious hero of Mark Lemon's drama of "Old
Parr." He was required to appear of the age of 120
years in the first act and 148 in the second. The story
dealt with the question of the authenticity of a certain
will proved at last upon the evidence of the fabulously
old man, his memory corresponding in length with his
years. The performance was pronounced "masterly
beyond all precedent," the "make-up" a marvellous
piece of portrait-painting. "There is something inex-
pressibly touching," wrote a critic of the time, "in the
delineation of the palsied hand, the fading memory, the
querulousness of an extreme old age." The play enjoyed
few repetitions, however, its course being suddenly inter-
rupted by the alarming illness of the chief performer.
Towards the close of the new drama, the newspapers
recorded: "Mr. Farren was observed to exhibit an unusual tremor of manner, and to sink back in his chair.
It was discovered that he had been attacked with a fit
and was unable to speak. He was conveyed to his
room, and medical assistance sent for : his right side and
arm proved to be completely stricken. This is the third
attack he has had of the same malady." This account,
happily, was of exaggerated character. It was some
months, however, before Farren resumed his professional
duties ; he did not reappear as *Old Parr*.

In 1848 he undertook the management of the Strand

Theatre, relinquishing that establishment for the newly
built Olympic in 1851. He was assisted by a strong
company, which included Mrs. Glover and Compton,
Mrs. Stirling and Leigh Murray, and at a later date the
famous Robson. He produced many new and interesting
dramas; he played through a long list of his most
admired characters; he introduced his sons Henry and
William to the public. It was understood, however, that
as a manager he had succeeded but indifferently; that .
the large fortune acquired by his exertions as an actor
had suffered somewhat by his speculations as an impresario. His own attractiveness had waned seriously; his
clear, resonant, staccato articulation had failed him; it
was now difficult to understand what he said. The
public dealt gently with him, remembering how great and
genuine an artist he had proved himself in the past; but
he played to audiences that grew steadily thinner and
thinner. It was hard; for he was a great actor still, at
heart; he continued in excellent health and spirits, a
very hale and hearty old man; he dressed with his old
perfect taste and skill; his command of movement,
gesture, and facial expression was what it had ever been,
but his painful infirmity of speech could not be concealed
or controlled. Old playgoers spared themselves the disappointment of seeing him again; young playgoers could
not credit that he had ever been great. I saw him for
the last time in 1851, I think, when he played *Lord*

Duberly in "The Heir-at-Law." He seemed to be acting admirably, but in an unknown tongue. Scarcely an
intelligible word could be picked from the confused
gabble of his utterance. He continued to appear, however, from time to time, until the close of his management of the Olympic, on the 22nd September, 1853, with
a performance of "The Clandestine Marriage." He
finally took leave of the public at the Haymarket Theatre
on the 16th July, 1855. The house was crowded to the
ceiling. All the leading actors of the time lent their
services, and appeared grouped round the old man.
"Miss Helen Faucit gracefully presented the veteran
with a laurel wreath, and Harley flung his arms about
the neck of his old stage companion." Mr. Morley
records that "Mr. Farren was unable to speak his own
good-bye; all had to be felt, and there was nothing to be
said."

Farren survived this leave-taking six years. He died
on the 24th September, 1861, at the age of seventy-five.
Henry Farren, an actor of great confidence and vigour,
but curiously lacking in grace and refinement, pre-
deceased his father. William Farren, the younger,
appearing before the public in the first instance as a
singer, has since established himself in general opinion
as a sound and intelligent performer : he has even obtained considerable acceptance in certain of the characters
once sustained so perfectly by his sire.

Alfred Bunn, who had been Farren's manager, writes of him that, "barring the question of pounds, shillings, and pence, and his taking you by the button-hole whenever he wants to convince you of an impossibility, Farren is a gentlemanly man and a very fine actor." With Bunn it was a grievance that his actors demanded of him such large salaries, and he prints the articles of agreement he entered into with Farren in 1835. His salary was fixed at £30 per week, but it rose presently to double that amount. Sundry of the conditions were very favourable to the actor : his salary was to continue, although the theatre might be closed on Christmas Day, Christmas Eve, the 30th January, and Whitsun Eve ; he was to have his benefit early, and a choice of night, on paying the charges, £210 ; he was to be entitled to write three double-box and three double-gallery orders on every night of dramatic performance ; no parts were to be allotted to him such as he deemed "unsuited to his talents or prejudicial to his theatrical reputation ;" of the following characters none were to be performed by any other performer but William Farren, except in case of his illness ; *Don Manuel, Moneytrap, Don Cæsar, Sir Francis Gripe, Dogberry, Old Dornton, Lord Priory, Sir Peter Teazle, Lord Ogleby, Sir Anthony Absolute, Sir Abel Handy*, and *Sir Harry Sycamore ;* and the parties to the agreement bound themselves to its performance in the sum of £1000 "as agreed and liquidated damages ;"

Mr. Bunn being careful to relate how the actor had really incurred this penalty upon one occasion by his stealthily quitting Drury Lane, and, without leave first asked or obtained, secretly performing for a benefit at Brighton. In these times, however, it will hardly be thought that the terms exacted by Farren were exorbitant: his position was unique; he was, as he said, "the only cock-salmon in the market." There is sound proof of Farren's eminence and importance in Macready's statement of his plan, "practicable and promising, if only Farren could be bound down," for establishing the drama at the Lyceum "under a new name and a proprietary of performers, the best of each class formed into a supervising committee, and receiving, over and above their salaries, shares in proportion to their rank of salary and a percentage proportionate to their respective advances of money," etc. But Farren held aloof, and the scheme came to naught.

CHAPTER VI.

MRS. GLOVER.

An Irish actor, calling himself Thomas Betterton, and fancifully claiming kindred with the famous English tragedian of that name, had for many years strolled the country as a member of itinerant companies, figuring now upon this provincial stage, now upon that. His real name was probably Butterton; he was born in Dublin; his father and grandfather had filled the office of sexton to St. Andrew's Church in that city. He was a skilled player, versatile, possessed of unbounded confidence in himself; he was prepared to shine alike in light comedy and heavy tragedy; he was an accomplished dancer; and he was the father of an Infant Phenomenon. Tate Wilkinson has related how, in 1786, his company in York was joined by Mr. Betterton from Edinburgh, to play the characters of *Archer, Jaffier,* etc. The actor, as Wilkinson writes, "had squandered a little fortune at Newry and other towns in Ireland;" had been "bred a dancing-master," and moved "with a grace," his person being "remarkably genteel and elegantly made;" he boasted a good voice, but did not sufficiently vary or modulate his tones; he had, moreover, "a rapid study, and many strong recommendations for the stage." At the same time, it was charged against Mr. Betterton that he was over-fond of himself, and rated his own abilities too highly; that his habits were extravagant, and that he always schemed and laboured "to manage his managers." With Wilkinson Mr. Betterton remained some years, however, bringing upon the stage his little daughter, Miss Julia Betterton, to be known to a later generation —and to become famous, indeed—as MRS. GLÓVER, the best comic actress of her time.

Julia Betterton was born at Newry on the 8th January, 1779. At the earliest period possible she was pressed into the service of the drama; she stepped, as it were, from her cradle on to the stage. Almost before she could stand she was required to represent Cupids and Fairies. *Cordelio*, the page, in the tragedy of "The Orphan," is said to have been the first "speaking part" she essayed. The celebrated Anne Bracegirdle, at the early age of six, and to the admiration of all beholders, had been the original *Cordelio*, a character described as "of great importance to the play, as giving greater scope for the display of talent than any other juvenile part." Little Miss Betterton further undertook the usual duties of what may be called the infantile repertory. During her

father's engagement with Tate Wilkinson she appeared
as the *Duke of York* to the *Richard III.* of George
Frederick Cooke; and when, on the occasion of his
benefit, that eminent tragedian condescended to personate *Glumdalca*, the Queen of the Giants, in Fielding's
burlesque of "Tom Thumb," the clever little girl Julia
Betterton was chosen to play the hero of the story. So
charmed was Cooke with the spirited performance of the
tiny actress, that he lifted her in his arms, we are told,
and, "placing her upon the palm of his hand, held her
forth to receive the rapturous applause of the audience."

The drama finds occupation for players of all ages.
At thirteen Miss Betterton was appearing with success
as the hoydens and school-girls of comedy and farce;
she was still in her teens when she first ventured to
personate the leading heroines of tragedy. Without
doubt she had been carefully instructed by her father,
who showed alacrity too in receiving and applying to his
own uses the earnings of his child. She had never sixpence "to call her own," as people said; it was Mr.
Betterton's custom punctually to appropriate the handsome salary she received from the managers. In 1795
Miss Betterton, "from Liverpool," first appeared in Bath,
then viewed as a sort of dramatic nursery, the favour
obtained there being accounted a sure criterion of merit,
and a foretaste of the popularity the performer might
rely upon enjoying in London. Her first character was

Elwina in Hannah More's tragedy of "Percy"—in part
an adaptation from the French, and now regarded as an
inordinately dull production; but from its first performance in 1777, "Percy" had been esteemed as a poetic
work that afforded excellent opportunities to the players.
That Miss Betterton set store upon her performance of
Elwina may be judged from the fact that she decided to
appear in that character when the time came for her
entrance upon the London stage. It was even thought
worth while to revive "Percy" in 1815 for the sake of
Miss O'Neill's *Elwina*, Hazlitt writing upon the occasion : "We shall not readily forgive Miss Hannah More's
heroine *Elwina* for having made us perceive, what we
had not felt before, that there is a considerable degree
of manner and monotony in Miss O'Neill's acting." For
Miss Betterton's benefit at Bath, in 1795, "Wild Oats"
was produced, when she played *Amaranth* to the *Rover*
of her father and the *Sim* of Elliston, the leading actor
of the theatre. During three seasons at Bath the actress
appeared as *Desdemona, Lady Macbeth,* the *Queen* in
"Richard III.," *Bellario* in "Philaster," *Ellen* in "A
Cure for the Heartache," *Julia* in "The Way to get
Married," *Marianne* in "The Dramatist," etc.

The fame of Miss Betterton's success in Bath reached
London, and Mr. Harris, the Covent Garden manager,
was forthwith moved to offer her an engagement. Probably Mr. Betterton conducted the negotiation on his

child's behalf, for there was considerable haggling over
the transaction.   Harris offered first £10 and then £12
per week, protesting that no performer engaged at his
theatre was in receipt of a higher salary.   Mr. Betterton,
perceiving the manager's eagerness, was in no haste to
arrive at an agreement.   At length the lady was secured
to the London stage for a period of five years upon a
salary beginning at £15 a week, and rising to £20:
terms then thought to be liberal even to extravagance.
It was perhaps a condition that Mr. Betterton should
also be employed.   He was no longer young, it is true,
but he was still a serviceable actor, and it was thought
he might render valuable assistance to his daughter.
She appeared at Covent Garden as *Elwina* on the 12th
October, 1797.   A few nights afterwards her father
presented himself to the London public as *Castalio* in
"The Orphan."   A little later, and Mr. and Miss Betterton were seen upon the stage together as *Belcour* and
Charlotte Rusport in "The West Indian."   For some
seasons Mr. Betterton continued a member of the
Covent Garden company, sustaining characters of considerable importance.   Opportunity was even found to
exhibit his skill as a dancer : he was selected by Mrs.
Abington to perform with her the mock minuet in
"High Life Below Stairs," presented on the occasion of
her benefit in 1798.

The success of the new *Elwina* was complete, but

there were difficulties in the way of her rapid advance. The Covent Garden company was so numerous that Miss Betterton was only occasionally called upon to appear. She found a formidable rival in Miss Campion, known also as Mrs. Spencer and afterwards as Mrs. Pope; while the two distinguished actresses, Mrs. Crawford and Mrs. Abington, had been persuaded to return to the stage for a while and resume the chief characters in tragedy and comedy respectively. There are princesses whose religious convictions are kept in solution, as it were, to be precipitated when the particular creed professed by the prince they are to marry has been clearly ascertained : in like manner Miss Betterton's histrionic inclinations were for some time held suspended. Probably her thoughts and wishes in the first instance were bent towards tragedy, but she had been duly instructed how to bear herself satisfactorily in comedy. Nature, too, had assuredly qualified her the more for success as a comic actress. Her beauty was remarkable, but it was not of a severe type. Her face did not readily lend itself to solemnity of expression; her features were dainty and pretty rather than regular; many found in her looks a resemblance to the brilliant archness, vivacity, and piquancy of Mrs. Abington. There were no tears in Miss Betterton's voice, and anxiety to impress often urged her towards exaggerations of tone and gesture. Her complexion was exquisitely fair; her luxuriant hair

was very dark of hue; her large blue eyes were shadowed
by the longest lashes; she was above the average height,
and most graceful of movement.   The circumstances in
which she was placed more and more impelled her
towards comedy; choice, indeed, was hardly permitted
her; and time may be said to have definitively settled the
matter.   As the years passed, the lady's form acquired
amplitude and substantiality, until it assumed quite un-
poetic proportions; her prosperous and portly air was
found wholly unsuited to characters of seriousness.
Gradually the sceptred pall of gorgeous tragedy may be
said to have slipped from her plump shoulders.

For some seasons she was content, however, to play
such parts, lively or severe, as the management chose to
assign her.   Her third character in London was *Portia*,
in "The Merchant of Venice."   Presently Cumberland
solicited her to play the heroine in his comedy of "False
Impressions."   She appeared, too, in "Curiosity," a new
drama written, as the playbills alleged, by "the late
King of Sweden."   She represented *Miranda* in the
"Busy Body;" *Miss Dorillon* in "Wives as they Were
and Maids as they Are;" and *Lydia Languish* in "The
Rivals."   Holcroft's "Deserted Daughter" was played
on her first benefit night, when she appeared as *Joanna*
to the *Mordant* of her father.   In March, 1800, when
she personated *Letitia Hardy* in "The Belle's Stratagem," the advertisements described her oddly enough as

" the late Miss Betterton." Two months afterwards, on her appearance as *Miss Walsingham* in "The School for Wives," she was for the first time announced in the bills as "Mrs. Glover, late Miss Betterton."

Her marriage brought the poor lady much unhappiness. It is said that her own inclinings and sentiments in the matter had been grossly and cruelly disregarded ; that her husband had been forced upon her by her father, whose selfish aims had determined his choice. Needy, shifty, unscrupulous, Mr. Betterton overreached himself, however. He believed his son-in-law to be a man of fortune ; but Mr. Glover was rich only in expectations which were not destined to be realized. The husband now preyed upon the wife much as the father had preyed upon the daughter ; the earnings of the actress seemed never to be safely her own, but always in danger of being swept into the pockets of others. Her happiest hours were probably passed upon the stage in the presence of the public ; for there, at any rate, she could forget her domestic discords, cares, and afflictions. In the private relations of life she suffered acutely, the while her own conduct and character remained unimpeached : she obtained, indeed, general respect for her patience, forbearance, and rectitude under very trying conditions. She was the victim of repeated scandals and squabbles. The husband who, after treating her shamefully, had finally abandoned her, leaving her wholly dependent for subsistence upon her own exertions, was now suing the treasurer of the theatre to obtain possession of her salary, and now, as a certain means of assailing her purse, endeavouring to tear her children from her, way-laying them in the street, or breaking into their mother's house to gain possession of them. The poor actress underwent a long course of persecution of this kind.

Of Mr. Betterton, sorely disappointed in the results of his daughter's marriage, especially in their relation to his own fortunes, little more need be said. Lord Byron reckons among the distresses he endured as a member of the Drury Lane committee of management in 1815, a visit he received from "Mrs. Glover's father, an Irish dancing-master of some sixty years," to plead that he might be allowed to appear as *Archer* in "The Beaux' Stratagem." The actor presented himself "dressed in silk stockings on a frosty morning, to show his legs, which were certainly good and Irish for his age, and had been still better." Failing to secure an engagement at Drury Lane, the veteran was content to figure at Sadler's Wells, under the direction of Mr. Howard Payne. Upon that humble stage Mr. Betterton is supposed to have played for the last time probably about 1821.

Meantime Mrs. Glover continued to serve the drama industriously. Her professional career extended over a period of some sixty-five years: from her first appearance at Covent Garden in 1797 to her farewell performance at Drury Lane in 1850 she occupied a distinguished position upon the London stage. Histrionic life so prolonged has been permitted to few. From the *Cordelios*, the *Prince Arthurs*, and *Tom Thumbs* of her childhood she proceeded to the interesting girlish heroines of theatrical romance, to represent presently the vivacious matrons, the buxom widows, and spirited women of quality who stand a little apart from the main interest of the drama, and to subside at last into the old ladies, the nurses, the dowagers and duennas, the useful background figures of so many tragedies and comedies. She was not of those actresses who, having been *Juliets* once, would be *Juliets* always.; nor did she, as many of our players do, fall into the mistake of deferring too long her portrayal of elderly characters. It has been remarked that "no class of performance upon the stage requires more vigour than the simulation of the passions and humours of age." Mrs. Glover was even charged with abandoning prematurely her more youthful impersonations. A critic writing in 1826, while expressing admiration for the strength of mind that had induced the resolution of the actress, proposed that she should postpone, even for eight or nine years, her representation of "the old women of the stage." It must, of course, be understood that in the theatre age is a conventional matter, and that tragedy and comedy have varying prescriptions on the subject. An actress, from the point

of view of the public, may still preserve a reputation
for youth, even though she undertake such decidedly
mature characters as *Volumnia* and *Hermione, Lady
Macbeth* and *Lady Randolph; Constance* and *Gertrude;*
but if she once presents herself as *Mrs. Candour* and
Mrs. Malaprop, Deborah Dowlas and *Dame Ashfield,
Mrs. Heidelberg* and the *Widow Warren*, there is a
general agreement that both on and off the stage she is
really stricken in years. Without doubt, however, Mrs.
Glover exercised sound judgment when she decided
that, while still middle-aged herself, she would portray
the old women of the drama ; the argument of her
expanded physical proportions asserting itself probably
in this case not less than in the question of her
abandonment of tragedy for comedy. A young American
artist—he was afterwards famous as Charles Robert
Leslie, R.A.—corresponding with his family in Philadelphia, described the production of Coleridge's tragedy
" Remorse " at Drury Lane in 1813, and thus wrote of
the actress who represented the heroine of the night :
" Mrs. Glover played *Alhadra* uncommonly well. . . .
This lady has not a tragic voice, and very far from
a tragic air. She was dressed well, however, and is a
commanding figure, though monstrously fat."

Born the year of Garrick's death, Mrs. Glover lived
through the palmiest days of the Kembles, and witnessed
the rising and the setting now of George Frederick

Cooke and now of Edmund Kean. When in 1816 Macready made his first appearance in London, he found, something to his dismay, that in support of his *Orestes* "a special engagement had been made with Mrs. Glover, the best comic actress then upon the stage, to appear as the weeping widowed *Andromache*." She had first essayed the part of the *Nurse* in "Romeo and Juliet" in 1822, when her daughter Phillis made "her first attempt on any stage" in the character of *Juliet* to the *Romeo* of Edmund Kean : she was playing *Nurse* again in 1829, when Charles Kean was the *Romeo*, and the *Juliet* Miss F. H. Kelly. She had appeared as *Mrs. Ford* in "The Merry Wives of Windsor" to the *Falstaff* of Cooke and the *Ford* of John Kemble; she had personated *Violante* in the "Wonder" to Charles Kemble's *Don Felix*, and *Tilburina* in "The Critic" to Elliston's *Puff* and Dowton's *Sir Fretful*. She was *Lady Allworth* to Edmund Kean's *Sir Giles Overreach*, when his terrible intensity affected her so powerfully that she fainted away—"not at all from flattery, but from emotion." Indeed, Mrs. Glover's last performances in tragedy were in support of Kean. She was his *Lady Macbeth*, *Volumnia*, *Goneril*, *Emilia;* the *Queen* to his *Richard*, the *Elvira* to his *Rolla*. She appeared as *Paulina* in "The Winter's Tale" to Macready's *Leontes* in 1823; she was the original *Mrs. Subtle* in "Paul Pry" in 1825. On one of her benefit nights she played

Hamlet; on another she even ventured to appear as
Falstaff. In 1821 she had been playing at the West
London Theatre, known to these times as the Prince of
Wales's, when the "Œdipus Tyrannus" of Sophocles
was impudently announced to be represented, "being
its first appearance these 2440 years." The play was
really a condensed edition of the tragedy, "Œdipus,
King of Thebes," by Dryden and Lee. A critic wrote :
"Mrs. Glover's delineation of *Jocasta* was truly powerful,
and met with deserved applause; but we have seen her
to greater advantage than in her Grecian costume."
In 1831 Madame Vestris secured the services of Mrs.
Glover for the Olympic Theatre. In 1837 Macready,
entering upon the management of Covent Garden,
records in his diary that he had "called upon Mrs.
Glover and agreed with her for £9 10s." The actress
continued at Covent Garden during the subsequent
management of Madame Vestris, and afterwards joined
the company of Mr. Webster at the Haymarket,
remaining there some seasons, and presenting the best
impersonations of her later period. It was at the
Haymarket she originated the characters of the *Widow
Green* in Sheridan Knowles's "Love Chase," *Lady
Franklin* in "Money," and *Miss Tucker* in "Time
Works Wonders," Douglas Jerrold's best comedy. She
appeared, too, in "Quid pro Quo," Mrs. Gore's prize
comedy; in "The Maiden Aunt" by Richard Brinsley

Knowles; "The School for Scheming," by Mr. Boucicault; and in comedies by Robert Bell, Lovell, and
others.

Hazlitt, reviewing Kean's *Richard*, found occasion to
mention the *Queen* of Mrs. Glover as too turbulent and
vociferous; he noted at another time the "very
agreeable frowns" of her *Lady Allworth*, and especially
admired her *Lady Amaranth*, in "Wild Oats," as "an
inimitable piece of quiet acting." He adds: "The
demureness of the character, which takes away all
temptation to be boisterous, leaves the justness of her
conception in full force; and the simplicity of her Quaker
dress is most agreeably relieved by the *embonpoint* of her
person." Of her *Mrs. Oakley*, in "The Jealous Wife,"
he writes less favourably: "She represented the passions
of the woman, but not the manner of the fine lady;" she
was apt to "deluge the theatre with her voice;" her
style of acting "amounted to the formidable;" and "her
expression of passion was too hysterical, and habitually
reminded one of hartshorn and water." In the course of
Leigh Hunt's dramatic criticisms notes of Mrs. Glover's
performances frequently occur. In 1802 the actress had
personated Miss Hardcastle, but in 1830 she was playing
Mrs. Hardcastle in "She Stoops to Conquer." Leigh
Hunt pronounced her "too easy and pleasant-looking
for the fidgety Mrs. Hardcastle; Mrs. Davenport might
have been as stout, but she looked in less joyous

condition, and then she dug her words in as if she were sticking pins." A little later, and Mrs. Glover is performing *Mrs. Malaprop:* she had played *Lydia Languish* in 1798, and *Julia* in 1811 ! Leigh Hunt writes : " Mrs. Glover we think a very good *Mrs. Malaprop,* even though we have seen Miss Pope in the character. It is not of so high an order of comedy as that lady's ; it wants her perfection of old-gentlewomanly staidness, and so wants the highest relish of contrast in its *malapropism ;* but for a picture of a broader sort, fine and flower-gowned and powdered, it is very good indeed. If Miss Pope looked as though she kept the jellies and preserves, Mrs. Glover looked as though she ate them." Upon a performance of Mrs. Glover in 1831, at the Queen's Theatre—for the little house in Tottenham Street now bore that title—Leigh Hunt remarks : " Mrs. Glover plays her part admirably well. We really think she acts better and better the older she grows ; and she is young enough too, in spite of a jovial person, to retain a countenance the good-humoured freshness of which surprised us when we saw it the other evening among the spectators at one of the large theatres. Mrs. Glover is still a good-looking woman on the stage, and she is better off. Her good humour must be the secret of her good looks."

The lady had a quick wit of her own, however, and could say her tart things. Mr. Vandenhoff, in his

"Dramatic Reminiscences," describes her as "hearty-mannered," but "quick-tempered, and not unfrequently indulging in strokes of sarcastic bitterness," with an air "large, autocratic, oracular," and "smacking of her profession." The same authority relates a conversation between Mrs. Glover and her contemporaries, Mrs. Orger and Mrs. Humby, touching the marriage of Madame Vestris and Charles Mathews. "They say," remarked Mrs. Humby, with a quaint air of assumed simplicity, "that before accepting him Vestris made a full confession of all the indiscretions of her life. What touching confidence!" "What needless trouble!" said Mrs. Orger. "What a wonderful memory!" exclaimed Mrs. Glover, concluding the discussion triumphantly. She is said to have been an admirable reader and reciter of Shakespeare; she had at one time projected the establishment of a school for youthful players, purposing to preside herself over certain of the classes. She did not live, however, to carry this plan into execution.

My own recollections of Mrs. Glover date from her performances at the Haymarket Theatre, under Mr. Webster's management, about the year 1845, and during subsequent seasons. I had opportunities of witnessing certain of her more famous impersonations, and though I may not pretend to estimate these critically, for I was but a juvenile playgoer, I may yet claim to remember them very distinctly. One's earlier impressions of

theatrical exhibitions are perhaps the more ineffaceable ;
it is the first play much rather than the fiftieth, or the
five hundredth, that retains its place in the mind. Youthful memory has no doubt a tendency to exaggerate and
overvalue; but I do not think my retrospect suffers
appreciably on this account, for my view of Mrs. Glover
was much the view of the accepted critics of the time.
As I remember the actress then, she was "more than
common tall," large of person, but to no unwieldy extent,
with some remains of beauty in regard to brightness of
eye and mobility of expression, animated of movement,
and without the slightest evidence of the infirmities of
age. She had abundant energy at command, and her
voice was strong, clear, and resonant. Her histrionic
method, remarkable for its force and breadth, was yet
curiously subtle : while theatrically most effective, it
never forfeited its exceeding naturalness. She seemed
always admirably unconscious of the presence of her
audience, and a special air of spontaneity distinguished
her manner upon the stage. She never for a moment
relaxed her hold of the characters she assumed; when
silent her looks and movements, her persistent attention
to the scene, greatly aided the representation ; and when
speech was required of her, the ringing distinctness of
her tones, her prompt and voluble utterance, her vivacity
of action, told irresistibly upon the house. It was difficult
to believe that she was simply repeating words she had

beforehand learnt by heart; her speeches were delivered
in so lifelike a manner, that they seemed invariably the
natural and original locutions of a ready-witted and
sharp-tongued woman. She was especially happy in the
enunciation of those "asides" of the stage which admit
the audience into the confidence of the actors. She
imparted an epigrammatic point to her every sentence.
Altogether, acting more vividly quaint and humorous, or
more convincing in its verisimilitude, I have never seen.
The time had passed for her attempting scenes of pathos
or of serious emotion; she appeared only in comedy.
But there was no lack of variety about her impersonations. Now she presented herself as old *Lady Lambert*
—the *Madame Pernelle* of Molière—the most simple-
minded, sanctified of gentlewomen, white-haired, black-
mittened, rich in lace lappets and edgings, silken skirts
and scarfs of sober hues, pearl, or dove, or lilac, settling
herself comfortably in her chair beneath the shadow of
Mawworm's screen to listen like the devoutest of Little
Bethelites to the absurdest of canting sermons. Now
she was seen as the seemingly genuine *Mrs. Candour*,
patched and powdered, hooped and sacqued and fur-
belowed, rustling at every step, a breathless gossip alert
for tattle, all starts and surprises and affected sympathy,
with a malicious subacid tincturing her discourse and
lending pungency to her innuendoes. And then as the
old weather-beaten "she-dragon" *Mrs. Malaprop*, with

her aspersed parts of speech, black-browed, fiercely rouged, formidable of presence, peremptory of gesture, glaring of dress, the personification of coarse vanity, vulgar ignorance, and tyrannical disposition, yet highly diverting withal. Nor did she portray less successfully the old ladies of a later time—the leading character in the little comedy of " My Wife's Mother," for instance— wearing the ample black satin dress, the blonde cap with pink ribbons, the lace pelerine, secured by a cameo brooch the size of a blister—the fashions of five and thirty years since. And how inimitable she was as Douglas Jerrold's *Miss Tucker*, the peevish, selfish, soured schoolmistress, ruined by the elopement of her boarders, with her ceaseless whine about the limited rights of " the people who live in other people's houses," full of pity for herself and anxiety about her own personal comforts, her prospects of marriage with the artful Professor Truffles, her new silk dress, and the lobster to be brought to her by the London carrier !

In 1849 Mrs. Glover accepted an engagement to appear upon the small stage of the Strand Theatre, of which establishment her old playfellow Farren had become lessee and director, and to sustain for the last time all the more important characters in her repertory. It is clear that her health was now seriously failing her ; but, excellent actress that she was, she contrived success- fully to conceal her weakened state from the audience.

She seemed as alert and energetic, as bright and humorous as ever, and by turns her *Mrs. Heidelberg*, *Dame Ashfield*, and *Widow Green*, her *Mrs. Temperance* in the " Country Squire," her *Mrs. Candour*, *Mrs. Malaprop*, and the rest, received from crowded houses the familiar tribute of hearty laughter and loudest applause. Without doubt, however, her exertions cost her dearly. She appeared for the last time at the Strand Theatre on June 8, 1850. A contemporary critic wrote of her closing performances: " The manner in which she has lately, under the infirmities of age, supported her professional position, has frequently been quoted as a marvel, so perfect and complete has been the continued possession of her extraordinary powers." Her farewell benefit took place at Drury Lane Theatre on the following 12th July, under the express patronage of the Queen. It was understood that protracted care for her family had drained the resources of the actress; that, in spite of her long and seemingly prosperous career, she retired upon very limited means. Every effort was made, therefore, that her benefit should really prove " a bumper at parting." The leading players of the time, William Farren, Charles Mathews, and Madame Vestris prominent among them, volunteered their services. The play was " The Rivals." Poor Mrs. Glover had been for a fortnight confined to her bed, painfully ill; but she stirred herself to appear upon an occasion so memorable, and her strong will triumphing for a while over her physical weakness, she repaired to the theatre and duly trod the stage once more, and for the very last time, in her famous character of *Mrs. Malaprop.* She was received with the utmost enthusiasm; but her debility increased distressingly as the play proceeded, and though she completed her performance, it became but too evident that she was unequal to the task of addressing to the public the few sad, fond words of farewell she had designed to utter. The speech was dispensed with, therefore; and, the comedy concluded, the curtain rose again, to discover Mrs. Glover seated on a chair, environed by her professional friends and associates. She bowed to the house in grateful acknowledgment of its sympathy and applause; the rest was silence. The end was, indeed, very near. She was carried home to die. One short week after her farewell to the stage the remains of the famous Mrs. Glover were interred in the churchyard of St. George's, Bloomsbury. The place her death left vacant upon the stage has not since been supplied, albeit thirty years have sped.

CHAPTER VII.

"SIR CHARLES COLDSTREAM."

OLD playgoers are very apt to be wet-blankets: they employ their memories of the past as a means of oppressing present experiences; they insufficiently allow for tare and tret, so to say, in regard to the long voyage from youth to age undergone by their judicial faculties and their powers of enjoyment. Some five and thirty years ago, I remember, it was usual for the elders of the time to disparage "Young Mathews," as they described an actor I was beginning to know and greatly to esteem—an artist whose accomplishments in later days became the theme of general admiration. But in the early part of his career "Young Mathews" suffered from the fact that he was not "Old Mathews," or " *The* Mathews," as many preferred to designate him. In the unanimous opinion of the senior playgoers of that period, the son was not to be compared with his father. To my thinking, no reason existed why the two actors should ever have been collated in this way, or pitted against each other. Indeed, had they not borne the same name and been sire and son, comparison could hardly have been instituted between them. Let me admit that I never saw the elder Mathews: he died in 1835, and scarcely appeared publicly in London after 1833. But clearly he was almost invariably, as his widow relates, an actor of "old men, countrymen, and quaint low comedy." He now and then undertook whimsical sprightly characters, originally sustained by Lewis, such as *Goldfinch* in "The Road to Ruin," and *Rover* in "Wild Oats." His *Rover* was "very bad," notes Genest in 1816: "his figure and manner totally disqualified him for his part;" but these efforts were departures from his ordinary "line of business" as an actor. At no time could he have been properly described as "a light comedian." When he was but twenty-eight he was assigned the part of *Sir Peter Teazle* at Drury Lane; there was no thought of his appearing as *Charles Surface.* In "John Bull" he was wont to play, not *Tom Shuffleton,* but *Sir Simon Rochdale.* But to the younger Mathews such characters as *Charles Surface* and *Tom Shuffleton* were allotted as a matter of course, and by a sort of natural right. He did not inherit his father's repertory, although he successfully emulated the paternal feat of "doubling" the parts of *Puff* and *Sir Fretful Plagiary* in "The Critic:" being probably superior to his senior as *Puff* and inferior as

Sir Fretful. But he never appeared, it need hardly be said, as *Mawworm*, as *Caleb Quotem*, as *Caleb Pipkin*, as *Falstaff*, as *Don Manuel*, as *Trinculo*, etc., characters in which the elder Mathews won very great applause. No doubt the son possessed much of his father's skill as a mimic, a personator or illustrator of eccentric character, a singer of what are called "patter" songs—he had often found sympathetic employment in contriving and arranging the "At Homes" of the elder comedian, and at one time, with the assistance of his second wife, he essayed an entertainment very much of the paternal pattern. The histrionic fame of Charles Mathews the Second, however, arose from gifts and achievements which were peculiarly and independently his own. His success was of a personal and individual sort, and owed little or nothing to preceding exertions and examples. His method as an actor was not founded upon the method of any other actor. He was essentially a light comedian—the lightest of light comedians; but it was difficult to classify his art in relation to the art of others or to established technical conventions. He was distinguished for an extraordinary vivacity, an airy grace, an alert gaiety that exercised over his audience the effect of fascination. Elegance and humour so curiously combined can hardly have been seen upon the stage except in this instance. No doubt there was always risk of awarding admiration not so much to the art of the

comedian as to the natural endowments of the man ;
and it must often have happened that Charles Mathews
was applauded for being something which he could not
possibly help being. At the same time it must not be
assumed that he could only appear in his own character,
or that his efforts upon the scene lacked variety. Certain
graces of manner peculiar to himself he could never
wholly discard ; but his power of representation enabled
him to exhibit distinct and finished portraits of personages so very different as *Sir Charles Coldstream* and
Sir Hugh Evans, *Lavater* and *Mr. Affable Hawk*, *Slender*
and *Dazzle*, *Young Wilding* and the villanous heroes of
" The Day of Reckoning" and " Black Sheep," to name
no others. (By the way, I may proffer a doubt as to
whether the elder Mathews could have successfully represented any of these characters.)

On the 27th December, 1803, Charles Mathews,
senior, wrote from Liverpool to his friend John Litch-
field, of the Council Office :—" It is with the most
exquisite pleasure I inform you that I am the father of
a fine boy. . . . I am happy beyond measure. ' Who
would not be a father?'" In due season the fine boy
was christened " Charles," after his father, and " James,"
after his grandfather — a respectable bookseller in the
Strand, holding rigidly Calvinistic opinions. It was decided forthwith that Charles James Mathews should
become a clergyman, " if he inclined to that profession

on attaining an age to choose for himself"—an important stipulation. The father had long borne among certain of his friends the nickname of "Stick," because of the original slenderness of his form and the stiffness of his mien. As a consequence, young Charles James was soon playfully called "Twig;" while upon the little rustic cottage at Colney Hatch, in which he passed his earliest years, the title of "Twig Hall" was bestowed. "The Twig was slight, and drooped in London air," writes his mother; and she proceeds to relate how Liston the comedian was a frequent visitor at "Twig Hall," and Twig's especial favourite as a playfellow. They were often to be seen earnestly engaged in the game of "hide and seek," Liston flitting from gooseberry bush to gooseberry bush, and the tiny child toddling and peering after him. "I could not suppress a laugh," writes Mrs. Mathews, "when I saw the bigger boy, as he crouched down, quite unconscious of a witness of his grave amusement, draw out his snuff-box and take a pinch of snuff to heighten his enjoyment." Mrs. Mathews, as Miss Jackson, a pupil of Michael Kelly, had at the beginning of the century "supported the first line of singing" in the theatrical company of Tate Wilkinson at York.

Charles James was presently placed upon the foundation of Merchant Taylors' School by Mr. Silvester, afterwards Sir John Silvester, the Recorder of London, a valued friend of the family. This was about 1813. He boarded with the Rev. Thomas Cherry, the head-master of the school, an arrangement deemed to be of marked advantage to the boy, seeing that he was still intended for the Church. But it became necessary, his health continuing delicate, and confinement in the heart of London affecting him injuriously, to place him under the care of Dr. Richardson, whose private seminary, in the Clapham Road, already contained the sons of Charles Kemble, Young, Terry, and Liston. It was about 1819 that the youth, greatly to the chagrin of his parents, avowed his desire to become an architect. Instead of proceeding to one of the universities, there-fore, to complete his education, he was articled for four years to Pugin, the architect, with whom, in furtherance of his studies, he journeyed to Paris.

Before he was out of his teens, young Mathews seems to have distinguished himself as an amateur actor. In 1822 he appeared at the English Opera House, the performance being of a private kind, when he presented a successful imitation of Perlet, the famous French comedian. It was said, indeed, that the skill and humour he displayed upon this occasion brought him the offer of an engagement from the manager of the French plays in London. In 1823 he accompanied Lord Blessington to Ireland, and afterwards to Naples. His lordship at this time was professing to be a liberal patron of architecture; but a projected new mansion to be built upon his estate of Mountjoy Forest, in the county of Tyrone, with Charles Mathews for its architect, lived only as a paper edifice, and never acquired the substantiality of stones or of bricks.   It was during his two years' residence with Lord and Lady Blessington at the Palazzo Belvedere, Naples, that the young man, feeling himself affronted by certain observations of Count d'Orsay, sent a challenge to that superb nobleman ; for in those days the duello was still supposed to afford a sort of solace to aggrieved honour.   No hostile meeting took place, however : upon the intervention of Lord Blessington, the Count hastened to make all requisite apologies to the ruffled architect.   But the matter was really serious while it lasted.

After two years more or less assiduous exercise of his profession in England and Wales, varied by literary and musical essays in regard to his father's "At Homes," and the composition of the popular song of "Jenny Jones," etc., Charles Mathews, with his friend James d'Egville, again left England for Italy, still bent upon architectural studies and improvement.   But at Florence he took a prominent part in the private theatricals given by Lord Normanby, played a great variety of characters, built a theatre for the amateurs, and even painted a drop-scene for it. At Venice he suffered from a virulent attack of fever.   "Charles was six months in bed at Venice," writes his mother, "and nearly the same period in England." The mercurial, sprightly, jaunty young gentleman doomed to nearly a year of bed! The Italian doctors would have detained him still longer in their hands; told him, indeed, that it was certain death for him to attempt to move. He resolved that he would die on the road if it must be so, but that he would assuredly make an effort to see his parents and his home once more. He purchased a travelling carriage, in which a bed was constructed, and, attended by Nanini, his faithful Italian servant, successfully accomplished his weary journey of fourteen hundred miles in nineteen days. His father wrote of him to a friend: "Charles has returned, the most exaggerated case of paralysis upon record—a voice only to indicate that the corpse was animated. . . . An attached gem of an Italian servant brought him home like a portmanteau or any other piece of goods. . . . It was the most afflicting sight I ever experienced to see him lifted from the carriage. The only evidence of the body being animate was the sound of his dear voice offering up thanksgiving to God for having granted him strength to reach home." It was eight months before the father, writing to the Rev. Thomas Speidell, was able to record his wonder and delight at the complete recovery of the invalid. "You will be pleased to hear that dear Charles surprised his mother and me by meeting or rather running to us without a stick!"

A little later, and Charles Mathews obtained the appointment of district surveyor. This is how Mr. Cyrus Jay, solicitor, has noted the event in his volume of Reminiscences : " Once when a young man I attended the Middlesex Sessions, Clerkenwell, with two barristers. . . . I observed that something was going to take place by so many magistrates being present, and I soon learnt that there was an election of a district surveyor for Hackney. There were many candidates, and among them Mr. Charles Mathews. It was a very pleasing sight to see the venerable chairman (Francis Const, Esq.) leave the bench to give his vote at a quarter to four, for the poll closed at four o'clock ; but something astonished me a great deal more, and that was to see him followed by the sixteen police magistrates, who, along with the venerable chairman whom they greatly esteemed and respected, one and all voted for Charles Mathews, which settled the contest, and Charles Mathews was duly elected. One of the unsuccessful candidates said to me, ' He will not hold the appointment a month, for he can make more money in a week than he will by his salary at Hackney.' And so it eventually turned out," etc. It was of the district of Bow and Bethnal Green, not of Hackney, that he became the surveyor, retaining the appointment for some six years.

It was not until the 7th of December, 1835, that Charles Mathews made his first appearance on the stage as an actor by profession. Meanwhile he had contributed to the theatre various plays, adaptations from the French, "The Wolf and the Lamb," "The Court Jester," and "My Wife's Mother," among them, and he was credited with "The Black Riband," described as one of the most attractive and best-written stories in Heath's "Book of Beauty" for 1834. Further, he had figured as an amateur actor at Woburn, playing *Mr. Simpson* in "Simpson and Co.," with the Duchess of Bedford as *Mrs. Simpson*, and for a while had undertaken his late father's share in the management of the Adelphi Theatre. An erroneous opinion prevailed that he had only waited for his father's death to adopt the theatrical profession, the step being directly opposed to the parental wishes. The elder Mathews was indeed credited with a declaration that "not even a dog of his should set foot upon the stage." But the fact was that for some time before his death the father had fully recognized his son's histrionic skill and capacity, had perceived, too, the slenderness of his chances of prospering as an architect, and had recommended him to become an actor in earnest. The venture was made at last with some suddenness, however. He appeared at the Olympic Theatre, then under the management of Madame Vestris, after little more than a fortnight's preparation, as *George Rattleton* in "The Humpbacked Lover," a little comedy of French origin, which he had specially altered to suit his own purposes; and in "The Old and Young Stager," a piece written for the occasion by Leman Rede, in which Liston also took part, delaying, it was said, his own farewell of the stage that he might introduce and assist the son of his old playfellow. The success of the new actor was most unquestionable. "His *entrée* was hailed with thunders of applause," writes a critic of the time; "his father's merits were not forgotten, and his own soon caused the shouts to be redoubled till the roof rang." As *George Rattleton*, he played with lively ease, treading the stage with the unembarrassed confidence of a practised actor, speaking and looking "like a man of sense and a gentleman." His singing, we are told, was excellent, being aided by "a rapid and clear enunciation —the family peculiarity." In the second play he seems to have carefully reproduced his father's manner. " *Tim Topple, the Tiger*, a character of the broadest farce, soon told us whose son he was. We recognized in a moment the comic timber out of which he was hewed. 'A chip of the old block,' vociferated a hundred glad voices," etc. The dialogue was of the punning sort, then much in favour. "The hits, many and good, were conveyed in stage-coach phraseology, with an occasional sprinkling of St. Giles's Greek, but applicable to the stage that goes without wheels, past and present. All that bore reference to the sun which had for ever set, and that which had just risen, was eagerly seized by the audience and

applauded to the echo. At the conclusion the call for
Mr. Mathews was universal. He came forward, led
most cordially by the glorious 'old stager' who, rich
in laurels himself, hailed the triumph of the youthful son
of his friend." Charles Mathews remained a member of
the Olympic company, appearing in a variety of plays,
counting among them his own farces of "The Ring-
doves," "Why did you die?" "Truth," "He would be
an Actor," etc. He won much applause also as *David
Brown* in Mr. Planché's "Court Favour," and as *Cherubino* in "The Two Figaros," an adaptation of a comedy
by M. Marteley, first played at the Français in 1794,
reintroducing the characters of Beaumarchais after a
supposed lapse of sixteen years. Thus *Cherubino* appears
as a colonel of dragoons, and the *Countess Almaviva* is
the mother of a marriageable daughter. At this time the
Olympic was only licensed for the performance of " bur-
lettas," and could not lawfully present entertainments of
much pretence. A critic likened the theatre to "a fashionable confectioner's shop, where, although one cannot absolutely make a dinner, one may enjoy a most agreeable
refection, consisting of jellies, cheese-cakes, custards, and
such trifles light as air, served upon the best Dresden
china in the most elegant style." Madame Vestris was
the first London manager who sought, with the aid of
choice fittings and decorations, to give the stage the
refined aspect of a drawing-room.

On the 21st March, 1838, Charles Mathews, much
to the consternation of his friends, was married to
Madame Vestris at the Church of St. Mary Abbots,
Kensington. The management of the Olympic was
entrusted to the friendly hands of Mr. Planché, and the
newly married couple crossed the Atlantic, bent upon a
theatrical tour through the United States. They were
not well received in America, however: their adventure
resulted, indeed, in something very like failure. It may
have been that their histrionic method was too uncon-
ventional, that the plays in which they appeared were
too unsubstantial, to suit the somewhat crude tastes of
the American public; but more probably there was a
predisposition to view coldly an actress with whose fame
scandal had been very busy, and whose history offered
many opportunities for reproach. In America it had
been usual to inquire perhaps too curiously into the
private lives of the artists seeking public applause.
Madame Vestris and Charles Mathews returned to England, disappointed perhaps, but by no means disheartened. In 1839 they entered upon the management
of Covent Garden Theatre, which Macready had just
vacated.

Certainly they conducted their new and arduous
enterprise with singular spirit and liberality. But management of the patent theatres in those days was almost
a sure road to ruin; lessee after lessee had retired from

the field to mourn his losses in private, or to make public his misfortunes in the Court of Bankruptcy. The English stage was not in favour with fashion; the Court gave little countenance save to Italian operas and French plays. For three seasons Charles Mathews and Madame Vestris carried on the contest with energy. In a parting address to the audience, delivered on the 30th April, 1842, the manager described the experiences of his wife and himself in connection with Covent Garden Theatre : " My partner and I have been its directors for three years, during which time we have endeavoured, at much personal and pecuniary sacrifice, to sow the seeds of that solid prosperity which we hoped would one day manifest itself in permanent satisfaction to you and in a golden harvest to ourselves; but, alas for 'the mutability of human affairs !' our first season was merely sowing—our second little more than hoeing—and though the third has been growing, we must leave to other hands the fourth, which might have been our mowing." Charles Mathews, involved to the amount of £30,000, sought relief in the Insolvent Debtors' Court, and obtained " the benefit of the act." The theatre had been open for three years at a nightly loss, it appeared, of £22 during the first season, £10 in the second, and £41 in the third ! Yet the public had been offered entertainments of special excellence and great variety. To a modern *impresario*, with his long " runs," his unchanging programme, and his small troop of players, the proceedings at Covent Garden from 1839 to 1842 must seem most amazing. The company was of great strength; the lessee and his wife were supported by William Farren, Bartley, George Vandenhoff, John Cooper, Walter Lacy, F. Matthews, Granby, Harley, Meadows, Wigan, Brougham, Selby, Bland, and W. H. Payne; by Mrs. Nesbitt, Mrs. Glover, Mrs. W. Lacy, Miss Cooper, Mrs. Selby, Mrs. Brougham, Mrs. Bland; and an operatic company that included Adelaide Kemble, and Messrs. Harrison Borrani, Stretton, Leffler, etc. Amongst the new plays produced were Jerrold's "Bubbles of the Day," Sheridan Knowles's "Old Maids," Leigh Hunt's "Legend of Florence," Mr. Boucicault's "London Assurance," and a second comedy, "The Irish Heiress," from the same pen, which lived but for two nights; of farces, ballets, pantomimes, and spectacles, there was no lack; the operas of "Norma," "Elena Uberti," "The Marriage of Figaro," and "La Sonnambula" were presented, to introduce Miss Kemble to an English audience; and the following plays were revived with liberal provision of appropriate scenery and costumes :—"Merry Wives of Windsor," "Midsummer Night's Dream," "Love's Labour's Lost," "Romeo and Juliet," "Comus," "Rule a Wife and have a Wife," "Wives as they were and Maids as they are," "She would and she would not," "The Clandestine Marriage," "The Critic,"

"Rivals," "School for Scandal," etc., etc.   It may be
added, that for six nights in the season of 1832-40
Charles Kemble returned to the stage by royal command,
the management profiting to the amount of £1500.

This was perhaps the most ambitious period of
Charles Mathews's histrionic career.   He was at this
time, indeed, most venturesome in regard to new impersonations, and greatly extended his repertory of parts.
He stepped from burletta into legitimate comedy, representing not merely the heroes of Sheridan, *Charles Surface* and *Puff*—in the " Rivals " he was content to play
Fag — but achieving great success as the *Slender* of
Shakespeare and the *Michael Perez* of Beaumont and
Fletcher, the *Atall* of Cibber and the *Sir Wilful Wit-
woud* of Congreve.   After the disasters at Covent Garden
he retreated with his wife to Drury Lane, then opening
under the management of Macready.   But here difficulties arose touching a proposal to reduce the salaries
of all the company ; and then Madame Vestris felt herself unable to accept the character of *Venus* in a revival
of Dryden's " King Arthur," with Purcell's music.   In
truth, the comedians were not comfortable under the
direction of the tragedian.   Accordingly they quitted
Macready, to be received with open arms by Mr. Webster
at the Haymarket.

The interregnum of five years occurring between the
closing of Covent Garden in 1842 and the opening

of the Lyceum under the management of Madame Vestris in 1847 was by no means uneventful. For one thing Charles Mathews had again to petition for legal relief in regard to his pecuniary liabilities, although but eighteen months had elapsed since he left the Insolvent Court "as free as air, to begin the world a new man," as he described himself in a public address to his creditors. For he took the world into his confidence: he was anxious that his position should be generally understood. He had, it appeared, renewed obligations which his first insolvency had legally cancelled; and then he had failed in his undertaking to pay certain instalments out of the professional earnings of himself and his wife. A sum of £900 he had sent up to London from the provinces on this account; but, as he avowed, the "mouths of his devourers seemed to open wider and wider in proportion to the magnitude of the food provided." He nevertheless expressed a hope that by putting aside £1300 per annum, to be paid by weekly instalments into the hands of a trustee, he might satisfy the largest portion of the rapidly increasing debt, "hourly swelling with hideous law costs and yawning interest." This arrangement was defeated, however, by the impatience of his creditors, who continued to bring actions against him, to thrust him into prison, and executions into his house. To avoid arrest and to fulfil his duties to the public, his managers, and his creditors themselves, he had been, as he said, driven

to subterfuges for which he despised himself, in order
that he might gain entrance to and exit from the theatres
at which he had been engaged. "In short," he concluded, "for a year and a half have I been harassed,
censured, sued, arrested, lectured, and drained of every
farthing I could muster, earn, or borrow, and no one
debt seems materially reduced by it; interest and law
will swallow up everything. . . . All I can say is, I have
done my best; I am driven from my home and my profession, to neither of which I am determined will I
return until I can present myself before the public freely
and independently as I have always done."

It need hardly be said that the actor did not find
his difficulties enduring or insupportable, and that he
duly continued his professional exertions. For some
seasons he was included with his wife in the company
at the Haymarket under Mr. Webster's rule. The year
1844 saw the production of the prize comedy concerning which much excitement prevailed among the
theatrical public. Mr. Webster had offered a prize of
£500 for the best comedy that should be sent to the
Haymarket Theatre, a committee of dramatists and
actors being appointed to examine and pronounce judgment in the matter. The manager's intentions were of
the best, and the sum named was held to be a handsome
price to pay for an original five-act comedy in those
days. Nearly a hundred comedies were forwarded to

the committee, who were supposed to be ignorant of the
names of the authors tendering their works for examina-
tion. The prize was awarded in respect of a comedy
entitled " Quid pro Quo, or, the Day of Dupes," which
proved to be written by Mrs. Charles Gore, the well-
known and fashionable novelist of that date. Possibly
it was perceived by Mr. and Mrs. Mathews that greater
expectation had been raised in regard to the prize
comedy than its representation could satisfy. They
prudently declined the parts of *Captain Sippet*, a weaker
Dazzle, and *Lady Mary Rivers*, a more vapid *Grace
Harkaway*, which the committee had requested them to
accept, and the characters were therefore sustained by
Mr. Buckstone and Miss Julia Bennett. " Quid pro Quo "
was condemned by the audience in the most unequivocal fashion. It lingered, however, for a while upon
the scene. Mrs. Nisbett was thought to be delightful as
an Eton boy *Lord Bellamont*, and excellent acting was
contributed by Mrs. Glover, by Farren, and Strickland,
and Mrs. Humby ; but the fact of the failure of the prize
comedy could not be concealed or controverted. Nor
did Mrs. Gore mend matters by declaring that " Quid
pro Quo " had been crushed because of her sex by the
opposition of rival dramatists connected with the press
as dramatic critics, who had previously condemned for a
like reason the plays of Lady Dacre, Lady Emmeline
Wortley, and Joanna Baillie. In truth, " Quid pro Quo "

failed because of its dulness and vulgarity : it was written apparently in emulation of "London Assurance," but it exhibited little of the wit or the skill in stage artifice of that successful work.

In 1844, Charles Mathews, who shone so often as the English representative of parts sustained in Paris by Arnal, Ravel, Levassor, and Bouffé, sauntered into the repertory of Frédéric Lemaître, and ventured to appear at the Haymarket in an adaptation of "Don Cæsar de Bazan." As the hero of this French melodrama, the English comedian certainly furnished warrant for the charge so often brought against his histrionic method that "it wanted weight." It was found that he had all Don Cæsar's levity, nothing of his gravity. But in another play borrowed from the French, the actor obtained one of his greatest successes : his *Sir Charles Coldstream* in "Used Up" greatly pleased the public, and continued for many years to be one of his most admired impersonations. Arnal had "created" the part, and the play underwent adaptation at other theatres as a farce for the low-comedy purposes of Wright and Keeley. But Mathews's performance owed little or nothing to Arnal ; the character of *Sir Charles Coldstream*, the languid English dandy, elegant of aspect and manner, superfine of dress, sublimely calm of speech, corresponded only in regard to certain of his adventures with the hero of "L'Homme Blasé." The adaptation had been made

originally by Mr. Boucicault, who had given in the title
of "Bored to Death;" but Mr. Mathews so amended
and embroidered it, that finally he claimed it as his own,
at the risk of a lawsuit with Mr. Webster, who professed
to own the copyright of the English play. But it was
soon manifest that, whoever might be responsible for the
adaptation or possessed of its copyright, there was but
one possible *Sir Charles Coldstream*. For a little while
Mr. Webster himself, in assertion of what he believed to
be his rights, essayed the impersonation; but the public
did not encourage the experiment. Recognized as an
excellent actor, it was also felt that he was not exhibiting
himself to advantage in the part of *Sir Charles Coldstream*, the peculiar possession of Charles Mathews.

It was in this year that Mr. Boucicault produced his
second best comedy, "Old Heads and Young Hearts,"
a production, however, falling far short of the merits of
"London Assurance," though composed of similar ingre-
dients, and finding occupation for a strong company of
comedians, including the original representatives of *Sir
Harcourt Courtly*, *Grace Harkaway*, and *Dazzle*—to
name no more. Recognized as only a poor relation of
the elder work, resembling it chiefly in regard to its
worst qualities, "Old Heads and Young Hearts" pleased
for a season, and may be reckoned as of very superior
worth to the other comedies by the same hand, such as
"The Irish Heiress," "The School for Scheming,"

"Alma Mater," "Mr. Peter Piper," "Love in a Maze,"
etc., which enjoyed no long life upon the stage, and are
now little remembered.   In the following season Mr.
and Mrs. Mathews appeared as the first representatives
of *Felix Goldthumb* and *Bessie Tulip* in Douglas Jerrold's
"Time works Wonders"—his best and most successful
comedy, making ample amends by its excess of wit for
any deficiencies of dramatic construction and interest.
It cannot be said, however, that Jerrold was altogether
successful in providing Charles Mathews with suitable
characters or with complete opportunities for histrionic
display.   The actor was not seen at his best either as
Captain Smoke in "Bubbles of the Day," or as *Felix
Goldthumb*, who is less connected than the more serious
Clarence Norman with the interest of "Time works
Wonders."   Jerrold was content to employ Charles
Mathews merely as the light comedian of convention.
But he was much more than this.   Throughout his career,
indeed, the actor might reasonably have complained of
the small pains taken by the dramatists to supply him
with suitable parts—to take the measure, as it were, of
his histrionic capacity.   His assumption of *Dazzle*, even,
had been something of an accident : the character had
not been designed for him.   *Dazzle* had been originally
called *O'Dazzle*, or some such name—an Irish character,
to be represented by Tyrone Power, probably.

During 1846 and the following year, Charles Mathews

and Madame Vestris fulfilled engagements at the
Princess's and other theatres, the lady taking leave of
her provincial friends before the opening of the Lyceum
under her management in October, 1847. The public
often amuses itself by exaggerating the age of those
prominently before it : in the general judgment Madame
Vestris was much older than she was in truth, and
Charles Mathews was often spoken of as though he had
married his mother. Bidding adieu to the Liverpool
public in 1847, Madame Vestris frankly referred to the
matter. "Believe me," she said, "my health rather
than my inclination induces this apparently sudden step.
Were I, indeed, as old as some good people are pleased
to fancy me, I ought to have retired years ago, not only
from the mimic scene, but from the scene of life itself.
The truth is, that I have been long before the public,
thanks to the kindness of the public; I appeared con-
spicuously before it at an earlier age than is usual ; and
I am not yet, I venture to assert, quite superannuated."
She declined to reveal publicly her exact age, however,
claiming the privilege of her sex ; and she concluded
with a request that the support she had so long enjoyed
might, on her closing her country accounts and her
retirement from business so far, be extended to her
"junior partner." "He has secured for himself my
good will, and has, I trust, entitled himself to yours. It
is he, therefore, who will in future undertake the travelling

department." It was not supposed at this time, however, that he would ever be travelling round the world.

Born in 1797, Madame Vestris was but six years older than her husband. As she had said, she had been long before the public. She had married the worthless Armand Vestris in 1813; two years later she had sung for his benefit at the Italian Opera House in the Haymarket, in Winter's "Il Ratto di Proserpina." Her first appearance on the English stage was in 1820, at Drury Lane, when she played *Lilla* in Cobb's opera, "The Siege of Belgrade." Armand Vestris died about 1825, but husband and wife had lived apart since 1816. When I first saw the lady she was playing *Oberon* at Covent Garden in a most poetically ornate revival of "The Midsummer Night's Dream," with much music interpolated and many scenic illusions. I was a child in the dress circle (there were no stalls then), much delighted with the play, yet looking forward to the pantomime which was to follow, and which took liberties, I think, with Horace Walpole's "Castle of Otranto." To me that representative of *Oberon*, wearing a glittering suit of fairy golden armour crowned by a classic casque with flowing plumes, was a vision of beauty, wondrously graceful of motion and musical of speech. When I again beheld Madame Vestris some few years later, it was with more critical eyes, and time, as I judged, had meanwhile dealt somewhat harshly with her: her beauty had waned

seriously. She should hardly have essayed the part of
the youthful schoolgirl *Bessie Tulip.* Her looks suffered,
I think, from the excess of art employed to preserve
them, just as the age of a building is sometimes
revealed by the freshness of the materials employed in
repairing it. She had never possessed the regularity of
feature and repose of face which may long and successfully resist the insidious unkindness of the fleeting years.
Her address as an actress, with her excellent taste in
costume, she yet retained, of course ; she was, as ever,
bright of glance, lively of manner ; as a singer she could
still be heard with pleasure, and she gave all possible
point to the speeches she was required to deliver—witty
herself, she relished the wit of others ; no actress has
ever spoken better than she did such lines of pleasant
facetiousness, for instance, as Mr. Planché was wont to
include in his fairy extravaganzas. But she did not look
young ; indeed, by the side of her husband she looked
almost old. But then he bore with such amazing
sprightliness his burden of thirty-five to forty years ; an
adolescent grace and buoyancy remained with him so
long ; time had in no degree rounded his shoulders or
out-curved his waistcoat ; he was always youthfully
slim of form and elastic of movement. One natural
defalcation art easily remedied. His hair had thinned
early in life. What a collection of auburn and flaxen
wigs he must have possessed ! He first revealed publicly

his calvity, converting it to the uses of his art, when he
first played *Affable Hawk* "with his own bald head," as
people said. But this was not until 1850. Certain
earlier of his performances have first to be mentioned.

During his engagements at the Princess's Theatre
Charles Mathews played many new parts, although his
position as a "star" would have justified his confining
himself to a fixed repertory. The manager liked to vary
his programme, and dealt largely in translations from
the French, hastily written and cheaply produced. The
company did not lack strength : numbered, indeed, many
excellent performers. "The Merry Wives of Windsor,"
in recognition of the success obtained with it at Covent
Garden, was revived : Madame Vestris reappearing as
Mrs. Page to the *Mrs. Ford* of Mrs. Stirling, the *Ford*
of James Wallack, the *Page* of Mr. Ryder, the *Falstaff*
of Granby, etc. Resigning the part of *Slender* to
Compton, Charles Mathews now undertook the character of *Sir Hugh Evans*, looking quaintly picturesque
in his cassock and bands, and performing with admirable
humour. He was an adept, as his singing of "Jenny
Jones" had proved, in delivering English after the
glib, clipped, tripping Welsh fashion. This was the
operatic edition of the comedy : *Ann Page* and *Master
Fenton* being personated by singers, and the action every
now and then undergoing suspension, in order that
Mrs. Page and her daughter might sing "I know a

bank," or that *Master Fenton* might introduce " Blow,
thou winter wind." The songs, by various composers,
all boasted Shakespeare's words, derived indiscriminately
from the plays and the poems, their appropriateness in
relation to the positions they occupied in the play being
very little considered. Another Covent Garden triumph
—Mr. Planché's fairy play of " Beauty and the Beast "—
was also essayed; and many farces and small comedies
were presented, including " A Sovereign Remedy," " A
Curious Case," " The Barber Bravo," and " Love's
Telegraph," an adaptation of " Le Gant et l'Eventail,"
in which Charles Mathews found congenial occupation.
About this time, too, he first undertook an exclusively
serious character. He appeared as *Lovelace* in a version
of " Clarissa Harlowe," by MM. Dumanoir, Clairville,
and Guillard, an adaptation, of course, of the novel of
Richardson.

I may speak with some hesitation of a play which
was produced more than thirty years ago, and which I,
a schoolboy critic, saw but once. As I remember it,
however, it was a sombre work, unlikely to gratify an
English audience, unsuited to our stage. Little success
attended its performance here, although, I believe, it had
prospered in Paris. But French critics have long been
wont to prize exceedingly the writings of Richardson.
Absorbed by regard for his skill as a narrator, they have
overlooked, or have not been capable of estimating, the

tediousness and diffuseness of his literary style. " Clarissa Harlowe " was thus found to be a name to conjure with in Paris. The play owned a French compactness of construction. In the first act Clarissa was seen oppressed by her family. Mr. Ryder played her father, I think; Mr. James Vining her brother. There was much preaching on the subject of filial disobedience; the characters were all attired in Quaker drabs and greys ; Clarissa wept : she did little but weep from the first scene to the last of the drama, as she endured the didactic efforts and exercises of her relatives. The second act was more lively, in Sir Anthony Absolute's sense of the word ; indeed, the proceedings of Lovelace might well have evoked the intervention of the Lord Chamberlain : and here, too, relief was afforded by the vivacity of a rural *soubrette*, very well played by the late Miss Marshall. The last act—the English play consisted of three acts only—was chiefly occupied with the sufferings, the sorrows, and the death of Clarissa, personated with much ingenuity and pathos by Mrs. Stirling, if I rightly remember. As *Lovelace*, Charles Mathews looked very handsome, and wore well his bag wig and tasteful court dress, carrying himself most gallantly. His aspect and mien were worthy of the Français. But at all times he was wont to appear at ease in costumes of fanciful or old-fashioned device ; he had never the awkward, inconvenienced air exhibited by many players when required to assume unaccustomed clothes. Still, his *Lovelace* was not accounted successful. He took great pains with the part, played with unusual care, was calm and composed, avoiding levity and flippancy, and fairly exhibiting the unworthiness of *Lovelace*, but failing wholly to convey the passion animating him. Something the performance may have gained in decorum by this very deficiency on the part of the actor. But the spectator became aware of the boundary of Charles Mathews's art in a certain direction: it was like coming suddenly upon the ring fence confining an estate. It was manifest that as a stage-lover Charles Mathews could not shine; he was wholly without fervour or earnestness; it was as much as he could do to be commonly serious; he could only woo the heroines of the theatre after the tepid, unreal, insincere fashion of the conventional walking gentleman : always heedful during his most ardent speeches to keep his curls and his costume unrumpled, and the white lining of his glossy hat well turned towards the pit. It was very certain that he could not adequately represent the *Lovelace* of Richardson. At the time this was of the less consequenee, seeing that Janin's play did not please, and had to be withdrawn after a few representations.

Something further I may here, perhaps, be permitted to add touching the aspect and costumes of the actor. He had never been carried away by what was once called "the moustache movement." He entertained an old actor's prejudices on the subject, holding that facial expression was in such wise injuriously affected. He would have sympathized with Macready's objections upon one of his Macduffs appearing "with a pair of well-grown moustaches." When it seemed to him that such a decoration was absolutely necessary to the character he assumed, Charles Mathews exercised his skill as an artist, and, with a camel's-hair brush, painted a moustache upon his upper lip. His appearance as *Lovelace* I have mentioned; but I may add that he was not less picturesque and elegant of presence when he wore a Kneller dress of green velvet as the *Duke of Buckingham* in Planché's "Court Beauties;" when he assumed mediæval trunks and hose as the hero of "The Captain of the Watch;" or what may be called the French-Revolutionary costume of *Lavater* and some other characters. But he was chiefly seen upon the stage in modern dress; to his audiences he was usually a gentleman of their own period. Mr. G. H. Lewes has written of him: "In our juvenile apprehensions he was the beau-ideal of elegance. We studied his costumes with ardent emotion. We envied him his tailor, and made him our pattern to live and to die." Thirty-five years ago men were more superfine of dress than they are just now. There were dandies still surviving, and D'Orsay was a power in the world of fashion. "Such a dress!" writes Haydon of D'Orsay in 1839; "with great-coat, blue satin cravat, hair oiled and curling, hat of the primest curve and purest water, gloves scented with *eau de Cologne*, or *eau de jasmin*, primrose in tint, skin in tightness," etc. Charles Mathews dressed much after the D'Orsay manner, persisting in it even after it had become a little old-fashioned. He long delighted in frock or "Newmarket cut" coats, olive green or light brown, claret or mulberry colour, with lawn wristbands turned back over the tight cuffs; in shawl-patterned waistcoats and profuse satin stocks confined by jewelled pins linked together; in the lightest and tightest of trousers, cut to fit the boot like a gaiter and closely strapped beneath the instep. He was the last man, I think, to wear trousers of this pattern upon the stage, although the late Mr. James Vining, a dandy of an earlier date, may have rivalled him in the matter. It almost seemed at last as though there were a conventional costume to be worn by light comedians irrespective of the fashion prevalent outside the theatre. But no doubt it was hard to surrender D'Orsay as a model, to turn away from so consummate an *arbiter elegantiarum.* Even Macready, about to personate *Alfred Evelyn*, in 1840, thought it well to take counsel of the Count concerning "his hatter, the mode of keeping accounts at the clubs at play, about servants," etc.

The Lyceum opened with a strong company, Mr.

and Mrs. Mathews being assisted by Mrs. and Miss
Fitzwilliam, Mrs. Yates, Mrs. Stirling, and Miss Louisa
Howard; Messrs. Leigh Murray, Frank Matthews, Selby,
Roxby, John Reeve, junior, Meadows, Buckstone, and
Harley. The theatre had been tastefully and elaborately
re-decorated; certain of the modelled figures, panels, and
medallions have survived until the present date. A new
system of lighting was introduced, and, for the first
time in an English theatre, draperies of white lace
adorned the private boxes. The scene-painter was
Mr. Beverley, and the stage appointments soon acquired
fame in right of their exceeding beauty and originality.
The entertainments were of the pattern which had
proved so successful at the Olympic under Madame
Vestris's management, with increase of importance and
magnificence. Little advantage, however, was taken of
the Act of 1844, which established free trade in theatrical exhibitions, and permitted the representation of
the legitimate drama upon all stages alike. Five-act
comedies were eschewed at the Lyceum, nor was the
slightest encouragement offered to native authors. The
management endured for some nine years or so, but
during that period scarcely an original work was produced. The theatre subsisted upon vaudevilles,
comedies, and melodramas, adapted from the French,
and upon a series of extravaganzas founded by Mr.
Planché upon the old French fairy tales. "The

Golden Branch," "King Charming," "The King of the Peacocks," "The Islands of Jewels," "The Prince of Happy Land," "The Good Woman in the Wood," and "Once upon a Time there were two Kings," were perhaps the most remarkable of these productions, which gradu-ally degenerated from vehicles of pun and poetry, song and dance and Christmas pleasantry, into mere spectacles, brilliant and yet barren. Mr. Planché has himself described how the scene-painter by degrees came to take the dramatist's place in the theatre. "Year after year Mr. Beverley's powers were taxed to outdo his former outdoings. The last scene became the first in the estimation of the management. The most com-plicated machinery, the most costly materials, were annually put into requisition, until their bacon was so buttered it was impossible to save it. As to me, I was positively painted out. Nothing was considered brilliant but the last scene. Dutch metal was in the ascendant." Mr. Planché fled from the Lyceum and found refuge again at the Olympic. Robson was playing there, proving himself a great burlesque actor, and something more—indeed, a very great deal more.

It must not be supposed, however, that Charles Mathews allowed himself to be effaced by his extrava-ganzas. He rarely took part in these, although he had won fame by his efforts of a grotesque sort in the kindred plays of "Riquet with the Tuft" and "The Golden

Fleece." At one time, Madame Vestris being ill, he appeared in her stead as *King Charming*, attired splendidly in robes of pink silk and a head-dress of pearls, diamonds, and bird-of-Paradise plumes, in imitation of the Nepaulese ambassador, a celebrity of the time. Upon another occasion he undertook Mr. Buckstone's duties, and assumed the character of *Box* in the famous farce of "Box and Cox." But in burlesque and low comedy he was not usually concerned, and the farces in which he appeared were always of a certain refinement, strongly flavoured with comedy, and affording him artistic opportunities. He was seen at his best, I think, during these Lyceum times. He was in excellent health and spirits, and his histrionic method, with all its gaiety and sprightliness, was distinguished by a steady force and incisiveness which it lacked somewhat in late years. He even took his audience by surprise, developing unexpected resources, and essaying characters of an unaccustomed sort. He shone in melodrama. Mr. Lewes has described his performance of the *Count D'Arental*, the villanous hero of the "Day of Reckoning," an adaptation by Mr. Planché of a rather commonplace French melodrama, owing its origin to the popularity of M. Sue's "Mystères de Paris." Certain of the *dramatis personæ*, indeed, in quest of adventure, assume blouses and visit a *tapis-franc*, avowedly after the manner of the Prince Rudolphe of that once famous romance, although with-

out his philanthropic intentions. The Count is a monster of perfidy and cruelty, hardened and consummate,
capable of any crime. Nevertheless his demeanour is
most calm, polite, gentlemanly; nothing in his aspect
reveals his really shameless and corrupt nature. He is
as unlike the conventional villain of melodrama as could
possibly be. A bankrupt *roué*, he treats his young, rich,
and beautiful wife with the most insulting coldness and
neglect. He suspects her of infidelity, and indeed hopes
that she may prove unfaithful : in such wise he may the
better 'prey upon her fortune, which meantime is pro-
tected by the French code. The lady's distresses are
great, and she seeks some consolation at the hands of
a devoted but platonic admirer. The Count simply
threatens to shoot her friend and to ruin her reputation ;
but his manner is still scrupulously polite. He listens
calmly to her appeals and protestations, does not inter-
rupt her for a moment, yet never swerves from his resolve
to secure her fortune or to slay her lover. This exhibition of intense and complete cruelty proved most
effective upon the scene. It may be added that the
Count's courage is unquestionable, although founded as
much upon scorn of his fellows, their follies and weak-
nesses, as upon his own strength of character and self-
reliance. When in the *tapis-franc* his rank is discovered
and his life threatened, he is not discomposed : he de-
spises his antagonists too much. He knows that his

own safety and their good opinion can be bought for a
dozen of wine. When the final duel is forced upon him,
and he tries to take an unfair advantage of his adversary,
he is not influenced by a cowardly regard for his own
safety, but by utter contempt for his plebeian foe, whom
he would sweep from his path as he would brush away
an insect that troubled him.

The play is of an unwholesome kind, with a disagree-
ably opaque moral atmosphere ; and neither upon its
first representation in 1851 nor upon its revival at the
Adelphi in 1868 did it greatly please the public. But it
enhanced considerably the histrionic fame of Charles
Mathews. It was well understood that the actor was
curiously deficient in tenderness ; that his art, however
winning, graceful, vivacious, and humorous, had no hold
whatever upon the serious emotions of his audience.
Even that semblance of feeling by means of which very
obtuse players, given a pathetic situation, have been able
to move their public, was beyond him. He could not
sound a pathetic note ever so gently. When in the little
comedy of " The Bachelor of Arts," for instance, he was
required but to exclaim " My poor father ! " and to hide
his face in his handkerchief as the drop-scene fell, the
effect was almost ludicrous from the actor's curious inability to portray emotion even of the simplest and
slightest kind. As Mr. Lewes has noted, not only were
strong displays of feelings—" rage, scorn, pathos, dignity,

vindictiveness, tenderness, and wild mirth—all beyond his means, but he could not even laugh with animal heartiness; he sparkled, he never exploded." In the *Count D'Arental*, as in some other characters, what may be called without offence the heartlessness of the actor was turned to theatrical account and made to serve tragic uses. His levity was no longer harmless and pleasant; it was now allied to villainy and infamous cruelty. The audience did not much relish, perhaps, the change involved in this experiment; yet it had its success from an artistic point of view and in relation to the fame of the actor.

"The Day of Reckoning" paved the way for "The Chain of Events," produced in the following year—"a drama in eight acts, occupying the whole evening"— adapted by Mr. Lewes from "La Dame de la Halle," a French play of prodigious elaboration, ingenuity, and tediousness, so successful in Paris that its performance at several London theatres seemed a managerial necessity. I retain no very distinct impressions of it, but I remember that it was most liberally equipped with scenery and costumes, with a very vivid effect of a storm at sea and shipwreck; that Miss Laura Keene, afterwards very favourably known in America, personated the heroine; that the characters wore hair-powder, and that Charles Mathews played a cool and calculating villain, who in the last scene committed suicide by leaping from

the balcony of a gambling-house, I think in the Palais
Royal. The " Chain of Events " enjoyed many representations, although the stage has seen nothing of it
since 1852. A still longer play, however, presented in
1853—"A Strange History, in nine chapters "—was withdrawn after a few performances. For this production
Mr. Lewes, in conjunction with Mr. Mathews, was also
responsible. It had, of course, a French origin, and
contained many wonderful incidents—the fall of an
avalanche, I remember, among its scenic effects. But
"A Strange History" oppressed, because of its strange-
ness, its prodigious length, and the numerous complexi-
ties of its plot. It was relieved of an act or two ; but
the public refused to accept it upon any terms, and, with
a sigh, for it had cost many pains and much money, the
management abandoned it altogether and for ever. It
made way for "The Lawyers," a successful version of
" Les Avocats."

But the greatest success at the Lyceum under the
rule of Charles Mathews was probably obtained by " The
Game of Speculation," first represented in October, 1851.
This version of " Mercadet," Balzac's posthumous
comedy, was prepared by Mr. Lewes, then assuming
the name of Slingsby Lawrence, "in less than thirteen
hours, and produced after only two rehearsals," as the
preface to the printed play informs us. " Mercadet "
had not been performed in Paris exactly as its author

had left it. The five acts of the original had been reduced to three; many scenes were omitted and some transposed. Mr. Lewes judiciously followed the abridged acting edition, rendering the dialogue in spirited English, and tampering in no respect with the nature of the plot. The only fault to be found with his adaptation relates to the characteristic names bestowed upon the *dramatis personæ: Affable Hawk, Prospectus, Earthworm, Hard-corn, Dimity,* etc. This was pursuant to a fashion long enjoying public favour and boasting the authority of the best writers; but injurious, nevertheless, to the illusions which it is the aim of fiction to produce, and imparting unreality to what otherwise would appear genuine and natural enough. Sydney Smith rightly condemned what he termed "appellative jocularity," as savouring of vulgarity and sinning against good taste.

The original *Mercadet* was Geoffroy, I think, but I never saw him, and I am without information as to his method of playing the part. When the comedy was transferred to the Théâtre Français, Got appeared as *Mercadet.* In the course of the visit of the Comédie to London in 1871, "Mercadet" was presented at our Opera Comique in the Strand, and our playgoers were provided with an opportunity of comparing the impersonations of two most accomplished comedians. Mr. Lewes has frankly avowed his preference for the performance of Charles Mathews. But in regard to rival histrionic portrayals the one first seen is likely to be the one more admired. The player who has pre-audience secures our vote and interest. His art impresses us to the prejudice of the later performer, whose merits are tested by a standard not of his choosing, and to which he may reasonably object. The *Mercadet* of Got differed màterially from the *Affable Hawk* of Charles Mathews. The one succeeded by sheer force of character, the other by exquisite charm of manner. Got represented a sort of George Hudson, a railway king, a blunt man of business, careless of dress, homely of bearing, rough of speech. He rather encouraged his creditors to dupe themselves than laboured to cajole them; he was somewhat ashamed of the roguery to which his embarrassments had driven him, and in his own home appeared as a respectable member of society, an affectionate husband and father. He was thoroughly in earnest; and when he threatened to drown himself in the Seine, it seemed certain that he would be as good as his word. The performance was, indeed, much heightened by the actor's adroit touches of pathos, and by the passionate excitement of his surprise and joy at the return of his missing partner and the redemption of his name from discredit. As *Affable Hawk*, Charles Mathews invested debt with a sort of diplomatic dignity. He carried the graces of the drawing-room on 'Change. His creditors were constrained to yield to the fascinations of address; wrath and importunity were subdued by placidity and elegance. He was little troubled with remorse; those who sought money of him were his natural enemies, and to be treated accordingly. Under such conditions trickery was allowable, and only open to reproach if failure attended it, and he did not intend to fail. He hinted at suicide in the Thames, but no one took the hint. A conviction prevailed that if ever he got into the water he would promptly get out again, much benefited by his brief immersion. It was difficult to withhold sympathy from the engaging adventurer who, treating debt as a fine art, bore his pecuniary burthens with such admirable gallantry and good humour, fighting against bankruptcy so courageously, and by superior intelligence and address, helped by a lucky accident, triumphing at last over creditors even less reputable and scrupulous than himself. The actor obtained great popularity by reason of his performance of *Affable Hawk*. The "Game of Speculation" underwent revival in many subsequent seasons; it has never been presented, however, without Charles Mathews for its hero. It was last played in London during his engagement at the Gaiety in 1873. Among other Lyceum successes may be counted the comedies and farces of "A Nice Firm," "A Bachelor of Arts," "Serve Him Right," "A Wonderful Woman," "A Practical Man," "An Appeal to the Public," "Aggravating Sam," "Little Toddlekins," "Cool as a Cucumber," etc.

But the experiences of the Lyceum management were not wholly of a prosperous sort. The expenses were very great, and now and then serious disasters befell the enterprise. The strong company gradually dispersed. Sometimes the band, in despair at the non-payment of their salaries, declined to enter the orchestra. It became notorious that the manager was in pecuniary straits, and he was charged with extravagant habits. Again he was constrained to invoke the aid of the law, and compound in such wise with his creditors. Performing in a little comedy called " My Heart's Idol," he was so unfortunate as to receive a wound in the hand while fighting a duel with Mr. George Vining, who also took part in the play. Forthwith appeared this epigram upon Charles Mathews's recent accident :

> " Poor Charley's misfortune the public deplore,
>   Metallic advances he never could stand;
>   The *tin* always slipped through his fingers before,
>   And now the *steel* goes through the rest of his hand !"

It was said, too, that his own embarrassments had taught him how to play *Affable Hawk*. Mr. Lewes, in reference to the opinion entertained by the public touching the actor, has recorded the utterance of an elderly gentleman in the boxes of the Lyceum after the fall of the curtain upon the " Game of Speculation :" " And to think of such a man being in difficulties ! There ought to be a public subscription got up to pay his

debts!"   He attacked the press in regard to the use and
abuse of "orders," and he entered into a literary duel
with Mr. Angus Reach, who, as the critic of the *Morning Chronicle*, had ventured to censure certain of the
Lyceum productions and representations.   In 1852
Charles Mathews further distinguished himself by pub-
lishing, in French and English, a pamphlet setting forth
the condition of our English theatres, and demonstrating
that the new copyright treaty with France would not
improve the prospects of French dramatists.   He alleged
that in the year 1851, out of 263 plays produced upon
the French stage, but eight had been appropriated by
London managers; the reason being that, as a rule,
French plays were too foolish or too indecorous to suit
English theatres.   The pamphlet was clever, saucy, and
amusing; as a piece of reasoning it was absurd.   Mr.
Charles Reade justly wrote of it: "The thing that
astonishes me is, how he could sit down, in the spring of
1852, with his pockets full of money made out of French
skulls, and try to create a general impression that their
pieces are too irrational and loose to be played in
England, either with or without that alteration, abridgment, and discolouration, which adapters say are so
difficult, and inventors, and even impartial observers,
know to be so easy—compared with invention."

On July 26, 1854, Madame Vestris was seen upon
the stage for the last time.   She appeared on the occa-

sion of her husband's benefit, as the heroine of "Sun-
shine through the Clouds," a version of Madame de
Girardin's famous " La Joie fait Peur." Her health had
been failing her for some time, and she had been able
only intermittently to take part in the Lyceum representations, employing herself chiefly in the direction of the
stage and the selection and arrangement of the costumes.
In these departments her taste and skill were invaluable
to the theatre. She died on August 8, 1856, at her
residence, Grove Lodge, Fulham. She left behind her
pleasant memories of her attractions, gifts, and accomplishments as actress and singer.

The Lyceum management at an end, Charles
Mathews renounced for ever the cares and responsibili-
ties of an *impresario*. He was content now to wander
as a "star," now to attach himself for a while to a
London company. For some seasons he served under
Mr. E. T. Smith at Drury Lane, appearing in " Married
for Money," an amended version of a comedy derived
by Poole from the French, and parodying the " Wizard
of the North " in an occasional piece called " The Great
Gun Trick :" even executing with remarkable neatness
certain sleight-of-hand tricks for which the Wizard, a
North Briton, whose real name was Anderson, had
become famous. The public was much amused ; but
the Wizard, who had undertaken the management of
Covent Garden, scarcely approved. He promptly re-

torted by producing a farce with the polite title of "Twenty Minutes with an Impudent Puppy," Mr. Leigh Murray being expressly engaged to personate Charles Mathews. The Strand Theatre ridiculed the contest in a farce, boasting the Shakespearian name of "A Plague on both your Houses." The joke and the conjuror's management ended seriously: Covent Garden was totally destroyed by fire on the morning of March 6, 1856, at the close of a very riotous and vulgar *bal masqué* given for Mr. Anderson's benefit.

From a visit to America Charles Mathews returned in 1858 with his second wife, an actress possessed of personal advantages and considerable histrionic ability, known in the United States as Mrs. Davenport. He reappeared at the Haymarket on October 11, and was received with enthusiasm. He resumed his old part of *Dazzle*, Mrs. Mathews making her *début* in England as *Lady Gay Spanker*, and forthwith obtaining the good opinion of the audience. Mr. and Mrs. Mathews remained some seasons at the Haymarket Theatre, then under the management of Mr. Buckstone. They appeared in new plays called "Everybody's Friend"— since known as "A Widow Hunt"—"A Tale of a Coat," "The Royal Salute," "The Overland Mail," "The Contested Election," "His Excellency," etc. In 1860 they accepted an engagement at Drury Lane, personating the hero and heroine of "The Adventures of a Billet-

Doux," an early adaptation of "Les Pattes de Mouche" of Victorien Sardou. They visited the provincial theatres, and later years found them fulfilling engagements now at the St. James's, now at the Adelphi, and now at the Olympic. In 1863 Charles Mathews played at the Variétés, Paris, in a French version, executed by himself, of the English farce of "Cool as a Cucumber," and in other plays.

Old actors usually shun new parts; but Charles Mathews did not shrink from histrionic experiments, although he had now numbered more than sixty years. He achieved great success by his performance of *Young Wilding*, in a revised edition of Foote's "Liar" at the Olympic, in 1867, Mrs. Mathews lending him valuable assistance as the heroine of the comedy. He appeared, too, as *Tangent* in a revival of Morton's comedy, "The Way to Get Married "—but the work proved to be hopelessly out of date—and in forgotten comedies of French origin, "From Grave to Gay," and "The Woman of the World." In a powerful drama called "Black Sheep," founded upon Mr. Edmund Yates's novel of the same name, his energetic impersonation of the murderer, *Stewart Routh*, stirred memories of his old success as the *Count D'Arental* of "The Day of Reckoning," and obtained for the production great favour. Early in 1870, after taking the chair at a grand dinner given in his honour, he departed to fulfil a very profitable engagement in Australia and the colonies. On October 7, 1872, he reappeared in England, at the Gaiety Theatre, playing his old parts in " The Critic " and " A Curious Case." As his manager, Mr. Hollingshead, has recorded : " His reception was the most enthusiastic burst of feeling I ever witnessed or can imagine ; and the one who seemed the least moved by it was the chief actor." He played for ten weeks, the receipts being larger than the theatre had ever known before, "amounting to nearly £1000 per week," says Mr. Hollingshead. He was re-engaged for the summer of 1873, and in the winter of that year he appeared for a night or two as *Tom Shuffleton* in " John Bull," in combination with Mr. Phelps, Mr. Toole, Mr. Hermann Vezin, and others. He fulfilled further engagements at the Gaiety in 1874 and 1875, returning there in 1876, after playing for a month in Calcutta, during the Prince of Wales's visit to India. In the following year he played for nine weeks at the Opera Comique Theatre. On the night of June 2, 1877, he made his last appearance on the boards of a London Theatre. His last new part was *Mr. Evergreen*, in "My Awful Dad," a farcical play he had contrived for himself out of foreign materials. Its success was great, and it enjoyed many representations both in London and the provinces.

He died at the Queen's Hotel, Manchester, on June 24, 1878, of bronchitis. He had been playing but a fortnight before, at Staleybridge, but his strength had declined—he was seventy-five—and he sank under the severity of his malady. To the last he had acted with an ease and a spirit which had gone far to compensate for certain physical deficiencies and infirmities which would take no denial. Time had not galloped with him, but it had not stood still with him. He was youthfully slight of figure to the last, and he moved about the scene with his old graceful restlessness ; but his voice had lost tone, the family gift of clearness of articulation was failing him, and if he looked younger than his years he looked old, nevertheless. It would be hard to charge him, however, with the veteran's foible of lagging superfluously upon the stage. He was wont to say that his profession kept him alive, that he was never so well or so happy as when he was acting. And he retained to the end power to please his audiences ; he had been drawing crowded houses within a few days of his death ; the managers still offered him engagements ; while, in addition to the army of old playgoers still eager to applaud him and the genuineness of his art, there had grown up a new public, curious to see something of an actor whose connection with the theatre stretched backward to a remote period, and who had won for himself so large a share of public favour. But those who have only seen Charles Mathews at seventy or so must not deem themselves qualified to pronounce judgment upon his merits. He was then, in truth, but the shadow of what he had been at forty, fifty, or even sixty.

I will not employ the old phrase, always hyperbolical, that his death eclipsed the gaiety of nations. But I am sure that very many felt their spirits sadly dashed when tidings came of the passing away of Charles Mathews. He had figured so prominently during so long a series of years in their theatrical pleasures ; he had contributed so largely to the harmless entertainment of the public. The special attractions and attributes of his acting had, indeed, evoked on his behalf an amount of personal sympathy and regard such as few actors have ever known. I do not, of course, rank him among those great players of the past whose names have become historical, whose triumphs have been achieved on poetic and heroic heights towards which he at no time pretended to mount ; but he will long be remembered, I venture to think, as an artistic comedian, singularly gifted and accomplished, comparable with the best of actors, English or foreign, of his class ; original, following in the footsteps of no earlier performer, and leaving no successors—unique, unrivalled, inimitable.

CHAPTER VIII.

CHARLOTTE CUSHMAN.

THE Pilgrim Fathers figure in American pedigrees almost as frequently and persistently as Norman William and his followers appear at the trunk of our family trees. Certainly, the *Mayflower* must have carried very many heads of houses across the Atlantic. It was not in the *Mayflower*, however, but in the *Fortune*, a smaller vessel of fifty-five tons, that Robert Cushman, Nonconformist, the founder of the Cushman family in America, sailed from England, for the better enjoyment of liberty of conscience and freedom of religion. In the seventh generation from Robert Cushman appeared Elkanah Cushman, who took to wife Mary Eliza, daughter of Erasmus Babbit, jun., lawyer, musician, and captain in the army. Of this marriage was born Charlotte Saunders Cushman, in Richmond Street, Boston, July 23rd, 1816, and other children.

Charlotte Cushman says of herself: "I was born a tom-boy." She had a passion for climbing trees, and for breaking open dolls' heads. She could not make dolls' clothes, but she could manufacture their furniture—could do anything with tools. "I was very destructive to toys and clothes, tyrannical to brothers and sister, but very social, and a great favourite with other children. Imitation was a prevailing trait." The first play she ever saw was "Coriolanus," with Macready in the leading part; her second play was "The Gamester." She became noted in her school for her skill in reading aloud. Her competitors grumbled: "No wonder she can read; she goes to the theatre!" Until then she had been shy and reserved, not to say stupid, about reading aloud in school, afraid of the sound of her own voice, and unwilling to trust it; but acquaintance with the theatre loosened her tongue, as she describes it, and gave opportunity and expression to a faculty which became the ruling passion of her life. At home, as a child, she took part in an operetta founded upon the story of "Bluebeard," and played *Selim*, the lover, with great applause in a large attic chamber of her father's house before an enthusiastic audience of young people.

Elkanah Cushman had been for some years a successful merchant, a member of the firm of Topliffe and Cushman, Long Wharf, Boston. But failure befell him, "attributable," writes Charlotte Cushman's biographer, Miss Stebbins, "to the infidelity of those whom he trusted as supercargoes." The family removed from Boston to Charlèstown. Charlotte was placed at a public school, remaining there until she was thirteen only. Elkanah Cushman died, leaving his widow and five children with very slender means. Mrs. Cushman opened a boarding-house in Boston, and struggled hard to ward off further misfortune. It was discovered that Charlotte possessed a noble voice of almost two registers—"a full contralto, and almost a full soprano : but the low voice was the natural one." The fortunes of the family seemed to rest upon the due cultivation of Charlotte's voice, and upon her future as a singer. " My mother," she writes, " at great self-sacrifice gave me what opportunities for instruction she could obtain for me ; and then my father's friend, Mr. R. D. Shepherd, of Shepherdstown, Virginia, gave me two years of the best culture that could be obtained in Boston at that time, under John Paddon, an English organist and teacher of singing." When the English singer, Mrs. Wood—better known, perhaps, as Miss Paton—visited Boston in 1835 or 1836, she needed the support of a contralto voice. Charlotte Cushman was sent for, and rehearsed duets with Mrs. Wood. The young beginner was advised to prepare herself for the operatic stage ; she was assured that such a voice would " lead her to any height of fortune she coveted." She became the articled pupil of Mr. Maeder, the husband of Clara

Fisher, actress and vocalist, and the musical director of Mr. and Mrs. Wood. Instructed by Maeder, Miss Cushman undertook the parts of the *Countess* in " The Marriage of Figaro," and *Lucy Bertram* in the opera of " Guy Mannering." These were her first appearances upon the stage.

Mrs. Maeder's voice was a contralto ; it became necessary, therefore, to assign soprano parts to Miss Cushman. Undue stress was thus laid upon her upper notes. She was very young, and she felt the change of climate when she went on with the Maeders to New Orleans. It is likely that her powers as a singer had been tried too soon and too severely; her operatic career was brought to a sudden close. Her voice failed her ; her upper notes departed, never to return ; she was left with a weakened and limited contralto register. Alarmed and wretched, she sought counsel of Mr. Caldwell, the manager of the chief New Orleans theatre. "You ought to be an actress, and not a singer," he said, and advised her to take lessons of Mr. Barton, his leading tragedian. Her articles of apprenticeship to Maeder were cancelled. Soon she was ready to appear as *Lady Macbeth* on the occasion of Barton's benefit. But an unexpected difficulty presented itself. She had no costume for the part, and she did not disclose the fact until after rehearsal upon the day before the performance, dreading lest some other actress, better provided with a wardrobe, should be summoned to appear in her stead. The manager upon her behalf applied for assistance to the tragedienne of the French theatre. " I was a tall, thin, lanky girl at that time, about five feet six inches in height. The Frenchwoman, Madame Closel, was a short fat person of not more than four feet ten inches, her waist full twice the size of mine, with a very large bust ; but her shape did not prevent her being a very great actress. The ludicrousness ot her clothes being made to fit me, struck her at once. She roared with laughter, but she was very good-natured, saw my distress, and set to work to see how she could help it. By dint of piecing out the skirt of one dress, it was made to answer for an underskirt, and then another dress was taken in in every direction to do duty as an overdress, and so make up the costume. And thus I essayed for the first time the part of *Lady Macbeth,* fortunately to the satisfaction of the audience, the manager, and all the members of the company."

The season ended, she sailed for Philadelphia on her way to New York. Presently she had entered into a three years' engagement with Mr. Hamblin, the manager of the Bowery Theatre, at a salary of twenty-five dollars a week for the first year, thirty-five for the second year, and forty-five for the third. Mr. Hamblin had received excellent accounts of the actress from his friend Mr. Barton of New Orleans, and had heard her rehearse scenes from "Macbeth," "Jane Shore," "Venice Preserved," "The Stranger," etc. To enable her to obtain a suitable wardrobe, he became security for her with his tradespeople, deducting five dollars a week from her salary until the debt was satisfied. All promised well; independence seemed secured at last. Mrs. Cushman was sent for from Boston; she gave up her boarding-house and hastened to her daughter. Miss Cushman writes: "I got a situation for my eldest brother in a store in New York. I left my only sister in charge of a half-sister in Boston, and I took my youngest brother with me." But rheumatic fever seized the actress; she was able to act for a few nights only, and her dream of good fortune came to a disastrous close. "The Bowery Theatre was burned to the ground, with all my wardrobe, all my debt upon it, and my three years' contract ending in smoke." Grievously distressed, but not disheartened, with her family dependent upon her exertions, she accepted an engagement at the principal theatre in Albany, where she remained five months, acting all the leading characters. In September, 1837, she entered into an engagement, which endured for three years, with the manager of the Park Theatre, New York. She was required to fulfil the duties of "walking lady" and "general utility," at a salary of twenty dollars a week.

During this period of her career she performed very

many characters, and toiled assiduously at her profession. It was then the custom to afford the public a great variety of performances, to change the plays nightly, and to present two and sometimes three plays upon the same evening. The actors were for ever busy studying new parts, and when they were not performing they were rehearsing. "It was a time of hard work," writes Miss Stebbins, "of ceaseless activity, and of hard-won and scantily accorded appreciation." Miss Cushman had no choice of parts, she was not the chief actress of the company; she sustained without question all the characters the management assigned to her. Her appearance as *Meg Merrilies*—she acquired subsequently great favour by her performance of this character—was due to an incident—the illness of Mrs. Chippendale, the actress who usually supported the part. It was in the year 1840; the veteran Braham was to appear as *Henry Bertram*. A *Meg Merrilies* had to be improvized. The obscure "utility" actress was called upon to take Mrs. Chippendale's place. She might read the part if she could not commit it to memory, but personate *Meg Merrilies* after some sort she must. She had never especially noticed the part, but as she stood at the side scene, book in hand, awaiting her moment of entrance, her ear caught the dialogue going on upon the stage between two of the gipsies, "conveying the impression that Meg was no longer to be feared or respected, that she was no longer in her right mind." This furnished her with a clue to the character, and led her to present it upon the stage as the weird and startling figure which afterwards became so famous. Of course the first performance was but a sketch of her later portrayals of *Meg Merrilies*, yet she had made a profound impression. " I had not thought that I had done anything remarkable," she wrote, " and when a knock came at my dressing-room door, and I heard Braham's voice, my first thought was : 'Now what have I done? He is surely displeased with me about something.' Imagine my gratification, when Mr. Braham said, ' Miss Cushman, I have come to thank you for the most veritable sensation I have experienced for a long time. I give you my word when I saw you in that first scene I felt a cold chill run all over me. Where have you learned to do anything like that?'"

Miss Cushman's *Meg Merrilies* was not perhaps the *Meg Merrilies* of Scott, but it was an extraordinary instance of histrionic art; startling in its weird power, its picturesqueness of aspect, and in a certain supernatural quality that seemed attendant upon it. There was something unearthly in the sudden apparition of Meg upon the scene—she had entered with a silent spring to the centre of the stage, and stood motionless, gazing at Harry Bertram, one bare gaunt arm outstretched to him, the other bearing a withered stick or bough of a tree.

The disguise was complete. The personality of the actress was not to be detected. An artist inquired of the actress : " How do you know where to put in those shadows, and make those lines which so accurately give the effect of age?" "I don't know," she answered ; "I only feel where they ought to come." The process of her make-up was likened to "the painting of a face by an old Dutch master, full of delicate and subtle manipulations." Wild locks of grey hair streamed away from the parchment-hued, worn, and withered face; upon her head she wore a turban of twisted rags, "arranged in vague and shadowy semblance to a crown ; her costume, seemingly a mass of incoherent rags and tatters, but full of method and meaning—a bit picked up here, another there, from the strangest materials." How she contrived to assume this strange dress was known only to herself and Sallie, her faithful servant, dresser, and assistant, during the whole course of her theatrical career. "At times," writes her biographer, "with so much wear and tear, some part of the costume would require renewal. The stockings, for example, would wear out, and then no end of trouble would come in preparing another pair, that the exact tint of age and dirt should be attained." This she accomplished by immersing them in a peculiar dye of her own concoction. The opera ended with a dirge, and the actress was thus allowed time to escape from the stage, wash the paint from her face, abandon

her head-dress and grey locks, and appear before the
curtain, obedient to the call of the house, in her own
person, with a pleasant, smiling, intelligent face. She
had a woman's desire, perhaps, that the audience should
not depart deeming her quite so uncomely of look as she
had pretended to be.

During her visits to England, Miss Cushman personated *Meg Merrilies* more often than any other
character. In America she was also famous for her
performance of *Nancy* in a melodrama founded upon
"Oliver Twist;" but this part she did not bring with her
across the Atlantic. She had first played *Nancy* during
her "general utility" days at the Park Theatre, when
the energy and pathos of her acting powerfully affected
her audience, and the tradition of her success in the part
long "lingered in the memory of managers, and caused
them ever and anon, as their business interests prompted,
to bring great pressure to bear upon her for a reproduction of it." Mr. George Vandenhoff describes *Nancy* as
Miss Cushman's "greatest part; fearfully natural, dreadfully intense, horribly real."

In the winter of 1842 Miss Cushman undertook the
management of the Walnut Street Theatre, Philadelphia,
which was then in rather a fallen state. Under her
energetic rule, however, the establishment recovered its
popularity. "She displayed at that day," writes Mr.
George Vandenhoff, who "starred" at the Walnut Street

Theatre for six nights to small audiences, "a rude, strong, uncultivated talent. It was not till after she had seen and acted with Mr. Macready—which she did the next season—that she really brought artistic study and finish to her performances." Macready arrived at New York in the autumn of 1843. He notes: "The Miss Cushman who acted *Lady Macbeth* interested me much. She has to learn her art, but she showed mind and sympathy with me—a novelty so refreshing to me on the stage." She discerned the opportunity for study and improvement presented by Macready's visit, and underwent the fatigue of acting on alternate nights in Philadelphia and New York during the term of his engagement at the Park Theatre. Her own success was very great. She wrote to her mother of her great reception ; of her being called out after the play ; of the "hats and handkerchiefs waved to me ; flowers sent to me," etc. In October, 1844, she sailed for England in the packet-ship *Garrick* She had little money with her. A farewell benefit taken in Boston, her native city, had not proved very productive, and she had been obliged "to make arrangements for the maintenance of her family during her absence." And, with characteristic prudence, she left behind her a certain sum, to be in readiness for her, in case failure in England should drive her promptly back to America.

No engagement in London had been offered her, but

she received, upon her arrival, a letter fromMacready, proposing that she should join a company then being formed to give representations in Paris. She thought it prudent to decline this proposal, however, so as to avoid entering into anything like rivalry with Miss Helen Faucit, the leading actress of the troupe. She visited Paris for a few days, but only to sit with the audience of the best French theatres. She returned to her dull lodgings in Covent Garden, "awaiting her destiny." She was fond in after years of referring to the struggles and poverty, the hopes and the despair, of her first sojourn in London. Her means were nearly exhausted. Sally, the dresser, used to relate: "Miss Cushman lived on a mutton-chop a day, and I always bought the baker's dozen of muffins for the sake of the extra one, and we ate them all, no matter how stale they were; and we never suffered from want of appetite in those days." She found herself reduced to her last sovereign, when Mr. Maddox, the manager of the Princess's Theatre, came to her with a proposal. The watchful Sally reported that he had been walking up and down the street for some time early in the morning, too early for a visit. "He is anxious," said Miss Cushman. "I can make my own terms." He wished her to appear with Forrest, the American tragedian, then visiting the London stage for the second and last time. She stipulated that she should have her opportunity first, and "alone." If successful, she was willing to appear in support of Forrest. So it was agreed.

If Mr. Vandenhoff's account is to be trusted, Miss Cushman had previously addressed herself to Maddox, requesting an engagement. This he had declined, deeming her plainness of face a fatal obstacle to her success upon the stage. But after an interval, employment becoming more than ever necessary to her, she returned to him, armed with letters from persons who were likely to have weight with him, and renewed her application. The manager, however, remained obdurate. "Repulsed, but not conquered, she rose to depart; but as she reached the door she turned and exclaimed: 'I know I have enemies in this country; but'—and here she cast herself on her knees, raising her clenched hand aloft—'so help me Heaven, I'll defeat them!' She uttered this with the energy of Lady Macbeth, and the prophetic spirit of Meg Merrilies." The manager, convinced of the force of her manner, at any rate, at once offered her an engagement. Her first appearance upon the English stage was made on the 14th February, 1845: she assumed the character of *Bianca*, in Dean Milman's rather dull tragedy of "Fazio." Her triumph was indisputable. Her intensity and vehemence completely carried away the house. As the pit rose at Kean's *Shylock*, so it rose at Charlotte Cushman's *Bianca*. She wrote to her mother in America: "All my successes put together, since I have been upon the stage, would not come near my success in London." The critics described, as the crowning effort of her performance, the energy and pathos and abandonment of her appeal to *Aldabella*, when the wife sacrifices her pride, and sinks, "huddled into a heap," at the feet of her rival, imploring her to save the life of *Fazio*. Miss Cushman, speaking of her first performance in London, was wont to relate how she was so completely overcome, not only by the excitement of the scene, but by the nervous agitation of the occasion, that she lost for the moment her self-command, and was especially grateful for the long-continued applause which gave her time to recover herself. When she slowly rose at last and faced the house again, the spectacle of its enthusiasm thrilled and impressed her in a manner she could never forget. The audience were standing, some had mounted on the benches; there was wild waving of hats and handkerchiefs, a storm of cheering, great showering of bouquets.

Her second character in London was *Lady Macbeth*, to the *Macbeth* of Edwin Forrest; but the American actor failed to please, and the audience gave free expression to their discontent. Greatly disgusted, Forrest withdrew, deluding himself with the belief that he was the victim of a conspiracy. Miss Cushman's success knew no abatement. She played a round of parts, assisted by James Wallack, Leigh Murray, and

Mrs. Stirling, appearing now as *Rosalind,* now as *Juliana*
in "The Honeymoon," as *Mrs. Haller,* as *Beatrice,* as
Julia in "The Hunchback." Her second season was
even more successful than her first. After a long
provincial tour she appeared in December, 1845, as
Romeo at the Haymarket Théatre, then under the
management of Mr. Webster, her sister Susan assuming
the character of *Juliet.* She had sent for her family to
share her prosperity, and had established them in a
furnished house at Bayswater. Miss Cushman's *Romeo*
was thus described at the time by the late Gilbert à
Beckett in a versified account of the performance :

> "What figure is that which appears on the scene?
> 'Tis Madame Macready—Miss Cushman, I mean.
> What a wondrous resemblance ! the walk on the toes,
> The eloquent, short, intellectual nose ;
> The bend of the knee, the slight sneer of the lip,
> The frown on the forehead, the hand on the hip.
> In the chin, in the voice, 'tis the same to a tittle,
> Miss Cushman is Mister Macready in little ;
> The lady before us might very well pass
> For the gentleman viewed the wrong way of the glass.
> No fault with the striking resemblance we find,
> 'Tis not in the person alone, but the mind," etc., etc.

This likeness to Macready—a likeness which applied
not merely to features and "trick of face," but also to
gait and gestures, tone of voice and method of elocution
—had been from the first observed; and no doubt
gained force when the actress personated a male

character. Macready was plain, and was conscious of
his plainness, as a curious entry in his diary for 1839
testifies. He writes: "Read a very strange note from
some woman, threatening to destroy herself for love of
me. The ugly never need despair after this. Answered
it shortly." Very shortly, no doubt. Charlotte Cushman
owned Macready's depression of nose, breadth and
prominence of brow, and protrusion of chin. Hers was
certainly a plain face; although her eyes—blue, or dark
grey, in colour—were large and luminous; her hair was
abundant, and of a fine chestnut hue; her complexion
was clear, and her expression strikingly intelligent,
mobile, and intense. She was tall of stature, angular of
form, and somewhat masculine in the boldness and
freedom of her movements. Her success as *Romeo* was
very great. The tragedy was played for eighty nights.
Her performance won applause even from those most
opposed to the representation of Shakespeare's hero by a
woman. For a time her intense earnestness of speech
and manner, the passion of her interviews with *Juliet*
the fury of her combat with *Tybalt*, the despair of her
closing scenes, bore down all opposition, silenced
criticism, and excited her audience to an extraordinary
degree. She appeared afterwards—but not in London—
as *Hamlet*, following an unfortunate example set by Mrs.
Siddons; and as *Ion* in Talfourd's tragedy of that name.

In America, towards the close of her career, she

even ventured to appear as *Cardinal Wolsey*—obtaining
great applause by her exertions in the character, and the
skill and force of her impersonation. But histrionic
feats of this kind trespass against good taste, do violence
to the intentions of the dramatist, and are, in truth, departures from the purpose of playing. Miss Cushman
had for excuse—in the first instance, at any rate—her
anxiety to forward the professional interests of her sister ;
who, in truth, had little qualification for the stage apart
from her good looks and her graces of manner. The
sisters had played together in Philadelphia in "The
Genoese"—a drama written by a young American—
when, to give support and encouragement to Susan in
her personation of the heroine, Charlotte undertook the
part of her lover. Their success prompted them to
appear in "Romeo and Juliet." Other plays, in which
both could appear, were afterwards selected—such, for
instance, as "Twelfth Night," in which Charlotte played
Viola to the *Olivia* of Susan—so that the engagement of
one might compel the engagement of the other. Susan,
however, quitted the stage in 1847, to become the wife
of Dr. Sheridan Muspratt, of Liverpool.

Charlotte Cushman called few new plays into being.
Dramas, entitled "Infatuation," by James Kenny, 1845,
and "Duchess Elinour," by the late H. F. Chorley,
1854, were produced for her, but were summarily condemned by the audience, being scarcely permitted

indeed a second performance in either case. Otherwise, she did not add to her repertory. For many years she led the life of a "star," fulfilling brief engagements here and there, appearing now for a term in London, and now travelling through the provinces, playing some half a dozen characters over and over again. Of these *Lady Macbeth, Queen Katherine,* and *Meg Merrilies* were perhaps the most frequently demanded. Her fame and fortune she always dated from the immediate recognition she obtained upon her first performance in London. But she made frequent visits to America; indeed, she crossed the Atlantic "upwards of sixteen times," says her biographer. In 1854 she took a house in Bolton Row, Mayfair, "where for some years she dispensed the most charming and genial hospitality," and, notably, entertained Ristori on her first visit to England in 1856. Several winters she passed in Rome, occupying apartments in the Via Gregoriana, where she cordially received a host of friends and visitors of all nations. In 1859 she was called to England by her sister's fatal illness; in 1866 she was again summoned to England to attend the death-bed of her mother. In 1860 she was playing in all the chief cities of America. Three years later she again visited America, her chief object being to act for the benefit of the sanitary commission, and aid the sick and wounded victims of the civil war. During the late years of her life she appeared before the public more as a dramatic reader than as an actress. There were long intervals between her theatrical engagements; she seemed to quit her profession only to return to it after an interval with renewed appetite, and she incurred reproaches because of the frequency of her farewells, and the doubt that prevailed as to whether her "last appearances" were really to be the "very last." Yet it is curious to note that at a very early period in her career she contemplated its termination; in the first instance because of the disappointments she had incurred, and afterwards by reason of her great good fortune. "You talk of quitting the profession in a year," her firm friend Colley Grattan, consul and novelist, writes to her in 1842; "I expect to see you stand very high indeed in it by that time. You must neither write nor think nor speak in the mood that beset you three days ago." And immediately after her first appearance in London, in 1845, she wrote to her mother: "I have given myself five years more, and I think at the end of that time I will have fifty thousand dollars to retire upon. That will, if well invested, give us a comfortable home for the rest of our lives, and a quiet corner in some respectable graveyard." It was not until 1874, however, that she took final leave of the New York stage, amid extraordinary enthusiasm, with many poetic and other ceremonies. She was the subject of addresses in prose and verse. Mr. Bryant, after an eloquent speech, tendered her a laurel wreath bound with white ribbon resting upon a purple velvet cushion, with a suitable inscription embroidered in golden letters; a torch-bearers' procession escorted her from the theatre to her hotel; she was serenaded at midnight, and in her honour Fifth Avenue blazed with fireworks. After this came farewells to Philadelphia, Boston, and other cities, and to these succeeded readings all over the country. It is to be said, however, that incessant work had become a necessity with her; not because of its pecuniary results, but as a means of obtaining mental relief, or comparative forgetfulness for a season. During the last five or six years of her life she was afflicted with an incurable and agonizing malady. Vainly she sought aid from medicine, from the German baths, from surgical operations under the advice of Sir James Simpson and Sir James Paget. She possessed originally a powerful constitution, with most indomitable courage; she knew that she had returned to her native land to die there. But she resolved to contest inch by inch the advance of death, and to make what remained to her of life as useful and valuable as might be, both to herself and to others. Under most painful conditions she toiled unceasingly, moving rapidly from place to place, and passing days and nights in railway journeys. In a letter to a friend, she writes: " I do get so dreadfully depressed about myself, and all things seem so hopeless to me at those times, that I pray God to take me quickly at any moment, so that I may not torture those I love by letting them see my pain. But when the dark hour passes, and I try to forget by constant occupation that I have such a load near my heart, then it is not so bad." She died almost painlessly at last on the 18th February, 1876. Even so late as the 3rd February she had been speaking of the possibility of her journeying to California to give a long-promised series of readings there. She was buried at Mount Auburn—she had expressed her wishes in this respect, and had even selected her pall-bearers, and ordered all the details of her funeral—within sight of her "dear Boston," as she called it, while admitting that in her native city "they never believed in me so much as they did elsewhere," and bestowed but niggard patronage upon her early benefits. Boston, however, duly honoured the later years, and cherishes the memory of the actress. The house in which she was born is now a public building devoted to educational purposes, and bears the name of "The Cushman School."

Charlotte Cushman may assuredly be accounted an actress of genius in right of her originality, her vivid power of depicting emotion, the vehemence and intensity of her histrionic manner. Her best successes were obtained in tragedy, although she possessed a keen sense of humour, and could deliver the witty speeches of

Rosalind or of *Beatrice* with excellent point and effect.
Her *Meg Merrilies* will probably be remembered as her
most impressive achievement. It was really, as she
played it, a character of her own invention; but, in
truth, it taxed her intellectual resources far less than
her *Bianca,* her *Queen Katherine,* or her *Lady Macbeth.*
Her physical peculiarities no doubt limited the range of
her efforts, hindered her advance as an actress, or urged
her towards exceptional impersonations. Her performances lacked femineity, to use Coleridge's word; but in
power to stir an audience, to touch their sympathies, to
kindle their enthusiasm, and compel their applause, she
takes rank among the finest players. It only remains to
add that Miss Stebbins's fervid and affecting biography
of her friend admirably demonstrates that the woman
was not less estimable than the actress; that Charlotte
Cushman was of noble character, intellectual, large and
tender-hearted, of exemplary conduct in every respect.
The simple, direct earnestness of her manner upon the
mimic scene, characterized her proceedings in real life.
She was at once the slave and the benefactress of her
family; she was devotedly fond of children; she was
of liberal and generous nature; she was happiest when
conferring kindnesses upon others; her career abounded
in self-sacrifice. She pretended to few accomplishments,
to little cultivation of a literary sort; but she could
write, as Miss Stebbins proves, excellent letters, now

grave, now gay, now reflective, now descriptive, always interesting, and altogether remarkable for sound sense, and for force and skill of expression. Her death was regarded in America almost as a national catastrophe. As Miss Stebbins writes, "the press of the entire country bore witness to her greatness, and laid their tributes upon her tomb."

CHAPTER IX.

FOR some years there figured as lessee and manager of Her Majesty's Theatre in the Haymarket, one M. Laporte, a French actor of a certain distinction, whose knowledge of the English tongue had even enabled him to appear with credit upon the London stage. At Drury Lane, in 1826, he had impersonated *Sosia* in " Amphitryon," *Wormwood* in " The Lottery Ticket," *La Nippe* in " The Lord of the Manor," *Blaisot* in " The Maid and the Magpie," and some other characters. M. Laporte underwent in full the customary trials and experiences of an operatic director in England. A cloud of Chancery suits lowered upon his house; he became greatly embarrassed; he was arrested for debt, and incarcerated in the Fleet—to encounter there by chance as his fellow-prisoner Mr. Chambers, an earlier manager of the theatre. He filed his petition, was relieved of his liabilities, and duly passed through the Court of Bankruptcy. At liberty again, he returned to the cares of management, which during his term of duress had been undertaken by his father.   But the old unfortunate times came back again, or a new sea of troubles seemed to rise and rage about him.   His expenses were enormous, yet his receipts steadily declined; he quarrelled desperately with his singers, whose demands grew more and more exacting; he raised his prices, he shortened his seasons; his patrons and subscribers were loud in their expressions of discontent.   The year 1841 was the last of M. Laporte's management of the opera; it was, indeed, the last of his life.   In the autumn, at his house on the banks of the Seine, near Corbeil, he expired suddenly of disease of the heart, leaving his executor, solicitor, and agent, Mr. Benjamin Lumley, to succeed him as impresario.   The year 1841 was the year, too, of the famous " Tamburini Row," of the first performance on the stage of Her Majesty's Theatre of French plays alternately with Italian operas, and of M. Laporte's resumption of his old profession, and reappearance in characters he had been wont long since to sustain in " Les Précieuses Ridicules " and " Le Dépit Amoureux." Moreover, 1841 was the year of the first introduction to the English public of the greatest of French actresses— Mademoiselle Rachel Felix.

Laporte had with little difficulty secured the services of the lady in England for the term of one month.

There had been subsidence for a while of the enthusiasm with which her performances during some three years had been received in Paris. Absence, it was thought, would make the hearts of her critics and the public grow fonder. No pains were spared to accord the actress a fervent welcome in London. Laporte had introduced certain foreign arts of management; he lavished attentions upon the press with a view to the conciliation of critical opinion, and he laboured hard to force the public judgment by means of fabricated applause. A chronicler of the operatic proceedings of forty years back writes : "Men and women, as notoriously hired for such mystification as the howlers at an Irish funeral, began to be seen in known places every night, obtruding their stationary raptures, which were paid for, at the serviceable times and places. The extent to which this nuisance grew was one, among other causes, of the decay of the old Italian opera," etc. It was decided that Rachel should make her first appearance in England on May 14, as *Hermione* in the "Andromaque" of Racine. To support her performance, certain players of very inferior quality had been gathered from the minor stages of France. At that period our playgoing public boasted little acquaintance with the French classical drama. It was not generally known in Her Majesty's Theatre that, while *Andromaque* appeared in the first act of the tragedy, the entrance of *Hermione* was deferred to the second act. So the audience rose with one accord, in their anxiety to greet Mademoiselle Rachel in *Hermione*, and wasted a whirlwind of mistaken applause upon the subordinate actress who represented *Andromaque.* Poor Mademoiselle Larcher was said to be completely overcome by the ardour and uproar of her welcome : she was quite unaccustomed to such turbulent expressions of public regard. And, as a result of this misdirection of enthusiasm, Rachel was allowed to steal almost unnoticed upon the scene : but the faintest plaudits attended the entrance of *Hermione.* Of course the error was rectified as soon as possible. The genius of the actress soon made itself felt, forced its way to the hearts of the audience. Her eventual success was indeed supreme. " The new idol," writes a biographer, " was hailed with fanatical admiration." On each night of her performance the theatre was crowded to excess. Fashion flew into the wildest raptures on her account : Rachel became the rage. Society, asking no questions or listening to no answers, threw wide open its arms and the doors of its drawing-rooms. The actress was received everywhere. She was invariably accompanied by her father and her elder sister, Sarah. " Her unaffected and even dignified simplicity," we are told, " her modesty, and the perfect decorum of her conduct, made her a great favourite with the fastidious English aristocracy." The aunts of the Queen "condescended to notice her;" she was invited to perform at Windsor Castle; was presented by the Duchess of Kent to her Majesty, and received most graciously. She appeared in the first act of "Bajazet," the third act of "Marie Stuart," and the fourth act of "Andromaque." When she seemed to suffer from cold, the Duchess of Kent removed her own magnificent yellow Indian shawl and wrapped it round the actress. The Queen presented her with a costly bracelet, composed of entwined diamond-headed serpents, and bearing the inscription, "Victoria to Mademoiselle Rachel." Her every movement was chronicled by the press. A slight illness afflicted her, and frequent bulletins were issued, informing the public concerning her state of health. Reappearing upon the stage, the Queen and the Queen Dowager being present, she was greeted and congratulated as though she had escaped from the tomb. She took leave of her London admirers on July 20, when she appeared as *Camille* in the "Horace" of Corneille. "Every formula of praise was exhausted by the press upon this occasion." According to one report, "her triumph had even extended to the heart of the manager, who was said to have offered her his hand!" This was probably but one of the many forms of puffing which the wily Laporte was wont to employ.

Rachel reappeared in London during the following

Season, engaged by Mr. Lumley, the new director of Her Majesty's Theatre. She brought with her a more efficient company of performers, including the accomplished Mademoiselle Rabut, afterwards known as Madame Fechter. Her success was still brilliant, if she found rival candidates for the favour of London in the famous comedians Bouffé and Déjazet. Moreover, Mr. Lumley is careful to record that she now owed her triumph rather to the good will of the general public than to the favour of the high and exclusive. He adds that his own relations with the actress were always of the pleasantest, and that the spirit of exaction and rapacity she was so often charged with was never obtruded upon her English manager. Between 1846 and 1853 Rachel fulfilled five successive engagements with Mr. Mitchell at the St. James's Theatre, and appeared in all the more important characters of her repertory. It could not be concealed, however, that society was less moved towards her than in 1841. The drawing-rooms were no longer open to her. She was not again the guest of the sovereign ; the royal duchesses held aloof. It is fair to say that in this matter London was but following the example of Paris. In the first instance, the most aristocratic *salons* had welcomed her entrance, the stateliest ladies of the Faubourg had sought her out to caress and adore her, the most distinguished personages in France had

paid her exceeding homage, not less in private than
in public. It was not only that she was the leading
representative of an intellectual art: she was an
upholder of the classic drama in its contest with the
romantic; she had restored Racine and Corneille,
after long years of neglect and exile, to their legitimate
home on the boards of the Français. Moreover, she
was charming in her own right, because of her graces
of aspect, her charming repose and reserve of manner,
the readiness of her wit, the sweetness of her smile, her
desire and her absolute power to please. Never, it was
said, did a new stage queen present herself in private
life with such instinctive tact as she. Her friend
Dr. Véron writes of her: " Son esprit vif et brillant,
ses reparties promptes, plaisantes, jamais blessantes,
se gardent bien cependant de se trop montrer et de
prendre trop de place; jamais je ne vis tant d'art
caché sous une simplicité si naïve, sous une réserve
de si bon goût." But the actress was playing a part
which she soon found to be wearisome and oppressive,
and which she at length completely abandoned. The
honours of high and learned society, however flattering,
were found tiresome enough after a year or so. She
ceased to prize the social position to which she had
been advanced. She could not be for ever acting—
leading one kind of private life to please the *salons*,
and another to please herself. It was sufficient if she

played her part well upon the stage.   Gradually the
miseries of her early life became publicly known, and
then there oozed out scandals touching her career and
her character away from the theatre and the drawing-
rooms.   " Her grand reserved manner, snatched up as
a dress," writes one of her critics, "could be flung
down by her as such at any moment."   And the same
authority adds, " She grew up to be a grasping, sensual,
selfish woman."   To one thing only was she true—not
her art, for of that she was willing to make sacrifice upon
occasion, and for due consideration.   But her family she
served with a curious constancy ; her good fortune was
ever shared with them ; they clung together—father and
mother, sisters and brother—with strong animal affection,
uniting always in their efforts to spoil the Egyptians and
to make money by whatever means, but faithful and
tender to each other in sickness, in sorrow, and in death.
When Rachel grasped, as grasp she did, it was that the
Felix family might profit equally with herself.

A correspondence exists between the careers of
Rachel and of Edmund Kean, while their methods
of acting present many curious points of resemblance.   Both were born in obscurity, of humble origin,
and passed through a childhood of suffering, a severe
novitiate, before arriving at good fortune.   The actress,
however, triumphed at seventeen ; Edmund Kean was
twenty-seven when the memorable night came for his

success as *Shylock* at Drury Lane. There was even likeness, or trace of likeness, in minor respects, such as the oriental character of face, slightness of form, dark brilliancy of eye, natural grace of gesture, and hoarseness of voice. Against each alike the doors of comedy were securely closed; they could find parts to play only in the more ruthless and passionate of tragedies. As Mr. G. H. Lewes has written: "Those who never saw Edmund Kean may form a very good conception of him if they have seen Rachel. She was very much as a woman what he was as a man. If he was a lion, she was a panther. . . . With a panther's terrible beauty and undulating grace she moved and stood, glared and sprang. . . . Her range, like Kean's, was very limited, but her expression was perfect within that range. Scorn, triumph, rage, lust, and merciless malignity she could represent in symbols of irresistible power; but she had little tenderness, no womanly, caressing softness, no gaiety, no heartiness. She was so graceful and so powerful that her air of dignity was incomparable; but somehow you always felt in her presence an indefinite suggestion of latent wickedness." Few new parts of lasting worth were given to the stage by either Rachel or Kean. To neither was a prolonged histrionic career permitted: Kean died at forty-six; Rachel at thirty-seven. Success brought to both maddening and disastrous influences; both sought diversion in irregularity, disdained the restrictions of refined society, and offended the public by the frequent scandals and frailties of their lives in private—it being understood, of course, that Kean is not to be charged with Rachel's avarice and rapacity, nor Rachel with Kean's vices of intemperance. Their sins were alike only in that they were sins. " Que j'ai besoin de m'encanailler ! " Rachel would exclaim as she quitted the *salons*.   In a like spirit Kean hurried from Lord Byron's dinner-table to take the chair at a pugilistic supper ; courted rather than fell into evil company, accepted tribute indeed most willingly of the noble and intellectual, who heaped rich gifts upon him, the while he scorned or feared their society.

Those who would find excuse for Rachel's trespasses must look to the corroding misery of her early vagabond life—misery of which it has been said that, while it pinched and withered her frame, it may well likewise have starved, contracted, and deadened the heart within it.   Almost she was trained to become what she became. Conscious to her finger-tips of her own genius, and yet to feel the urgent want of food and fuel and sufficiency of clothing !   As a child she had been starved alike in body and mind—squalor and penury had schooled her into enmity and mutiny against society and its prescriptions.   She was, as some beautiful creature of prey, only treacherously tame, prompt to return to the old wild ways, to hunt and combat for the means of livelihood, to turn fiercely against and to rend those who but seemed to block the pathway, and to regard all around as natural foes and proper victims. The opportunity she yearned for was so long denied her, seemed at times so completely past her praying for, no wonder she was sickened and soured by disappointment and deferred hope. When success really came, it found her unprepared to bear it becomingly; her nature was perverted, her heart was warped and cramped; it was as though some cruel poison already pervaded her system, or some rank corruption, mining all within, infected her unseen.

The Parisians adored her for a while. She was irresistible; they could not but flock to her, crowding the theatre every night she played, and overwhelming her with applause. She made them her slaves, not her friends. They revenged upon her their servitude by reviling her. She was not an amiable woman : she did not conciliate. She knew her value, and at last she was able to make others know it : she exacted it, indeed, to the last farthing. She was unsympathetic, hard, cynical, avaricious, sordid, unscrupulous. An actress of unsurpassed genius, she soared high indeed; a woman, she grovelled very low. It is the Paris manner, perhaps, to shatter the old idols, the better to pave the roadways leading to newer objects of worship. Rachel was savagely satirized, libelled, and lampooned. The grave had scarcely closed over her when scandalous chronicles of her life, reprints of her least eligible letters, all kinds or damaging reports, were issuing from the press, and efforts were made on every side to assail her memory and tear her fame to tatters. Yet she was probably the greatest actress France has ever known.

It is told that Rachel Felix was born on March 24, 1821, at Munf, near the town of Aarau, in the canton of Aargau; the burgomaster of the district simply noting in his books that upon the day stated, at the little village inn, the wife of a poor pedlar had given birth to a female child. The entry included no mention of family name or religion, and otherwise the event was not registered in any civil or religious record. The father and mother were Abraham Felix, a Jew born in Metz, but of German origin, and Esther Haya, his wife. They had wandered about the Continent during many years, seeking a living and scarcely finding it. Several children were born to them by the wayside, as it were, on their journeyings hither and thither; Sarah in Germany, Rebecca in Lyons, Dinah in Paris, Rachel in Switzerland; and there were other infants who did not long survive their birth, succumbing to the austerities of the state of life to which they had been called. For a time, perhaps because of their numerous progeny, M. and Madame Felix settled in Lyons. Madame Felix opened a small shop and dealt in second-hand clothes; M. Felix gave lessons in German to the very few pupils he could obtain. About

1830 the family moved to Paris. They were still miserably poor. The children Sarah and Rachel, usually carrying a smaller child in their arms or wheeling it with them in a wooden cart, were sent into the streets to earn money by singing at the doors of cafés and estaminets. A musical amateur, one M. Morin, noticed the girls, questioned them, interested himself about them, and finally obtained their admission into the Government School of Sacred Music in the Rue Vaugirard. Rachel's voice did not promise much, however ; as she confessed she could not sing, she could only recite. She had received but the scantiest and meanest education ; she read with difficulty ; she was teaching herself writing by copying the manuscript of others. Presently she was studying elocution under M. St. Aulaire, an old actor retired from the Français, who took pains with the child, instructing her gratuitously and calling her " ma petite diablesse." The performances of M. St. Aulaire's pupil were occasionally witnessed by the established players, among them Monval of the Gymnase and Samson of the Comédie. Monval approved and encouraged the young actress, and upon the recommendation of Samson she entered the classes of the Conservatoire, over which he presided, with Michelot and Provost as his co-professors.

At the Conservatoire Rachel made little progress. All her efforts failed to win the good opinion of her preceptors. In despair, she resolved to abandon alto-

gether the institution, its classes and performances. She
felt herself neglected, aggrieved, insulted. " Tartuffe "
had been announced for representation by the pupils ;
she had been assigned the mute part of *Flipote* the
serving-maid, who simply appears upon the scene in the
first act that her ears may be soundly boxed by *Madame
Pernelle!* To this humiliation she would not submit.
She hurried to her old friend St. Aulaire, who consulted
Monval, who commended her to his manager, M. Poirson. She entered into an engagement to serve the
Gymnase for a term of three years upon a salary of 3000
francs. M. Poirson was quick to perceive that she was
not as so many other beginners were; that there was
something new and startling about the young actress.
He obtained for her first appearance, from M. Paul
Duport, a little melodrama in two acts. It was called
" La Vendéenne," and owed its more striking scenes to
" The Heart of Midlothian." After the manner of Jeanie
Deans, Généviève, the heroine of the play, footsore
and travel-stained, seeks the presence of the Empress
Josephine to implore the pardon of a Vendéan peasant
condemned to death for following George Cadoudal.
" La Vendéenne," produced on April 24, 1837, and
received with great applause, was played on sixty succes-
sive nights, but not to very crowded audiences. The
press scarcely noticed the new actress. The critic of the
Journal des Débats, however, while rashly affirming that

Rachel was not a phenomenon and would never be extolled as a wonder, carefully noted certain of the merits and characteristics of her performance. " She was an unskilled child, but she possessed heart, soul, intellect. There was something bold, abrupt, uncouth, about her aspect, gait, and manner. She was dressed simply and truthfully in the coarse woollen gown of a peasant girl; her hands were red, her voice was harsh and untrained, but powerful; she acted without effort or exaggeration; she did not scream or gesticulate unduly; she seemed to perceive intuitively the feeling she was required to express, and could interest the audience greatly, moving them to tears. She was not pretty, but she pleased," etc. Bouffé, who witnessed this representation, observed, "What an odd little girl! Assuredly there is something in her. But her place is not here." So judged Samson also, becoming more and more aware of the merits of his former pupil. She was transferred to the Français to play the leading characters in tragedy, at a salary of 4000 francs a year. M. Poirson did not hesitate to cancel her agreement with him. Indeed, he had been troubled with thinking how he could employ his new actress. She was not an *ingénue* of the ordinary type; she could not be classed among soubrettes. There were no parts suited to her in the light comedies of Scribe and his compeers, which constituted the chief repertory of the Gymnase.

It was on the 12th of June, 1838, that Rachel, as *Camille* in " Horace," made her first appearance upon the stage of the Théâtre Français. The receipts were but 750 francs; it was an unfashionable period of the year; Paris was out of town; the weather was most sultry. There were many Jews in the house, it was said, resolute to support the daughter of Israel, and her success was unequivocal; nevertheless, a large share of the applause of the night was confessedly carried off by the veteran Joanny, who played *Horace.* On the 16th June Rachel made her second appearance, personating *Emilie* in the " Cinna " of Corneille. The receipts fell to 550 francs. She repeated her performance of *Camille* on the 23rd; the receipts were only 300 francs !—the poorest house, perhaps, she ever played to in Paris. She afterwards appeared as *Hermione* in " Andromaque," *Aménaïde* in " Tancrède," *Eriphile* in " Iphigénie," *Monime* in " Mithridate," and *Roxane* in " Bajazet," the receipts now gradually rising, until in October, when she played *Hermione* for the tenth time, 6000 francs were taken at the doors, an equal amount being received in November, when, for the sixth time, she appeared as *Camille.* Paris was now at her feet. In 1839, called upon to play two or three times per week, she essayed but one new part, *Esther* in Racine's tragedy of that name. The public was quite content that she should assume again and again the characters in which she had already triumphed. In

1840 she added to her list of impersonations *Laodie* and *Pauline* in Corneille's "Nicomède" and "Polyeucte," and *Marie Stuart* in Lebrun's tragedy. In 1841 she played no new parts. In 1842 she first appeared as *Chimène* in "Le Cid," as *Ariane,* and as *Frédégonde* in a wretched tragedy by Le Mercier.

Rachel had saved the Théâtre Français, had given back to the stage the masterpieces of the French classical drama. It was very well for Thackeray to write from Paris in 1839 that the actress had "only galvanized the corpse, not revivified it. . . . Racine will never come to life again and cause audiences to weep as of yore." He predicted: "Ancient French tragedy, red-heeled, patched, and beperiwigged, lies in the grave, and it is only the ghost of it that the fair Jewess has raised." But it was something more than a galvanized animation that Rachel had imparted to the old drama of France. During her career of twenty years, her performances of Racine and Corneille filled the coffers of the Français, and it may be traced to her influence and example that the classic plays still keep their place upon the stage and stir the ambition of the players. But now the committee of the Français had to reckon with their leading actress, and pay the price of the prosperity she had brought them. They cancelled her engagement and offered her terms such as seemed to them liberal beyond all precedent. But the more they offered, so much the more was demanded.

In the first instance, the actress being a minor, negotia-
tions were carried on with her father, the committee de-
nouncing in the bitterest terms the avarice and rapacity
of M. Felix.   But when Rachel became competent to
deal on her own behalf, she proved herself every whit as
exacting as her sire.   She became a *sociétaire* in 1843,
entitled to one of the twenty-four shares into which the
profits of the institution were divided.   She was rewarded,
moreover, with a salary of 42,000 francs per annum; and
it was estimated that by her performances during her
congé of three or four months every year she earned a
further annual income of 30,000 francs.   She met with
extraordinary success upon her provincial tours; enormous
profits resulted from her repeated visits to Holland and
Belgium, Germany, Russia, and England.   But, from
first to last, Rachel's connection with the Français was
an incessant quarrel.   She was capricious, ungrateful,
unscrupulous, extortionate.   She struggled to evade her
duties, to do as little as she possibly could in return for
the large sums she received from the committee.   She
pretended to be too ill to play in Paris, the while she
was always well enough to hurry away and obtain great
rewards by her performances in the provinces.   She wore
herself out by her endless wanderings hither and thither,
her continuous efforts upon the scene.   She denied herself all rest, or slept in a travelling carriage to save time
in her passage from one country theatre to another.

Her company complained that they fell asleep as they
acted, her engagements denying them proper opportunities of repose. The newspapers at one time set forth
the acrimonious letters she had interchanged with the
committee of the Français. Finally she tended her resignation of the position she occupied as *sociétaire;* the
committee took legal proceedings to compel her to return
to her duties; some concessions were made on either
side, however, and a reconciliation was patched up.

The new tragedies, "Judith" and "Cléopatre," written
for the actress by Madame de Girardin, failed to please;
nor did success attend the production of M. Romand's
"Catherine II.," M. Soumet's "Jeanne d'Arc," in which,
to the indignation of the critics, the heroine was seen at
last surrounded by real flames! or "Le Vieux de la
Montagne" of M. Latour de St. Ybars. With better
fortune Rachel appeared in the same author's "Virginie,"
and in the "Lucrèce" of Ponsard. Voltaire's "Oreste"
was revived for her in 1845 that she might play *Electre.*
She personated Racine's "Athalie" in 1847, assuming
long white locks, painting furrows on her face, and dis-
guising herself beyond recognition, in her determination
to seem completely the character she had undertaken.
In 1848 she played *Agrippine* in the "Britannicus" of
Racine, and, dressed in plain white muslin, and clasping
the tri-coloured flag to her heart, she delivered the
"Marseillaise" to please the Revolutionists, lending

the air strange meaning and passion by the intensity of
her manner, as she half chanted, half recited the words,
her voice now shrill and harsh, now deep, hollow, and
reverberating—her enraptured auditors likening it in
effect to distant thunder.

To the dramatists who sought to supply her with
new parts Rachel was the occasion of much chagrin and
perplexity.   After accepting Scribe's "Adrienne Lecouvreur" she rejected it absolutely, only to resume it
eagerly, however, when she learnt that the leading
character was to be undertaken by Mademoiselle Rose
Chéri. His "Chandelier" having met with success, Rachel
applied to De Musset for a play. She was offered, it
seems, "Les Caprices de Marianne ; " but meantime the
poet's "Bettine" failed, and the actress distrustfully
turned away from him.   An undertaking to appear in the
"Medea " of Legouvé landed her in a protracted lawsuit.
The courts condemned her in damages to the amount of
200 francs for every day she delayed playing the part of
Medea after the date fixed upon by the management for
the commencement of the rehearsals of the tragedy.   She
paid nothing, however, for the management failed to fix
any such date. M. Legouvé was only avenged in the
success his play obtained, in a translated form, at the
hands of Madame Ristori.   In lieu of "Medea," Rachel
produced "Rosemonde," a tragedy by M. Latour de St.
Ybars, which failed completely.   Other plays written for

her were the "Valéria" of MM. Lecroix and Maquet, in which she personated two characters : the *Empress Messalina*, and her half-sister *Lysisca*, a courtesan; the "Diane" of M. Augier, an imitation of Victor Hugo's "Marion Delorme;" "Lady Tartuffe," a comedy by Madame de Girardin ; and "La Czarine," by M. Scribe. She appeared also in certain of the characters originally contrived for Mademoiselle Mars, such as *La Tisbe* in Victor Hugo's "Angelo" and the heroines of Dumas' "Mademoiselle de Belle-Isle" and of "Louise de Lignerolles" by MM. Legouvé and Dinaux.

The classical drama of France has not found much favour in England. We are all, perhaps, apt to think with Thackeray disrespectfully of the "old tragedies—well-nigh dead, and full time too—in which half a dozen characters appear, and shout sonorous Alexandrines for half a dozen hours;" or we are disposed to agree with Mr. Matthew Arnold, that, their drama being fundamentally insufficient both in substance and in form, the French, with all their gifts, have not, as we have, an adequate form for poetry of the highest class. Those who remember Rachel, however, can testify that she breathed the most ardent life into the frigid remains of Racine and Corneille, relumed them with Promethean heat, and showed them to be instinct with the truest and intensest passion. When she occupied the scene, there could be no thought of the old artificial times of hair-

powder and rouge, periwigs and patches, in connection
with the characters she represented. *Phèdre* and
Hermione, Pauline and *Camille,* interpreted by her
genius, became as real and natural, warm and palpitating,
as *Constance* or *Lady Macbeth* could have been when
played by Mrs. Siddons, or as *Juliet* when impersonated
by Miss O'Neill. Before Rachel came, it had been
thought that the new romantic drama of MM. Hugo and
Dumas, because of its greater truth to nature, had given
the *coup de grâce* to the old classic plays ; but the public,
at her bidding, turned gladly from the spasms and the
rant of "Angelo" and "Angèle," "Antony" and
"Hernani," to the old-world stories, the formal tragedies
of the seventeenth-century poet-dramatists of France.
The actress fairly witched her public. There was something of magic in her very presence upon the scene.
None could fail to be impressed by the aspect of the
slight, pallid woman, who seemed to gain height by
reason of her slenderness, who moved towards her
audience with such simple natural majesty, who wore
and conducted her fluent classical draperies with such
admirable and perfect grace. It was as though she had
lived always so attired in tunic, peplum, and pallium—
had known no other dress,—not that she was of modern
times playing at antiquity. The physical traditions of
her race found expression or incarnation in her. Her
face was of refined Judaical character, the thin nose

slightly curved, the lower lip a trifle full, but the mouth exquisitely shaped, and the teeth small, white, and even. The profuse black-brown hair was smoothed and braided from the broad, low, white, somewhat over-hanging brow, beneath which in shadow the keen black eyes flashed out their lightnings, or glowed luridly like coals at a red heat. Her gestures were remarkable for their dignity and appropriateness; the long, slight arms lent themselves surprisingly to gracefulness; the beauti-fully formed hands, with the thin tapering fingers and the pink filbert nails, seemed always tremblingly on the alert to add significance or accent to her speeches. But there was eloquence in her very silence and complete repose. She could relate a whole history by her changes of facial expression. She possessed special powers of self-control; she was under subjection to both art and nature when she seemed to abandon herself the most absolutely to the whirlwind of her passion. There were no undue excesses of posture, movement, or tone. Her attitudes, it was once said, were those of "a Pythoness cast in bronze." Her voice thrilled and awed at its first note, it was so strangely deep, so solemnly melodious, until, stirred by passion as it were, it became thick and husky in certain of its tones; but it was always audible, articulate, and telling, whether sunk to a whisper or raised clamorously. Her declamation was superb, if, as critics reported, there had been decline in this matter during those later years of her life to which my own acquaintance with Rachel's acting is confined. I saw her first at the Français in 1849, and I was present at her last performance at the St. James's Theatre in 1853, having in the interval witnessed her assumption of certain of her most admired characters. And it may be true, too, that, still resembling Kean, she was more and more disposed, as the years passed, to make "points;" to slur over the less important scenes, and reserve herself for a grand outburst or a vehement climax, sacrificing thus many of the subtler graces, refinements, and graduations of elocution for which she had once been famous. To English ears, it was hardly an offence that she broke up the sing-song of the rhymed tirades of the old plays and gave them a more natural sound, regardless of the traditional methods of speech of Clairon, Le Kain, and other of the great French players of the past. Less success than had been looked for attended Rachel's invasion of the repertory of Mademoiselle Mars, an actress so idolized by the Parisians that her sixty years and great portliness of form were not thought hindrances to her personation of the youthful heroines of modern comedy and drama. But Rachel's fittest occupation, and her greatest triumphs, were found in the classical poetic plays. She, perhaps, intellectualized too much the creations of Hugo, Dumas, and Scribe; gave them excess of majesty. Her histrionic style was too exalted

and ideal for the conventional characters of the drama
of her own time: it was even said of her that she could
not speak its prose properly or tolerably. She disliked
the hair-powder necessary to *Adrienne Lecouvreur* and
Gabrielle de Belle-Isle, although her beauty, for all its
severity, did not lose picturesqueness in the costumes
of the time of Louis XV. As *Gabrielle* she was more
girlish and gentle, pathetic and tender, than was her
wont, while the signal fervour of her speech addressed to
Richelieu, beginning, "Vous mentez, Monsieur le Duc,"
stirred the audience to the most excited applause.

Rachel was seen upon the stage for the last time at
Charleston, on the 17th December, 1856. She played
Adrienne Lecouvreur. She had been tempted to America
by the prospect of extravagant profits. It had been
dinned into her ears that Jenny Lind, by thirty-eight
performances in America, had realized 1,700,000 francs.
Why might not she, Rachel, receive as much? And
then, she was eager to quit Paris. There had been
strange worship there of Madame Ristori, even in the
rejected part of *Medea!* But already Rachel's health
was in a deplorable state. Her constitution, never very
strong, had suffered severely from the cruel fatigues, the
incessant exertions, she had undergone. It may be, too,
that the deprivations and sufferings of her childhood now
made themselves felt as overdue claims that could be
no longer denied or deferred. She forced herself to

play, in fulfilment of her engagement, but she was languid, weak, emaciated; she coughed incessantly, her strength was gone; she was dying slowly but certainly of phthisis.   And she appeared before an audience that applauded her, it is true, but cared nothing for Racine and Corneille, knew little of the French language, and were urgent that she should sing the "Marseillaise" as she had sung it in 1848 !   It was forgotten, or it was not known in America, that the actress had long since renounced revolutionary sentiments to espouse the cause of the Second Empire.   She performed all her more important characters, however, at New York, Phila-delphia, and Boston.   Nor was the undertaking com-mercially disappointing, if it did not wholly satisfy expectation.   She returned to France possessed of nearly 300,000 francs as her share of the profits of her forty-two performances in the United States; but she returned to die.   The winter of 1856 she passed at Cairo.   She returned to France in the spring of 1857, but her physicians forbade her to remain long in Paris.   In September she moved again to the South, finding her last retreat in the villa Sardou, at Cannet, a little village in the environs of Cannes.   She lingered to the 3rd January, 1858.   The Théâtre Français closed its doors when news arrived of her death, and again on the day of her funeral.   The body was embalmed and brought to Paris for interment in the cemetery of Père la Chaise,

the obsequies being performed in accordance with the
Jewish rites. The most eminent of the authors and
actors of France were present, and funeral orations were
delivered by MM. Jules Janin, Bataille, and Auguste
Maquet. Victor Hugo was in exile, or, as Janin
announced, the author of "Angelo" would not have
withheld the tribute of his eulogy upon the sad occasion.
By her professional exertions Rachel was said to have
amassed a sum of £100,000 sterling.

Dr. Véron, who, with French frankness, wrote of the
actress in her lifetime, doubted whether he had secured
for her the more of censure or of esteem. But he urged
that her early life should be taken into account: "Il faut
se rappeler d'où elle est partie, où elle est arrivée, pour
lui tenir compte du long chemin semé de ronces et
d'épines, plein de périls et d'abîmes, que dans son
enfance et sa première jeunesse elle eut à parcourir
presque sans guides, sans le nécessaire et sans appui. A
côté de quelques mauvais sentiments qu'elle réprime,
restes impurs d'une vie errante à travers d'épaisses brous-
sailles et de pernicieux marais, on trouve en elle de
nobles instincts, le sentiment des grandes et belles
choses, une passion ardente pour les plaisirs de l'esprit,
une intelligence supérieure, une aimable philosophie, et
toutes les séductions d'une élégance et d'une distinction
naturelles."

CHAPTER X.

CHARLES KEAN.

THE son of an eminent father may be supposed to enter upon the race for fame under favourable conditions; but he carries, assuredly, a heavy weight. He must submit to invidious comparisons; expectation being perhaps unfairly raised concerning him, disappointment becomes unavoidable, and a measure even of disparagement ensues. The warmth of his first welcome gradually abates, and he finds himself painfully exposed to the cold blasts of criticism. He is liable to censure both for being like and unlike his progenitor. In the one case he is contemned as a poor copy of a great original; in the other it is charged against him that he departs presumptuously from an admirable example. It is hard for him to please. He has almost to wait until a new generation has arisen that can judge him without reference to his sire, can accept him for himself and for his own merits, and not because of his pedigree, the accident of his birth, and the excellence of his predecessor.

In a speech delivered at a public dinner some few years after his first hard-won success as an actor, Charles Kean described pathetically the disadvantages under which he had laboured at the outset of his career. "Thrown before the public by untoward circumstances at the early age of sixteen and a half, encompassed by many difficulties, friendless and untutored, the efforts of my boyhood were criticized in so severe and spirit-crushing a strain as almost to unnerve my energies and drive me despairingly from the stage. The indulgence usually extended to novices was denied to me. I was not permitted to cherish the hope that time and study could ever enable me to correct the faults of youthful inexperience. The very resemblance I bore my late father was urged against me as an offence, and condemned as being 'strange and unnatural.' Sick at heart, I left my home and sought the shores of America. To the generous inhabitants of that far land I am indebted for the first ray of success that illumined my clouded path."

Charles John Kean was born at Waterford on January 18, 1811, when his father's position and prospects seemed hopeless enough. He was engaged at a salary of five and twenty shillings a week, the leading member of a company playing now at Swansea, now at Carmarthen, now at Haverfordwest, and thence crossing to Ireland. He figured in tragedy, in comedy; he sang, he danced; he was accounted "one of the best harlequins in Wales or the West of England," and a skilled "getter-up of pantomimes;" he was stage manager, and he taught fencing. With all these advantages and accomplishments, he had suffered much from indigence and even the pangs of hunger. Three years later, and Edmund Kean had appeared at Drury Lane Theatre; the pit had risen at him; his success was prodigious; Fortune showered her gifts upon him. This abrupt turning of the tide, this sudden bound from poverty to wealth, from obscurity to fame, proved terribly trying. What wonder that the poor player, who had endured so heroically the buffets of Fortune, sank under the weight of her rewards! For three months he had been idle in London, earning nothing, waiting, hoping, watching, praying for his opportunity to appear at Drury Lane. He had no money; he could not pay the rent of his humble lodgings in Cecil Street. "He lived—he, his wife and child—in the most penurious way," writes his biographer; "they had meat once a week *if possible.*" Help from the pawnbroker was needed to obtain for him substantial food on the night of his first personation of *Shylock* in London. He returned home after that triumphant performance wild with joy, as he cried to his poor, trembling wife, breaking down with the excess of her anxiety, "Oh, Mary! my fortune is made: you shall ride in your carriage!" Presently he exclaimed, "Oh, that Howard were alive now!" Howard was his first-

born son, who died in 1813. Then the little child,
Charles Kean, was lifted from his cradle, as though to
share in the family happiness, and to be kissed by his
father as he said, "Now, my boy, you shall go to Eton!"
The child figures curiously in these early scenes of
Edmund Kean's triumph. Mr. Whitbread, one of the
Drury Lane managers, calls to express his sense of the
actor's services to the theatre, and places a draft for
£50 into the baby hands of Charles Kean. The actor's
benefit is announced, and an eye-witness relates that
"money was lying about the room in all directions."
Charles Kean, "a fine little boy, with rich curling hair,
was playing with some score of guineas on the floor;
banknotes were in heaps on the mantelpiece, table, and
sofa. . . . I think the receipts of that benefit amounted
to £1150." Yet, a little while before, the actor had
lacked pence wherewith to buy bread!

On the eve of his venture at Drury Lane, Kean had
exclaimed, "If I succeed, I think I shall go mad!"
There was more of truthful prophecy in this utterance
than he was conscious of at the time. Mrs. Kean duly
rode in her carriage. Charles Kean, after preparatory
courses at the schools of Mr. Styles of Thames Ditton
and Mr. Polehampton at Worplesdon, entered Eton as
an oppidan in June, 1824, to rise to the upper division,
to obtain credit by his Latin verses, and to distinguish
himself as second Captain of the Long Boats. The

further career of Edmund Kean need hardly be re-counted. His fortune came and went, slipping through his fingers into the mud. He had received princely rewards : he squandered them like a boor or a savage. Since Garrick's time, no actor had earned so much in so brief a period. But riotous living and reckless extrava-gance made waste alike of the man and his money. The plea of absolute insanity seemed the only explana-tion of the terrible excesses of his later years. He was little more than thirty-five when his physical powers showed unmistakable signs of premature decay; his mind was shattered, his memory was gone, he could learn no new parts; his means were exhausted, he was living precariously from day to day upon the earnings which his growing infirmities rendered more and more uncertain.

Charles Kean had been brought up to believe himself the heir to a prodigious fortune. He desired to enter the army; his father had proposed the navy as a prefer-able service; his mother's wish was that he should become a clergyman. There was no thought of his adopting the profession of the stage. But in 1827 came an offer of a cadetship in the East India Company's ser-vice. Edmund Kean urged peremptorily that his son should accept this offer, and prepare to quit England forthwith. Mrs. Kean, in broken health, helpless, de-jected, miserable, implored her son not to leave her.

For three years she had been living apart from her husband because of his dissoluteness, violence, and vicious excesses. Her state was pitiable. The poor allowance of £200 a year which he had agreed to pay her upon separating himself from her, Kean, in one of his fits of ungovernable fury, had threatened to suspend. It was hard for the Eton boy of sixteen to decide what course he should adopt. He determined at length upon accepting the cadetship if his father would secure an income of £300 to Mrs. Kean for three years. " I will not leave her sick and helpless, as she now is," said the son, "without some assurance that provision has been made for her support." But if he had the will, Kean had no longer the power to give effect to such a proposition. He lived from hand to mouth; he had saved no money; his profligate habits absorbed all he received.

Charles Kean was removed from Eton and left to depend entirely upon his own resources. He was thrown, indeed, penniless upon the world. Kean lent his son no further assistance — even to the amount of sixpence. What was the boy to do? Nor had he only his own welfare to consider. The cruel, crazy husband now entirely withdrew the small income he had pledged himself to pay the suffering wife. Mother and son were absolutely destitute. No wonder the boy listened to a proposal made by Mr. Price, the American lessee of Drury Lane Theatre. The offer seemed to drop from the clouds. Charles Kean signed an engagement for three years to appear upon the stage in certain leading characters, with a salary of £10 a week for the first year, to be increased to £11 and £12 during the second and third years, should success attend his efforts. He was such a boy at the time that there was discussion whether he should be announced in the playbills as *Master* Kean or as Mr. Kean, *Junior.*

He had seen his father act, and he could fence well—he had been taught by Angelo at Eton—otherwise he knew little enough of the player's art. No word of instruction had he ever received from Edmund Kean. Once, when a boy of twelve or so, he had ventured upon some recitation of a theatrical sort in the presence of his father, who, after listening moodily for some time with a scowl of disapproval upon his face, said at last, "There—that will do. Good-night. It is time to go to bed. No more—a—*acting*, Charles!" He was resolved, he said, to be the first and last tragedian of the name of Kean. "That boy will be an actor, if he tries; and if he *should*," he cried passionately, "*I'll cut his throat!*" It is not to be supposed that he meant what he said. Kean was much addicted to mountebank exhibitions and speeches.

Charles Kean made his first essay as an actor at Drury Lane on the 1st October, 1827, when he personated *Young Norval* in the tragedy of "Douglas."

He was so new to the stage that a dress rehearsal had been ordered that he might "face the lamps" for the first time, and accustom himself to his theatrical dress. The house was filled to overflowing. Young Norval does not appear until the opening of the second act, when he should enter after the retainers of Lord Randolph have brought forward as their prisoner Norval's faithless servant, "the trembling coward who forsook his master." The audience, unfortunately, over-anxious to greet the new tragedian cordially, wasted their enthusiasm in applauding the subordinate representative of the servant, mistaking him for Charles Kean, who thus encountered but a half-hearted and uncomfortable sort of welcome. Disconcerted somewhat, the youth recovered himself presently, proceeding with his part and obtaining, as it seemed, the approval of the audience, who rewarded his efforts with encouraging cheers, and called him before the curtain at the conclusion of the tragedy. It was clear that he had not triumphed, but he had not absolutely failed. Edmund Kean was not present. A friend supplied him with an account of the performance. It was the cue of the elder Kean's friends at this time to undervalue his son, and even to censure him in that he had become an actor in opposition to the wishes and even the commands of his father. "When Charles first came on the stage," Edmund Kean was informed, "he trembled exceedingly, supported himself on his sword, and appeared to have much ado to retain his self-possession. He bowed to the audience several times gracefully, and like a young gentleman of education. He regained his composure wonderfully. . . . His voice is altogether puerile, his appearance that of a well-made genteel youth of eighteen. His speech, 'My name is Norval,' he hurried, and spoke as though he had a cold, or were pressing his finger against his nose. His action on the whole was better than could have been expected from a novice, in many instances graceful." The newspapers dealt severely with the young actor. No allowance was made for the circumstances in which his effort was made, for his youth and inexperience. No word of encouragement was offered him, nor was there admission of the possibility of undeveloped faculties. The schoolboy attempt was judged as the performance of a mature and practised actor. "Not simple disapproval or qualified censure, but sentence of utter incapacity, stern, bitter, crushing, and conclusive." The poor lad was nearly heart-broken. He proposed to Mr. Price that his engagement should be cancelled. But the American manager gallantly stood by the youngest member of his company, counselled perseverance and renewed effort. "Douglas" was played six nights. Charles Kean then appeared as *Selim* in "Barbarossa," as *Frederick* in "Lovers' Vows," and *Lothair* in "Monk" Lewis's forgotten tragedy of "Adelgitha." He earned little applause, however, and played to dwindling audiences. His services being no longer needed at Drury Lane, the season drawing towards its close, he journeyed to Dublin, where, in April, 1828, his *Young Norval* met with a most indulgent reception. From Ireland, after some months' stay, he passed to Scotland, and, while fulfilling an engagement at Glasgow, effected a reconciliation with his father, then leading a secluded life in the house he had built for himself in the Isle of Bute. Edmund Kean even volunteered to play for his son's benefit, and they met on the stage for the first time in the Glasgow Theatre on the 1st October, 1828—the anniversary, as it chanced, of Charles Kean's first appearance in London. They appeared as *Brutus* and *Titus* in Howard Payne's tragedy of "Brutus." In the last pathetic scene, when Brutus, overpowered by his emotions, falls upon the neck of Titus with an agonized cry of "Embrace thy wretched father!" the audience, we are told, after sitting for some time suffused in tears, broke forth into loud and prolonged applause. "We're doing the trick, Charley!" whispered Edmund Kean to his son.

In December, 1828, Charles Kean reappeared at Drury Lane, personating *Romeo* for the first time. He was improved, it was held, by his experiences in the provinces, but he attracted little attention. On "Boxing Night," 1828, by way of prelude to the indispensable

pantomime, " Lovers' Vows " was repeated, when Charles
Kean's *Frederick* received valuable assistance from the
Amelia Wildenheim of Miss Ellen Tree — the future
Mrs. Charles Kean : they now met upon the stage for
the first time. In the summer Charles Kean appeared
with his father in Cork and Dublin, sustaining the
characters of *Titus, Bassanio, Welborn, Iago, Icilius,* and
Macduff. In the autumn he accepted an engagement at
the Haymarket, his performance of *Sir Edward Mortimer* in " The Iron Chest " winning hearty applause from
the audience and the decided approval of the critical
journals. " For the first time," notes his biographer,
" he felt that he had succeeded."

In 1830 he was a member of an English company
visiting Amsterdam. The expedition proved altogether
unfortunate ; the manager, a needy adventurer, de-
camped, leaving his players in a sadly poverty-stricken
plight, to return home as best they could. During the
same year Charles Kean made his first journey to
America, where he met with the most fervent of wel-
comes. He was absent two years and a half, returning
to England early in 1833, to fulfil an engagement at
Covent Garden, then under the management of M.
Laporte, at a salary of £30 per week. He reappeared
in London as *Sir Edward Mortimer.* He was but
coldly received, however, and played to thin houses.
Laporte, a shrewd impresario, then bethought him of

engaging Edmund Kean, and presenting father and son together upon the stage for the first time in London. Accordingly, "Othello" was announced for representation on the 25th March, 1833, with Edmund Kean as *Othello,* Charles Kean as *Iago,* and Miss Ellen Tree as *Desdemona.* This was Edmund Kean's last appearance upon the stage. He was now the merest wreck of what he had been. He had been wretchedly weak and ill, and cold and shivering all day long. There had been no rehearsal. The play began. He was very feeble; he could scarcely walk across the stage. "Charles is getting on," he observed; "he's acting very well; I suppose that's because he's acting with me." Brandy was freely administered to him, but his strength was fast failing him. This was so plain to those upon the stage, that a servant was directed to air another dress, so that Mr. Warde, a respectable tragedian of the second rank, might be prepared to assume the character should Kean be unable to complete his performance. Before the third act commenced he said to his son, "Mind, Charles, that you keep well before me in this act. I don't know that I shall be able to kneel; but if I do, be sure that you lift me up." The play proceeded. He delivered the famous "Farewell" with all his wonted pathos; but when he attempted the outburst, "Villain, be sure," etc., he staggered and sank into his son's arms. His acting was over for ever. "I am dying, Charles;

speak to them for me," he whispered; and in a fainting state he was borne from the stage. He lingered some three weeks, dying at Richmond on the 15th May, 1833.

Charles Kean remained at Covent Garden until the close of the season, winning applause in his first original part, *Leonardo Gonzaga,* in Sheridan Knowles's successful play of "The Wife." There seemed no prospect of a renewal of his engagement, however; nor was he to be tempted to Drury Lane by an offer of £15 per week— half the salary he had received at Covent Garden. It was plain to him that there was as yet no abiding-place for him upon the London stage; he had insufficiently impressed the public, while the press still treated him with a sort of scornful reprehension. But the provinces were open to him; he knew that he could obtain profitable engagements enough out of London. "I will not return," he said to Mr. Dunn, the Drury Lane treasurer, "until I can command my own terms—£50 per night." "Then, bid farewell to London for ever," replied Mr. Dunn, "for the days of such salaries are gone for ever." But five years later Charles Kean, in his own carriage, was driving to Drury Lane, engaged for a stated number of performances, upon his own terms—£50 per night. He played *Hamlet* twenty-one times, *Richard III.* seventeen times, and *Sir Giles Overreach* five times, and attracted crowded audiences. During his absence from London he had earned £20,000 by his provincial engagements. He had visited Hamburg with an English company, under the direction of Mr. Barham Livius, one of the earliest translators of Weber's " Der Freischütz ; " but the authorities interfered, prohibiting the performances of the "foreign intruders" as injurious to the exhibitions of native talent. In 1839 Charles Kean fulfilled his second engagement in America, reappearing at the Haymarket in the following year. He was married to Miss Ellen Tree, in Dublin, on the 29th January, 1842. The fact of this union was for some time withheld from the public; and, by an odd chance, the bride and bridegroom, who had been wedded in the morning, appeared at night upon the stage in the comedy of " The Honeymoon." A little later, and they were supporting a new play at the Haymarket—" The Rose of Arragon " —one of the least attractive works of Sheridan Knowles. Miss Ellen Tree had made her first appearance upon the stage at Covent Garden in 1823, when she was scarcely seventeen. She played *Olivia* in " Twelfth Night," the occasion being the benefit of her sister, Miss M. Tree, who represented *Viola*.

It was in 1850 that Charles Kean, having for his partner the favourite comedian Robert Keeley, became lessee of the Princess's Theatre in Oxford Street, and first undertook the cares and toils of management. The preceding years had been occupied with protracted engagements in America and the provinces. For two seasons Mr. and Mrs. Charles Kean had appeared at the Haymarket, less as "stars" than as permanent members of a strong company, content to play such parts as the management might assign to them. They brought with them Mr. Lovell's drama of " The Wife's Secret," which had enjoyed many representations in America. They appeared in the new plays of " Strathmore," by Dr. Marston ; " The Loving Woman," by Mark Lemon ; " Leap Year," by Mr. Buckstone ; and in " King René's Daughter," an adaptation from the Danish of Henrik Herz ; and they sustained many of their accustomed Shakesperian characters. Charles Kean no longer priced his performances at £50 per night : nevertheless, as an actor, he had risen greatly in general estimation. In 1848 he had been selected by the Queen to conduct the dramatic representations at Windsor Castle, which were continued annually at the Christmas season some ten years, with interruptions in 1850 owing to the death of the Queen Dowager, and in 1855 because of the Crimean War and the national gloom it had induced. Early in 1851 Macready retired from the stage, and it must be said that for many years the admirers and private friends of Macready had been among the most hostile of Charles Kean's critics. He was now to be viewed as in some sort the last of the " legitimate " tragedians ; perhaps he was also to be accounted the least of them. He had survived the wreck of the patent houses; he was almost the only representative of the long line of players who had played "leading business," appeared in high tragedy, upon the stages of Drury Lane and Covent Garden. The one establishment was now devoted to the uses of Italian Opera; the other had sunk to the level of a minor theatre—had been turned into a circus, a promenade concert room. The Act of 1843 had absolutely abolished the theatrical protective system, and instituted free trade in the drama. It was not surprising, perhaps, that in stage politics Charles Kean should be an extreme Tory. He had lived to see the swift decline of that poetic drama and that school of heroic acting which at the outset of his career had seemed so firmly founded. He could not believe that the period was one of transition only. He could discover no hope upon the horizon. To his thinking the drama was lost, and lost for ever. "The change is going on every night," he said before the Parliamentary Committee on Theatrical Licences in 1866; "we are going deeper into the mire." There were no actors. There was no supply of young actors. There was no training for them, no possibility of educating them. "Actors," he said, "cannot spring into experience without going through a training. In my boyhood we never considered that a man had gone through his probation until he had been on the stage for seven years; but now an actor plays the leading parts of Shakespeare before he has been on the stage two years!" He had forgotten, apparently, his own boyish attempts. He deprecated the licensing of more theatres; there were already too many. "If you go on licensing theatres, you will drive the higher class of drama off the stage—the art will vanish." He held that "the greatest blow the drama ever received was the doing away with the patent theatres: from this it had never recovered, and never would." The remedy—if the state of things really needed a remedy—should have been, not less, but more patent theatres, in correspondence with the increase of the population.

But for the nullifying of the patents by the Act of 1843, however, Charles Kean could not have played Shakespeare at the Princess's Theatre, and it was with every disposition to make the best of the position of affairs that he entered upon his managerial career. "We can't now," he said at the time, "be bound by the old rules and keep troubling ourselves about what John Kemble didn't like or Macready wouldn't do. I've thrown away the dignity of a tragedian. I'm prepared now to undertake any part. I'll play low comedy if need be. I *did* appear as a footman at the Haymarket only a little time ago." This was in the comedy of "Leap Year"—the footman proving to be a lover in disguise, however. The entertainments of the Princess's were therefore various enough, and Charles Kean advanced further towards melodrama than he had ever ventured in his earlier years: low comedy he was not really required to undertake. The partnership with Mr. Keeley did not long endure, although the firm closed their first season of thirteen months with a net profit of £7000: it was the year of the first Great Exhibition in Hyde Park. In the November of 1851 the Princess's Theatre reopened under the sole direction of Charles Kean.

New plays of pretence were forthcoming at any rate during the earlier years of Charles Kean's management, before he devoted himself so exclusively to his richly embellished revivals of Shakespeare. At the Princess's were first produced Douglas Jerrold's dramas of "St. Cupid" and "A Heart of Gold," Dr. Marston's "Anne Blake," Mr. Lovell's "Trial of Love," Mr. Slous's "Templar," "The First Printer," by Mr. Charles Reade and Tom Taylor, and Mr. Boucicault's "Love in a Maze;" and to these are to be added the plays of foreign origin, "The Duke's Wager," a version of "Mademoiselle de Belle-Isle," "Louis XI.," "The Corsican Brothers," "Pauline," "The Courier of Lyons," "Marco Spada," "Faust and Marguerite," etc. It is curious that out of this list certain of the foreign plays only have secured any hold upon the English stage, or undergone the honour of reproduction. A revival in 1853 of Lord Byron's "Sardanapalus" attracted great attention, not because of the tragedy's intrinsic merits, but in that Mr. Layard's excavations and discoveries at Nineveh had been ingeniously turned to account by the stage-decorator. A spectacle was provided, rich in winged bulls, costumes, armour and arms, and curiosities of Assyrian architecture, such as Lord Byron assuredly had not dreamt of. *Sardanapalus*, very dusky of skin, and wearing a long and elaborately plaited beard, was personated by Charles Kean, Mrs. Kean appearing as the Ionian *Myrrha*. In his revivals of Shakespeare, Charles Kean had for his predecessors the Kembles and Macready, if he had to deal with a much smaller stage and a weaker company than were at their disposal. But he advanced beyond their example. He was so far true to the poet's text that, while condensing it, he did not garble or adulterate it; but he made it more and more an excuse for displaying the arts of the scene-painter, the costumier, and the stage-machinist. All was admirably contrived, the utmost pains being taken to secure archæological correctness and to content antiquarian critics. But the play seemed sometimes to grow pale and faint because of the weighty splendour of its adornments. As Macready expressed it, "the text allowed to be spoken was more like a running commentary upon the spectacles exhibited than the scenic arrangements an illustration of the text. It has, however, been popular," he added, "and the main end answered." The Shakesperian plays revived at the Princess's Theatre in this costly, luxurious, and resplendent fashion, were " King John," " Macbeth," " King Henry VIII.," " The Winter's Tale," King Lear," " A Midsummer Night's Dream," " King Richard II.," "The Tempest," "The Merchant of Venice," " Much Ado about Nothing," and " King Henry V." " Richard III." was also produced, but, sad to relate, in deference to the memories of Garrick, Kemble, Cooke, and Edmund Kean, the text was Colley Cibber's, and not Shakespeare's !

These revivals succeeded because of their magnificence as spectacles or pageants, yet it is to be said that with them Charles Kean's exertions as an actor were invariably well received; he found, indeed, much and faithful admiration; he had fairly conquered his public. His term of management over, he was enabled to figure again prosperously as a " star," and to sustain the great Shakesperian characters upon country and colonial stages with but the slightest aid from the scenic artist or the stage manager. He had fought hard to retrieve the errors of what may be called his first histrionic manner, and to subdue the prejudices excited against him by his raw and boyish efforts, his premature appearance upon the stage. By dint of assiduous and wary labour, helped by his genuine love of his art, he had become a skilled and finished actor. He had persevered with himself not less than with his audience. He forced from them their applause, having first forced himself to deserve it. And he worked with trying, harsh, ungrateful materials. Nature had not been kind to him. He was low of stature, and, although he acquired a certain grace and dignity of bearing, he was inelegant of form. The early description of him as one who " spoke as though he had a cold, or were pressing his finger against his nose," remained true to the last : his pronunciation of certain words was thus affected, and something of ludicrousness or caricature seemed often to haunt his elocution. His voice was strong, however ; he was capable of feats of rapid enunciation, and he could indulge at times in a sort of passionate vociferousness that was highly effective if it occasionally degenerated into rant. Lockhart, writing in 1838, commended "the sweet melancholy" tones of the actor's voice ; and, while admitting he "would never declaim like Kemble," held that "his whisper was as effective as ever Mrs. Siddons's was." But there was little charm in Charles Kean's oratory ; it lacked musical variety, it was too prosaic, and here and there was marred by errors of emphasis or odd jerks and spasms of the voice. He was far happier in his delivery of short sentences, sharp questions, or stinging replies. His face, plain of feature, was immobile of expression, although his heavy-lidded eyes were bright and pene-trating. He was versed in all stage accomplishments,

was adroit of attitude, fenced well, gesticulated with
address, making good use of his small and shapely
hands. An air of refinement attended him, and for all his
lack of comeliness he always wore the look of a gentleman. For the more stately of Shakespeare's heroes he
was deficient in physical attributes; his *Othello* and
Macbeth, for instance, seemed too insignificant of presence, although in *Wolsey* and *Lear* he fought successfully with Nature and became picturesque. His *Hamlet*
was admired for its polish and carefulness; it was indeed
a thoroughly thoughtful and artistic performance, while
its theatrical efficiency was beyond question. As *Richard*
and *Shylock*, he simply followed as closely as he could
his father's interpretation of those characters. A certain
supreme energy and chivalric exaltation of manner
always carried him successfully through such parts as
Hotspur and *Henry V.* In comedy he was often excellent. The habitual sadness of his face lent a strong
effect to his smiles, while his peculiarities of voice could
be readily turned in the direction of drollery. His
Mr. Ford in "The Merry Wives of Windsor," his *Duke
Aranza, Don Felix*, and *Mr. Oakley*, were admirable examples of comic impersonation; his *Benedick*, although
he could not look the character, was full of humorous
animation and intelligence. Perhaps the main secret of
his success lay in his earnestness of manner and his
incisiveness of delivery, seconded by his special power of

self-control.   He had learnt the value of repose in acting, of repressing all excitement of attitude and gesture, and he imported into modern tragedy a sort of drawing-room air little known upon the English stage before his time.   In this wise he did not the less, but rather the more, impress his audience.   There was at times what has been called " a deadly quiet " about his acting which exercised a curious silencing and chilling influence over the spectators ; they became awed, were set shuddering, and remained spell-bound, they scarcely knew how or why.   It was particularly in plays of the French school, such as " Pauline " and " The Corsican Brothers," that these qualities of his art manifested themselves.   At the same time he never sank to the level of conventional melodrama, but rather lifted it to the height of tragedy.   He might appear in highly coloured situations, but he betrayed no exaggeration of demeanour ; his bearing was still subdued and self-contained.   His solemn fixedness of facial expression, the sorrow-laden monotony of his voice—defects in certain histrionic circumstances—were of advantage in the effect of concentration and intensity they imparted to many of his performances.   He was thus enabled to distinguish himself greatly in what may be called " one-idea-ed " parts, of which his *Mr. Ford* in comedy and his *Louis XI.* in tragedy may be taken as examples.   His claim to be remembered as an actor may be found to depend upon these characteristics or peculiarities of his professional method, which, being individual and personal, "differentiate" him from earlier and later players.

Charles Kean's management of the Princess's Theatre closed in 1859. In the July of that year a banquet was held in his honour at St. James's Hall, the Duke of Newcastle of that day presiding, and Mr. Gladstone, then Chancellor of the Exchequer in Lord Palmerston's administration, making a speech upon the occasion. Many eminent personages were assembled, including certain of the actor's contemporaries at Eton College. Mr. Kean's later years were devoted to the fulfilment of various engagements in London and the provinces, America and the colonies. But he did not extend his repertory, he undertook no new characters; he was content to repeat again and again the performances which had already secured him so large a share of public favour. His "grand tour" was on a scale such as earlier actors, however prone to stroll, could scarcely have contemplated, and included California and Australia. It may be said, indeed, that, aided by his wife and a small company travelling with him, he played in every part of the habitable globe occupied by English-speaking inhabitants and possessed of a stage upon which players could present themselves.

Charles Kean died, after a brief illness, at his house in London, on the 22nd January, 1868.

CHAPTER XI.

A NOTE ON FECHTER.

I FIRST saw the late Charles Fechter in Paris a long time since, when Prince Louis Bonaparte presided over the second French Republic and the barrel-organs were still busy grinding out "Mourir pour la Patrie ;" when the charming Rose Chéri was the accepted heroine of sentimental comedy, and the incomparable Rachel Felix was the absolute tragedy-queen of the Théâtre Français; when Lamartine's "Toussaint L'Ouverture" was in course of representation at the Porte St. Martin, much lamp-black being consumed by the personators of the natives of St. Domingo, and Mélingue was strutting and fretting in the portentous play of "Urbain Grandier" at Alexander Dumas' Théâtre Historique ; when Auriol was a famous clown and Gavarni the most admired of caricaturists ; and when a good many of us were " young and curly" who are now old, and grey or bald, as the case may be. Charles Fechter was rather to be re-

marked for his good looks than his good acting in those
days. He played at the Ambigu Comique parts not
very taxing to the intellect, such as *Phœbus*, in an
elaborate acting-edition of "Nôtre Dame," and *Amaury*
in a long melodrama, "Les Quatre Fils Aymon," familiar
to some Englishmen as the theme of one of Balfe's
operas. The young player was much slimmer of figure
than he became in later times; his handsome face—it
had always an English look, to my thinking—was less
fleshy; his manner was very bright and gay, with an air
of romance and picturesqueness about it peculiar to the
man. But he did not impress the public very deeply.
It was not, I think, until 1852, when he appeared as
Armand Duval in "La Dame aux Camélias, to the
Marguerite Gautier of Madame Doche, that his merits
were fairly asserted or recognized. The facts of his
theatrical career subsequently have been often recited,
and are well known. He became famous as the best
stage-lover of his time.

It chanced that he was born in England; but English
was to him always a foreign language, and the feat of
his success upon our stage has hardly received its meed
of applause. Charles Mathews won much admiration
by his performance of two characters in French before a
Parisian audience, but the effort was quite of an exotic
sort. It stirred curiosity and amused, and there was an

end of it.   No one knew better than Mathews himself
that there was no abiding-place for him upon French
boards; he was there merely as a visitor, liable at any
moment to discover that he was outstaying his welcome.
But Charles Fechter firmly established himself in
England; he remained here for nearly ten years.   He
performed a long list of characters, he became a London
manager, he played in Shakespeare, and took high rank
among our best players.   The English public greatly
admired him, and but for his ambition to extend his
fame, and the favour awarded him in America, it is
probable that he would have remained among us, a
leading, esteemed, and prosperous actor to the last.   It
is true that he always spoke English with a strong
foreign accent, and that he was never able to deliver
English blank-verse with due regard to its rhythmical
properties.   He reduced it to plain prose.   And these
were grave defects.   But with every actor appearing in
the poetic or heroic drama there is always something
the audience have to "get over," to grow accustomed
to, to become reconciled with and to forget.   It may be
defect of face or of figure, tricks of manner, faults of
gesture and deportment.   In Fechter's case, his accent,
the havoc he made of the blank-verse, and a certain
"throaty" quality of voice, had to be forgiven him.   In
later years, too, the size of his waist had to be over-

looked. But, discount having been allowed in these
respects, Fechter's acting was full of charm. There was
a French redundancy of gesture, no doubt, and he had
a way of looking not immediately towards the persons he
addressed, but at some imagined point—a yard, perhaps,
above their heads. Presumably he thought his fine eyes
were thus seen to the best advantage. But he suited the
action to the word with singular appropriateness; he
was very graceful of movement; he never relaxed his
grasp of the character he represented; he was refined,
fervent, pathetic, passionate. He appeared with success
in what are called "coat-and-waistcoat" plays; but he
was best pleased, I think, to figure in dramas permitting
an exhibition of his taste and skill in costume. He
liked a romantic story with a chivalrous hero attired in a
picturesque dress. Of course he was more effective in
some parts than in others; certain of Lemaître's characters suited him very indifferently, and his *Othello* won
little approval; but his success was great as *Ruy Blas*,
as *Henri de Lagardère*, as *Claude Melnotte*, *Obenreizer*,
Edgar of Ravenswood, and as *Hamlet*. His term of
management commenced most happily with "The Duke's
Motto," and he thrived greatly for some seasons; but he
was not well advised in his choice of new productions.
"Bel Demonio," "The King's Butterfly," and "The
Watch-Cry" were but poor plays.

He was very inventive in the matter of stage business, and desirous always of substituting new business for old. He professed that it had been to him an unceasing labour of love for twenty years to reform the scenic representation of Shakespeare. He denounced "tradition" as a "worm-eaten and unwholesome prison, where dramatic art languishes in fetters," forgetting that it is the great players who legislate for the stage in this regard, and hand it down its traditions. Did he not look forward to his own innovations becoming in time traditions? Fechter's *Hamlet* will long be reckoned by playgoers among the best *Hamlets* they have ever known. I have seen perhaps a score of *Hamlets*, including the *Hamlets* of Macready, of Charles Kean, of Emil Devrient, and Salvini: it seems to me that Fechter's *Hamlet* ranks with the worthiest of these. He had special physical qualifications; his manner was natural and charming. As Mr. G. H. Lewes wrote at the time: "Fechter is lymphatic, delicate, handsome, and with his long flaxen curls, quivering, sensitive nostrils, fine eye, and sympathetic voice, perfectly represents the graceful Prince. His aspect and bearing are such that the eye rests on him with delight; our sympathies are completely secured," etc. It must be remembered, however, that failure in the part of *Hamlet* has been of rare occurrence, and that applause has been carried off by *Hamlets* of

but meagre histrionic capacity. Macready pronounced
as the result of his experience that "no actor possessed
of moderate advantages of person, occasional animation,
and some knowledge of stage business, can entirely fail
in the part of *Hamlet*. The interest of the story, and the
rapid succession of startling situations growing out of it,
compel the attention of the spectator, and irresistibly
engage his sympathy." The success of Fechter in *Hamlet*
really owed little to his innovations, his neglect of traditions; although a certain amused curiosity prevailed
for a while concerning the new French *Hamlet* who wore
a flaxen wig. I will not venture to discuss at length his
new views and readings, his new stage business, but
these have been fully placed upon record. It was the
firm belief of Fechter's *Hamlet*, in defiance of general
opinion to the contrary, that *Queen Gertrude* was
Claudius's accomplice in the murder of her husband.
In the time of Fechter's *Hamlet* it was the fashion in
Denmark to wear a medallion portrait, swinging from a
gold chain, round the neck. Fechter's *Hamlet* wore thus
a portrait of his father; the *Queen* wore a portrait of
Claudius; Guildenstern was similarly adorned. Usually
there is not a pin to choose between *Rosencrantz* and
Guildenstern; the unfortunate gentlemen are alike odious
to *Hamlet*, and they are slaughtered off the stage, at
the instigation of that prince, after they have been well

murdered in the presence of the house by their histrionic
representatives.   But to Fechter's *Hamlet Rosencrantz*
was less hateful than *Guildenstern ; Rosencrantz* wore no
portrait round his neck.   When Fechter's *Hamlet* spoke
his first speech, and compared the late king to Hyperion
and *Claudius* to a satyr, he produced and gazed fondly
at his father's picture ; when he mentioned his uncle's
"picture in little" he illustrated his meaning by handling
the medallion worn by *Guildenstern ;* in the closet
scene he placed his miniature of his father side by
side with his mother's miniature of *Claudius ;* when at
the close of their interview *Gertrude* outstretched her
arm, and would embrace her son, he held up sternly
the portrait of his father ; the wretched woman recoiled
and staggered from the stage ; *Hamlet* reverentially
kissed the picture as he murmured, " I must be cruel,"
etc.   In the play-scene Fechter's *Hamlet*, when he rose
at the discomfiture of *Claudius*, tore the leaves from the
play-book and flung them in the air ; in the scene with
Ophelia, Fechter's *Hamlet* did not perceive that the
King was watching him ; had he known *that* he would
have been so convinced of his uncle's guilt, that the play
would have been unnecessary.   In the fourth act, if
Fechter's *Hamlet* had not been well guarded, he would
have killed the King then and there.   In the last scene
a gallery ran at the back of the stage, with short flights

of stairs on either side; all exits and entrances were made by means of these stairs. Upon the confession of *Laertes*, the King endeavoured to escape up the right-hand staircase; *Hamlet*, perceiving this, rushed up the left-hand stairs, and encountering *Claudius* in the centre of the gallery, there despatched him.

THE END.

PRINTED BY WILLIAM CLOWES AND SONS, LIMITED, LONDON AND BECCLES.

CHATTO & WINDUS'S
LIST OF BOOKS.

NEW FINE-ART WORK. Large 4to, bound in buckram, 21s.

Abdication, The; or, Time Tries All.
An Historical Drama. By W. D. SCOTT-MONCRIEFF. With Seven Etchings by JOHN PETTIE, R.A., W. Q. ORCHARDSON, R.A., J. MAC WHIRTER, A.R.A., COLIN HUNTER, R. MACBETH, and TOM GRAHAM.

Crown 8vo, Coloured Frontispiece and Illustrations, cloth gilt, 7s. 6d.

Advertising, A History of.
From the Earliest Times. Illustrated by Anecdotes, Curious Specimens, and Notices of Successful Advertisers. By HENRY SAMPSON.

Crown 8vo, cloth extra, with 639 Illustrations, 7s. 6d.

Architectural Styles, A Handbook of.
From the German of A. ROSENGARTEN by W. COLLETT-SANDARS.

Crown 8vo, with Portrait and Facsimile, cloth extra, 7s. 6d.

Artemus Ward's Works:
The Works of CHARLES FARRER BROWNE, better known as ARTEMUS WARD. With Portrait, Facsimile of Handwriting, &c.

Crown 8vo, cloth extra, 7s. 6d.

Bankers, A Handbook of London;
With some Account of their Predecessors, the Early Goldsmiths: together with Lists of Bankers from 1677 to 1876. By F. G. HILTON PRICE.

Bardsley (Rev. C. W.), Works by:
English Surnames: Their Sources and Significations. By CHARLES WAREING BARDSLEY, M.A. Crown 8vo, cloth extra, 7s. 6d.

Curiosities of Puritan Nomenclature. By CHARLES W. BARDSLEY. Crown 8vo, cloth extra, 7s. 6d.

Crown 8vo, cloth extra, Illustrated, 7s. 6d.

Bartholomew Fair, Memoirs of.
By HENRY MORLEY. New Edition, with One Hundred Illustrations.

Imperial 4to, cloth extra, gilt and gilt edges, 21s. per volume.

Beautiful Pictures by British Artists:

A Gathering of Favourites from our Picture Galleries. In Two Series.
The FIRST SERIES including Examples by WILKIE, CONSTABLE, TURNER, MULREADY, LANDSEER, MACLISE, E. M. WARD, FRITH, Sir JOHN GILBERT, LESLIE, ANSDELL, MARCUS STONE, Sir NOEL PATON, FAED, EYRE CROWE, GAVIN O'NEIL, and MADOX BROWN.
The SECOND SERIES containing Pictures by ARMITAGE, FAED, GOODALL, HEMSLEY, HORSLEY, MARKS, NICHOLLS, Sir NOEL PATON, PICKERSGILL, G. SMITH, MARCUS STONE, SOLOMON, STRAIGHT, E. M. WARD, and WARREN.
All engraved on Steel in the highest style of Art. Edited, with Notices of the Artists, by SYDNEY ARMYTAGE, M.A.

" *This book is well got up, and good engravings by Jeens, Lumb Stocks, and others, bring back to us Royal Academy Exhibitions of past years.*"—TIMES.

Small 4to, green and gold, 6s. 6d. ; gilt edges, 7s. 6d.

Bechstein's As Pretty as Seven,

And other German Stories. Collected by LUDWIG BECHSTEIN. With Additional Tales by the Brothers GRIMM, and 100 Illustrations by RICHTER.

One Shilling Monthly, Illustrated.

Belgravia for 1882.

A New Serial Story, entitled "All Sorts and Conditions of Men," written by WALTER BESANT and JAMES RICE, Authors of " Ready-Money Mortiboy," &c., and Illustrated by FRED. BARNARD, will be begun in the JANUARY Number of BELGRAVIA ; this Number will contain also the First Chapters of a New Novel, entitled "**The Admiral's Ward**," by Mrs. ALEXANDER, Author of "The Wooing o't." &c. ; and the first of a series of Twelve Papers, entitled " About Yorkshire," by KATHARINE S. MACQUOID, illustrated by T. R. MACQUOID.

. *The FORTY-FIFTH Volume of BELGRAVIA, elegantly bound in crimson cloth, full gilt side and back, gilt edges, price 7s. 6d., is now ready.—Handsome Cases for binding volumes can be had at 2s. each.*

Demy 8vo, with Illustrations, 1s.

Belgravia Annual.

With Stories by WILKIE COLLINS, F. W. ROBINSON, DUTTON COOK, PERCY FITZGERALD, J. ARBUTHNOT WILSON, HENRY W. LUCY D. CHRISTIE MURRAY, JAMES PAYN, and others.   [*Nov.* 10.

Folio, half-bound boards, India Proofs, 21s.

Blake (William):

Etchings from his Works. By W. B. SCOTT. With descriptive Text.

Crown 8vo, cloth extra, gilt, with Illustrations, 7s. 6d.

Boccaccio's Decameron;

or, Ten Days' Entertainment. Translated into English, with an Introduction by THOMAS WRIGHT, Esq., M.A., F.S.A. With Portrait, and STOTHARD'S beautiful Copperplates.

Demy 8vo, Illustrated, uniform in size for binding.

Blackburn's (Henry) Art Handbooks:

Academy Notes, 1875. With 40 Illustrations. 1*s.*
Academy Notes, 1876. With 107 Illustrations. 1*s.*
Academy Notes, 1877. With 143 Illustrations. 1*s.*
Academy Notes, 1878. With 150 Illustrations. 1*s.*
Academy Notes, 1879. With 146 Illustrations. 1*s.*
Academy Notes, 1880. With 126 Illustrations. 1*s.*
Academy Notes, 1881. With 128 Illustrations. 1*s.*
Grosvenor Notes, 1878. With 68 Illustrations. 1*s.*
Grosvenor Notes, 1879. With 60 Illustrations. 1*s.*
Grosvenor Notes, 1880. With 56 Illustrations. 1*s.*
Grosvenor Notes, 1881. With 74 Illustrations. 1*s.*
Pictures at the Paris Exhibition, 1878. 80 Illustrations. 1*s.*
Pictures at South Kensington. With 70 Illustrations. 1*s.*
The English Pictures at the National Gallery. 114 Illusts. 1*s.*
The Old Masters at the National Gallery. 128 Illusts. 1*s.* 6*d.*
Academy Notes, 1875-79. Complete in One Volume, with
nearly 600 Illustrations in Facsimile. Demy 8vo, cloth limp, 6*s.*
A Complete Illustrated Catalogue to the National Gallery.
With Notes by H. BLACKBURN, and 242 Illusts. Demy 8vo, cloth limp, 3*s.*

UNIFORM WITH "ACADEMY NOTES."

Royal Scottish Academy Notes, 1878. 117 Illustrations. 1*s.*
Royal Scottish Academy Notes, 1879. 125 Illustrations. 1*s.*
Royal Scottish Academy Notes, 1880. 114 Illustrations. 1*s.*
Royal Scottish Academy Notes, 1881. 104 Illustrations. 1*s.*
Glasgow Institute of Fine Arts Notes, 1878. 95 Illusts. 1*s.*
Glasgow Institute of Fine Arts Notes, 1879. 100 Illusts. 1*s.*
Glasgow Institute of Fine Arts Notes, 1880. 120 Illusts. 1*s.*
Glasgow Institute of Fine Arts Notes, 1881. 108 Illusts. 1*s.*
Walker Art Gallery Notes, Liverpool, 1878. 112 Illusts. 1*s.*
Walker Art Gallery Notes, Liverpool, 1879. 100 Illusts. 1*s.*
Walker Art Gallery Notes, Liverpool, 1880. 100 Illusts. 1*s.*
Royal Manchester Institution Notes, 1878. 88 Illustrations. 1*s.*
Society of Artists Notes, Birmingham, 1878. 95 Illusts. 1*s.*
Children of the Great City. By F. W. LAWSON. 1*s.*

Bowers' (G.) Hunting Sketches:

Canters in Crampshire. By G. BOWERS. I. Gallops from
Gorseborough. II. Scrambles with Scratch Packs. III. Studies with
Stag Hounds. Oblong 4to, half-bound boards, 21*s.*
Leaves from a Hunting Journal. By G. BOWERS. Coloured in
facsimile of the originals. Oblong 4to, half-bound, 21*s.*

Crown 8vo, cloth extra, gilt, 7*s.* 6*d.*

Brand's Observations on Popular Antiquities,

chiefly Illustrating the Origin of our Vulgar Customs, Ceremonies, and
Superstitions. With the Additions of Sir HENRY ELLIS. An entirely
New and Revised Edition, with fine full-page Illustrations.

Bret Harte, Works by:

Bret Harte's Collected Works. Arranged and Revised by the Author. Complete in Five Vols., crown 8vo, cloth extra, 6s. each.

Vol. I. COMPLETE POETICAL AND DRAMATIC WORKS. With Steel Plate Portrait, and an Introduction by the Author.

Vol. II. EARLIER PAPERS—LUCK OF ROARING CAMP, and other Sketches —BOHEMIAN PAPERS—SPANISH and AMERICAN LEGENDS.

Vol. III. TALES OF THE ARGONAUTS—EASTERN SKETCHES.

Vol. IV. GABRIEL CONROY.

Vol. V. STORIES—CONDENSED NOVELS, &c.

The Select Works of Bret Harte, in Prose and Poetry. With Introductory Essay by J. M. BELLEW, Portrait of the Author, and 50 Illustrations. Crown 8vo, cloth extra, 7s. 6d.

An Heiress of Red Dog, and other Stories. By BRET HARTE. Post 8vo, illustrated boards, 2s. ; cloth limp, 2s. 6d.

The Twins of Table Mountain. By BRET HARTE. Fcap. 8vo, picture cover, 1s. ; crown 8vo, cloth extra, 3s. 6d.

The Luck of Roaring Camp, and other Sketches. By BRET HARTE. Post 8vo, illustrated boards, 2s.

Jeff Briggs's Love Story. By BRET HARTE. Fcap. 8vo, picture cover, 1s. ; cloth extra, 2s. 6d.

Small crown 8vo, cloth extra, gilt, with full-page Portraits, 4s. 6d.

Brewster's (Sir David) Martyrs of Science.

Small crown 8vo, cloth extra, gilt, with Astronomical Plates, 4s. 6d.

Brewster's (Sir D.) More Worlds than One,

the Creed of the Philosopher and the Hope of the Christian.

A HANDSOME GIFT-BOOK.—Small 4to, cloth extra, profusely Illustrated, 6s.

Brushwood.

By T. BUCHANAN READ. Illustrated from Designs by FREDERICK DIELMAN.

THE STOTHARD BUNYAN.—Crown 8vo, cloth extra, gilt, 7s. 6d.

Bunyan's Pilgrim's Progress.

Edited by Rev. T. SCOTT. With 17 beautiful Steel Plates by STOTHARD, engraved by GOODALL ; and numerous Woodcuts.

Demy 8vo, cloth extra, 7s. 6d.

Burton's Anatomy of Melancholy :

A New Edition, complete, corrected and enriched by Translations of the Classical Extracts.

Crown 8vo, cloth extra, gilt, with Illustrations, 7s. 6d.

Byron's Letters and Journals.

With Notices of his Life. By THOMAS MOORE. A Reprint of the Original Edition, newly revised, with Twelve full-page Plates.

Demy 8vo, cloth extra, 14s.

Campbell's (Sir G.) White and Black :

Travels in the United States. By Sir GEORGE CAMPBELL, M.P.

Demy 8vo, cloth extra, with Illustrations, 7s. 6d.

Caravan Route (The) between Egypt and

Syria. By His Imperial and Royal Highness the ARCHDUKE LUDWIG SALVATOR of AUSTRIA. With 23 full-page Illustrations by the Author.

Post 8vo, cloth extra, 1s. 6d.

Carlyle (Thomas) On the Choice of Books.

With a Life of the Author by R. H. SHEPHERD. Entirely New and Revised Edition.

Crown 8vo, cloth extra, 7s. 6d.

Century (A) of Dishonour:

A Sketch of the United States Government's Dealings with some of the Indian Tribes.

Crown 8vo, cloth extra, with Illustrations, 7s. 6d.

Chap-Books.—A History of the Chap-Books

of the Eighteenth Century. By JOHN ASHTON. With nearly 400 Illustrations, engraved in facsimile of the originals. [*In the press.*

*** A few Large-Paper copies will be carefully printed on hand-made paper, for which early application should be made.

Large 4to, half-bound, profusely Illustrated, 28s.

Chatto and Jackson.—A Treatise on Wood

Engraving: Historical and Practical. By WILLIAM ANDREW CHATTO and JOHN JACKSON. With an Additional Chapter by HENRY G. BOHN; and 450 fine Illustrations. A reprint of the last Revised Edition.

Small 4to, cloth gilt, with Coloured Illustrations, 10s. 6d.

Chaucer for Children:

A Golden Key. By Mrs. H. R. HAWEIS. With Eight Coloured Pictures and numerous Woodcuts by the Author.

Demy 8vo, cloth limp, 2s. 6d.

Chaucer for Schools.

By Mrs. HAWEIS, Author of "Chaucer for Children."

Crown 8vo, cloth limp, with Map and Illustrations, 2s. 6d.

Cleopatra's Needle:

Its Acquisition and Removal to England. By Sir J. E. ALEXANDER.

Crown 8vo, cloth extra, gilt, 7s. 6d.

Colman's Humorous Works:

"Broad Grins," "My Nightgown and Slippers," and other Humorous Works, Prose and Poetical, of GEORGE COLMAN. With Life by G. B. BUCKSTONE, and Frontispiece by HOGARTH.

Demy 8vo, cloth, 16s.

Dutt's India, Past and Present;

with Minor Essays on Cognate Subjects. By SHOSHEE CHUNDER DUTT, Rái Báhádoor.

Crown 8vo, cloth boards, 6s. per Volume.

Early English Poets.

Edited, with Introductions and Annotations, by Rev. A. B. GROSART.

1. **Fletcher's (Giles, B.D.) Com-** plete Poems: Christ's Victorie in Heaven, Christ's Victorie on Earth, Christ's Triumph over Death, and Minor Poems. With Memorial-Introduction and Notes. One Vol.

2. **Davies' (Sir John) Complete** Poetical Works, including Psalms I. to L. in Verse, and other hitherto Unpublished MSS., for the first time Collected and Edited. Memorial-Introduction and Notes. Two Vols.

3. **Herrick's (Robert) Hesperi-** des, Noble Numbers, and Complete Collected Poems. With Memorial-Introduction and Notes, Steel Portrait, Index of First Lines, and Glossarial Index, &c. Three Vols.

4. **Sidney's (Sir Philip) Com-** plete Poetical Works, including all those in "Arcadia." With Portrait, Memorial-Introduction, Essay on the Poetry of Sidney, and Notes. Three Vols.

Imperial 8vo, with 147 fine Engravings, half-morocco, 36s.

Early Teutonic, Italian, and French Masters

(The). Translated and Edited from the Dohme Series, by A. H. KEANE, M.A.I. With numerous Illustrations.

"*Cannot fail to be of the utmost use to students of art history.*"—TIMES.

Crown 8vo, cloth extra, gilt, with Illustrations, 6s.

Emanuel On Diamonds and Precious

Stones ; their History, Value, and Properties ; with Simple Tests for ascertaining their Reality. By HARRY EMANUEL, F.R.G.S. With numerous Illustrations, Tinted and Plain.

Crown 8vo, cloth extra, with Illustrations, 7s. 6d.

Englishman's House, The:

A Practical Guide to all interested in Selecting or Building a House, with full Estimates of Cost, Quantities, &c. By C. J. RICHARDSON. Third Edition. With nearly 600 Illustrations.

Crown 8vo, cloth extra, with nearly 300 Illustrations, 7s. 6d.

Evolution, Chapters on;

A Popular History of the Darwinian and Allied Theories of Development. By ANDREW WILSON, Ph.D., F.R.S. Edin. &c. [*In preparation.*

Crown 8vo, cloth extra, 6s.

Evolutionist (The) At Large.

By GRANT ALLEN.

By the same Author. Crown 8vo, cloth extra, 6s.

Vignettes from Nature.

By GRANT ALLEN.   [*In preparation.*

Folio, cloth extra, £1 11s. 6d.

Examples of Contemporary Art.

Etchings from Representative Works by living English and Foreign Artists. Edited, with Critical Notes, by J. COMYNS CARR.

"*It would not be easy to meet with a more sumptuous, and at the same time a more tasteful and instructive drawing-room book.*"—NONCONFORMIST.

Crown 8vo, cloth extra, with Illustrations, 6s.

Fairholt's Tobacco :

Its History and Associations; with an Account of the Plant and its Manufacture, and its Modes of Use in all Ages and Countries. By F. W. FAIRHOLT, F.S.A. With Coloured Frontispiece and upwards of 100 Illustrations by the Author.

Crown 8vo, cloth extra, 7s. 6d.

Familiar Allusions :

A Handbook of Miscellaneous Information; including the Names of Celebrated Statues, Paintings, Palaces, Country Seats, Ruins, Churches, Ships, Streets, Clubs, Natural Curiosities, and the like. By WILLIAM A. WHEELER, Author of "Noted Names of Fiction;' and CHARLES G. WHEELER. [*In the press.*

Crown 8vo, cloth extra, with Illustrations, 4s. 6d.

Faraday's Chemical History of a Candle.

Lectures delivered to a Juvenile Audience. A New Edition. Edited by W. CROOKES, F.C.S. With numerous Illustrations.

Crown 8vo, cloth extra, with Illustrations, 4s. 6d.

Faraday's Various Forces of Nature.

New Edition. Edited by W. CROOKES, F.C.S. Numerous Illustrations.

Crown 8vo, cloth extra, with Illustrations, 7s. 6d.

Finger-Ring Lore :

Historical, Legendary, and Anecdotal. By WM. JONES, F.S.A. With Hundreds of Illustrations of Curious Rings of all Ages and Countries.

"*One of those gossiping books which are as full of amusement as of instruction.*"—ATHENÆUM.

Gardening Books :

A Year's Work in Garden and Greenhouse : Practical Advice to Amateur Gardeners as to the Management of the Flower, Fruit, and Frame Garden. By GEORGE GLENNY. Post 8vo, cloth limp, 2s. 6d.

Our Kitchen Garden : The Plants we Grow, and How we Cook Them. By TOM JERROLD, Author of "The Garden that Paid the Rent," &c. Post 8vo, cloth limp, 2s. 6d.

Household Horticulture : A Gossip about Flowers. By TOM and JANE JERROLD. Illustrated. Post 8vo, cloth limp, 2s. 6d.

My Garden Wild, and What I Grew there. By FRANCIS GEORGE HEATH. Crown 8vo, cloth extra, 5s.

One Shilling Monthly.

Gentleman's Magazine (The), for 1882.

The JANUARY Number of this Periodical will contain the First Chapters of a New Serial Story, entitled "Dust," by JULIAN HAWTHORNE, Author of "Garth," &c. "Science Notes," by W. MATTIEU WILLIAMS, F.R.A.S., will also be continued monthly.

⁎ *Now ready, the Volume for* JANUARY *to* JUNE, *1881, cloth extra, price 8s. 6d.; and Cases for binding, price 2s. each.*

Demy 8vo, illuminated cover, 1s.

Gentleman's Annual, The.

Containing Two Complete Novels. [*Nov.* 15.

THE RUSKIN GRIMM.—Square 8vo, cloth extra, 6s. 6d. ; gilt edges, 7s. 6d.

German Popular Stories.

Collected by the Brothers GRIMM, and Translated by EDGAR TAYLOR. Edited with an Introduction by JOHN RUSKIN. With 22 Illustrations after the inimitable designs of GEORGE CRUIKSHANK. Both Series Complete.

"*The illustrations of this volume . . . are of quite sterling and admirable art, of a class precisely parallel in elevation to the character of the tales which they illustrate; and the original etchings, as I have before said in the Appendix to my 'Elements of Drawing,' were unrivalled in masterfulness of touch since Rembrandt (in some qualities of delineation, unrivalled even by him). . . . To make somewhat enlarged copies of them, looking at them through a magnifying glass, and never putting two lines where Cruikshank has put only one, would be an exercise in decision and severe drawing which would leave afterwards little to be learnt in schools.*"—Extract from Introduction by JOHN RUSKIN.

Post 8vo, cloth limp, 2s. 6d.

Glenny's A Year's Work in Garden and

Greenhouse : Practical Advice to Amateur Gardeners as to the Management of the Flower, Fruit, and Frame Garden. By GEORGE GLENNY.

· "*A great deal of valuable information, conveyed in very simple language. The amateur need not wish for a better guide.*"—LEEDS MERCURY.

Crown 8vo, cloth gilt and gilt edges, 7s. 6d.

Golden Treasury of Thought, The:

An ENCYCLOPÆDIA OF QUOTATIONS from Writers of all Times and Countries. Selected and Edited by THEODORE TAYLOR

New and Cheaper Edition, demy 8vo, cloth extra, with Illustrations, 7s.6d.

Greeks and Romans, The Life of the,

Described from Antique Monuments. By ERNST GUHL and W. KONER. Translated from the Third German Edition, and Edited by Dr. F. HUEFFER. With 545 Illustrations.

Square 16mo (Tauchnitz size), cloth extra, 2s. per volume.

Golden Library, The :

Ballad History of England. By W. C. BENNETT.

Bayard Taylor's Diversions of the Echo Club.

Byron's Don Juan.

Emerson's Letters and Social Aims.

Godwin's (William) Lives of the Necromancers.

Holmes's Autocrat of the Breakfast Table. With an Introduction by G. A. SALA.

Holmes's Professor at the Breakfast Table.

Hood's Whims and Oddities. Complete. With all the original Illustrations.

Irving's (Washington) Tales of a Traveller.

Irving's (Washington) Tales of the Alhambra.

Jesse's (Edward) Scenes and Occupations of Country Life.

Lamb's Essays of Elia. Both Series Complete in One Vol.

Leigh Hunt's Essays : A Tale for a Chimney Corner, and other Pieces. With Portrait, and Introduction by EDMUND OLLIER.

Mallory's (Sir Thomas) Mort d'Arthur : The Stories of King Arthur and of the Knights of the Round Table. Edited by B. MONTGOMERIE RANKING.

Pascal's Provincial Letters. A New Translation, with Historical Introduction and Notes, by T. M'CRIE, D.D.

Pope's Poetical Works. Complete.

Rochefoucauld's Maxims and Moral Reflections. With Notes, and an Introductory Essay by SAINTE-BEUVE.

St. Pierre's Paul and Virginia, and The Indian Cottage. Edited, with Life, by the Rev. E. CLARKE.

Shelley's Early Poems, and Queen Mab, with Essay by LEIGH HUNT.

Shelley's Later Poems : Laon and Cythna, &c.

Shelley's Posthumous Poems, the Shelley Papers, &c.

Shelley's Prose Works, including A Refutation of Deism, Zastrozzi St. Irvyne, &c.

White's Natural History of Selborne. Edited, with Additions, by THOMAS BROWN, F.L.S.

Crown 8vo, cloth extra, gilt, with Illustrations, 4s. 6d.

Guyot's Earth and Man ;

or, Physical Geography in its Relation to the History of Mankind. With Additions by Professors AGASSIZ, PIERCE, and GRAY ; 12 Maps and Engravings on Steel, some Coloured, and copious Index.

Hake (Dr. Thomas Gordon), Poems by :

Maiden Ecstasy. Small 4to, cloth extra, 8s.
New Symbols. Crown 8vo, cloth extra, 6s.
Legends of the Morrow. Crown 8vo, cloth extra, 6s.

Medium 8vo, cloth extra, gilt, with Illustrations, 7s. 6d.

Hall's (Mrs. S. C.) Sketches of Irish Character.

With numerous Illustrations on Steel and Wood by MACLISE, GILBERT, HARVEY, and G. CRUIKSHANK.

"*The Irish Sketches of this lady resemble Miss Mitford's beautiful English sketches in 'Our Village,' but they are far more vigorous and picturesque and bright.*"—BLACKWOOD'S MAGAZINE.

Haweis (Mrs.), Works by:

The Art of Dress. By Mrs. H. R. HAWEIS. Illustrated by the Author. Small 8vo, illustrated cover, 1s.; cloth limp, 1s. 6d.

"A well-considered attempt to apply canons of good taste to the costumes of ladies of our time. . . . . Mrs. Haweis writes frankly and to the point, she does not mince matters, but boldly remonstrates with her own sex on the follies they indulge in. . . . . We may recommend the book to the ladies whom it concerns."—ATHENÆUM.

The Art of Beauty. By Mrs. H. R. HAWEIS. Square 8vo, cloth extra, gilt, gilt edges, with Coloured Frontispiece and nearly 100 Illustrations, 10s. 6d.

The Art of Decoration. By Mrs. H. R. HAWEIS. Square 8vo, handsomely bound and profusely Illustrated, 10s. 6d.

*** *See also* CHAUCER, *p. 5 of this Catalogue.*

Crown 8vo, cloth extra, 5s.

Heath (F. G.)—My Garden Wild,

And What I Grew there. By FRANCIS GEORGE HEATH, Author of "The Fern World," &c.

SPECIMENS OF MODERN POETS.—Crown 8vo, cloth extra, 6s.

Heptalogia (The); or, The Seven against Sense.

A Cap with Seven Bells.

" The merits of the book cannot be fairly estimated by means of a few extracts; it should be read at length to be appreciated properly, and, in our opinion, its merits entitle it to be very widely read indeed."—ST. JAMES'S GAZETTE.

Cr. 8vo, bound in parchment, 8s.; Large-Paper copies (only 50 printed), 15s.

Herbert.—The Poems of Lord Herbert of

Cherbury. Edited, with an Introduction, by J. CHURTON COLLINS.

Complete in Four Vols., demy 8vo, cloth extra, 12s. each.

History of Our Own Times, from the Accession

of Queen Victoria to the General Election of 1880. By JUSTIN MCCARTHY, M.P.

"Criticism is disarmed before a composition which provokes little but approval. This is a really good book on a really interesting subject, and words piled on words could say no more for it."—SATURDAY REVIEW.

New Work by the Author of " A HISTORY of OUR OWN TIMES."

Four Vols. demy 8vo, cloth extra, 12s. each.

History of the Four Georges.

By JUSTIN MCCARTHY, M.P.   *[In preparation.*

Crown 8vo, cloth limp, with Illustrations, 2s. 6d.

Holmes's The Science of Voice Production

and Voice Preservation : A Popular Manual for the Use of Speakers and Singers. By GORDON HOLMES, L.R.C.P.E.

▓▓▓ ▀▀▀ Crown 8vo, cloth extra, gilt, 7s. 6d.

Hood's (Thomas) Choice Works,

In Prose and Verse. Including the CREAM OF THE COMIC ANNUALS.
With Life of the Author, Portrait, and Two Hundred Illustrations.

▓▓ ▀▀▀ Square crown 8vo, cloth extra, gilt edges, 6s.

Hood's (Tom) From Nowhere to the North

Pole : A Noah's Arkæological Narrative. With 25 Illustrations by
W. BRUNTON and E. C. BARNES.

" The amusing letterpress is profusely interspersed with the jingling rhymes
which children love and learn so easily. Messrs. Brunton and Barnes do full
justice to the writer's meaning, and a pleasanter result of the harmonious co-
operation of author and artist could not be desired."—TIMES.

Crown 8vo, cloth extra, gilt, 7s. 6d.

Hook's (Theodore) Choice Humorous Works,

including his Ludicrous Adventures, Bons-mots, Puns, and Hoaxes;
With a new Life of the Author, Portraits, Facsimiles, and Illustrations.

Crown 8vo, cloth extra, 7s.

Horne's Orion :

▓▓▓ An Epic Poem in Three Books. By RICHARD HENGIST HORNE.
▀▀▀ With a brief Commentary by the Author. With Photographic Portrait
▓▓▓ from a Medallion by SUMMERS. Tenth Edition.

Crown 8vo, cloth extra, 7s. 6d.

Howell's Conflicts of Capital and Labour

Historically and Economically considered. Being a History and
Review of the Trade Unions of Great Britain, showing their Origin,
Progress, Constitution, and Objects, in their Political, Social, Eco-
nomical, and Industrial Aspects. By GEORGE HOWELL.

" This book is an attempt, and on the whole a successful attempt, to place the
work of trade unions in the past, and their objects in the future, fairly before the
public from the working man's point of view."—PALL MALL GAZETTE.

Demy 8vo, cloth extra, 12s. 6d.

Hueffer's The Troubadours :

A History of Provencal Life and Literature in the Middle Ages. By
FRANCIS HUEFFER.

Crown 8vo, cloth extra, 6s.

Janvier.—Practical Keramics for Students.

By CATHERINE A. JANVIER.

" Will be found a useful handbook by those who wish to try the manufacture
or decoration of pottery, and may be studied by all who desire to know something
of the art."—MORNING POST.

A NEW EDITION, Revised and partly Re-written, with several New
Chapters and Illustrations, crown 8vo, cloth extra, 7s. 6d.

Jennings' The Rosicrucians :

Their Rites and Mysteries. With Chapters on the Ancient Fire and
Serpent Worshippers. By HARGRAVE JENNINGS. With Five full-
page Plates and upwards of 300 Illustrations.

Jerrold (Tom), Works by:

Household Horticulture: A Gossip about Flowers. By TOM and JANE JERROLD. Illustrated. Post 8vo, cloth limp, 2s.6d.

Our Kitchen Garden: The Plants we Grow, and How we Cook Them. By TOM JERROLD, Author of "The Garden that Paid the Rent," &c. Post 8vo, cloth limp, 2s. 6d.

"The combination of hints on cookery with gardening has been very cleverly carried out, and the result is an interesting and highly instructive little work. Mr. Jerrold is correct in saying that English people do not make half the use of vegetables they might ; and by showing how easily they can be grown, and so obtained fresh, he is doing a great deal to make them more popular."—DAILY CHRONICLE.

Two Vols. 8vo, with 52 Illustrations and Maps, cloth extra, gilt, 14s.

Josephus, The Complete Works of.

Translated by WHISTON. Containing both "The Antiquities of the Jews" and "The Wars of the Jews."

Small 8vo, cloth, full gilt, gilt edges, with Illustrations, 6s.

Kavanaghs' Pearl Fountain,

And other Fairy Stories. By BRIDGET and JULIA KAVANAGH. With Thirty Illustrations by J. MOYR SMITH.

"Genuine new fairy stories of the old type, some of them as delightful as the best of Grimm's 'German Popular Stories.' . . . . For the most part the stories are downright, thorough-going fairy stories of the most admirable kind. . . . Mr. Moyr Smith's illustrations, too, are admirable."—SPECTATOR.

Square 8vo, cloth extra, with Illustrations, 6s.

Knight (The) and the Dwarf.

By CHARLES MILLS. With numerous Illustrations by THOMAS LINDSAY.

Crown 8vo, illustrated boards, with numerous Plates, 2s. 6d.

Lace (Old Point), and How to Copy and

Imitate it. By DAISY WATERHOUSE HAWKINS. With 17 Illustrations by the Author.

Crown 8vo, cloth extra, gilt, with Portraits, 7s. 6d.

Lamb's Complete Works,

In Prose and Verse, reprinted from the Original Editions, with many Pieces hitherto unpublished. Edited, with Notes and Introduction, by R. H. SHEPHERD. With Two Portraits and Facsimile of a Page of the "Essay on Roast Pig."

"A complete edition of Lamb's writings, in prose and verse, has long been wanted, and is now supplied. The editor appears to have taken great pains to bring together Lamb's scattered contributions, and his collection contains a number of pieces which are now reproduced for the first time since their original appearance in various old periodicals."—SATURDAY REVIEW.

Crown 8vo, cloth extra, with numerous Illustrations, 10s. 6d.

Lamb (Mary and Charles):

Their Poems, Letters, and Remains. With Reminiscences and Notes by W. CAREW HAZLITT. With HANCOCK's Portrait of the Essayist, Facsimiles of the Title-pages of the rare First Editions of Lamb's and Coleridge's Works, and numerous Illustrations.

"*Very many passages will delight those fond of literary trifles; hardly any portion will fail in interest for lovers of Charles Lamb and his sister.*"—STANDARD.

Small 8vo, cloth extra, 5s.

Lamb's Poetry for Children, and Prince

Dorus. Carefully Reprinted from unique copies.

"*The quaint and delightful little book, over the recovery of which all the hearts of his lovers are yet warm with rejoicing.*"—A. C. SWINBURNE.

Crown 8vo, cloth extra, 6s.

Lares and Penates;

Or, The Background of Life. By FLORENCE CADDY.

"*The whole book is well worth reading, for it is full of practical suggestions. . . . . We hope nobody will be deterred from taking up a book which teaches a good deal about sweetening poor lives as well as giving grace to wealthy ones.*"— GRAPHIC.

Crown 8vo, cloth, full gilt, 6s.

Leigh's A Town Garland.

By HENRY S. LEIGH, Author of "Carols of Cockayne."

"*If Mr. Leigh's verse survive to a future generation—and there is no reason why that honour should not be accorded productions so delicate, so finished, and so full of humour—their author will probably be remembered as the Poet of the Strand.*"—ATHENÆUM.

SECOND EDITION.—Crown 8vo, cloth extra, with Illustrations, 6s.

Leisure-Time Studies, chiefly Biological.

By ANDREW WILSON, F.R.S.E., Lecturer on Zoology and Comparative Anatomy in the Edinburgh Medical School.

"*It is well when we can take up the work of a really qualified investigator, who in the intervals of his more serious professional labours sets himself to impart knowledge in such a simple and elementary form as may attract and instruct, with no danger of misleading the tyro in natural science. Such a work is this little volume, made up of essays and addresses written and delivered by Dr. Andrew Wilson, lecturer and examiner in science at Edinburgh and Glasgow, at leisure intervals in a busy professional life. . . . Dr. Wilson's pages teem with matter stimulating to a healthy love of science and a reverence for the truths of nature.*"—SATURDAY REVIEW.

Crown 8vo, cloth extra, with Illustrations, 7s. 6d.

Life in London;

or, The History of Jerry Hawthorn and Corinthian Tom. With the whole of CRUIKSHANK's Illustrations, in Colours, after the Originals.

Crown 8vo, cloth extra, 6s.

Lights on the Way:

Some Tales within a Tale. By the late J. H. ALEXANDER, B.A. Edited, with an Explanatory Note, by H. A. PAGE, Author of "Thoreau: A Study."

Crown 8vo, cloth extra, with Illustrations, 7s. 6d.

Longfellow's Complete Prose Works.

Including "Outre Mer," "Hyperion," "Kavanagh," "The Poets and Poetry of Europe," and "Driftwood." With Portrait and Illustrations by VALENTINE BROMLEY.

Crown 8vo, cloth extra, gilt, with Illustrations, 7s. 6d.

Longfellow's Poetical Works.

Carefully Reprinted from the Original Editions. With numerous fine Illustrations on Steel and Wood.

Crown 8vo, cloth extra, 5s.

Lunatic Asylum, My Experiences in a.

By a SANE PATIENT.

"*The story is clever and interesting, sad beyond measure though the subject is. There is no personal bitterness, and no violence or anger. Whatever may have been the evidence for our author's madness when he was consigned to an asylum, nothing can be clearer than his sanity when he wrote this book; it is bright, calm, and to the point.*"—SPECTATOR.

Demy 8vo, with Fourteen full-page Plates, cloth boards, 18s.

Lusiad (The) of Camoens.

Translated into English Spenserian verse by ROBERT FFRENCH DUFF, Knight Commander of the Portuguese Royal Order of Christ.

Mallock's (W. H.) Works:

Is Life Worth Living? By WILLIAM HURRELL MALLOCK. New Edition, crown 8vo, cloth extra, 6s.

"*This deeply interesting volume. . . . . It is the most powerful vindication of religion, both natural and revealed, that has appeared since Bishop Butler wrote, and is much more useful than either the Analogy or the Sermons of that great divine, as a refutation of the peculiar form assumed by the infidelity of the present day. . . . . Deeply philosophical as the book is, there is not a heavy page in it. The writer is 'possessed,' so to speak, with his great subject, has sounded its depths, surveyed it in all its extent, and brought to bear on it all the resources of a vivid, rich, and impassioned style, as well as an adequate acquaintance with the science, the philosophy, and the literature of the day.*"—IRISH DAILY NEWS.

The New Republic; or, Culture, Faith, and Philosophy in an English Country House. By W. H. MALLOCK. Post 8vo, cloth limp, 2s. 6d.

The New Paul and Virginia; or, Positivism on an Island. By W. H. MALLOCK. Post 8vo, cloth limp, 2s. 6d.

Poems. By W. H. MALLOCK. Small 4to, bound in parchment, 8s.

A Romance of the Nineteenth Century. By W. H. MALLOCK. Second Edition, with a Preface. Two Vols., crown 8vo, 21s.

Macquoid (Mrs.), Works by :

In the Ardennes. By KATHARINE S. MACQUOID. With 50 fine Illustrations by THOMAS R. MACQUOID. Uniform with "Pictures and Legends." Square 8vo, cloth extra, 10s. 6d.

"*This is another of Mrs. Macquoid's pleasant books of travel, full of useful information, of picturesque descriptions of scenery, and of quaint traditions respecting the various monuments and ruins which she encounters in her tour. . . . To such of our readers as are already thinking about the year's holiday, we strongly recommend the perusal of Mrs. Macquoid's experiences. The book is well illustrated by Mr. Thomas R. Macquoid.*"—GRAPHIC.

Pictures and Legends from Normandy and Brittany. By KATHARINE S. MACQUOID. With numerous Illustrations by THOMAS R. MACQUOID. Square 8vo, cloth gilt, 10s. 6d.

Through Normandy. By KATHARINE S. MACQUOID. With 90 Illustrations by T. R. MACQUOID. Square 8vo, cloth extra, 7s. 6d.

"*One of the few books which can be read as a piece of literature, whilst at the same time handy in the knapsack.*"—BRITISH QUARTERLY REVIEW.

Through Brittany. By KATHARINE S. MACQUOID. With numerous Illustrations by T. R. MACQUOID. Sq. 8vo, cloth extra, 7s. 6d.

"*The pleasant companionship which Mrs. Macquoid offers, while wandering from one point of interest to another, seems to throw a renewed charm around each oft-depicted scene.*"—MORNING POST.

Mark Twain's Works :

The Choice Works of Mark Twain. Revised and Corrected throughout by the Author. With Life, Portrait, and numerous Illustrations. Crown 8vo, cloth extra, 7s. 6d.

The Adventures of Tom Sawyer. By MARK TWAIN. With 100 Illustrations. Small 8vo, cloth extra, 7s. 6d. CHEAP EDITION, illustrated boards, 2s.

A Pleasure Trip on the Continent of Europe : The Innocents Abroad, and The New Pilgrim's Progress. By MARK TWAIN. Post 8vo, illustrated boards, 2s.

An Idle Excursion, and other Sketches. By MARK TWAIN. Post 8vo, illustrated boards, 2s.

The Prince and the Pauper. By MARK TWAIN. With nearly 200 Illustrations. Crown 8vo, cloth extra, 7s. 6d. Uniform with "A Tramp Abroad." [*In the press.*

The Innocents Abroad ; or, The New Pilgrim's Progress : Being some Account of the Steamship "Quaker City's" Pleasure Excursion to Europe and the Holy Land, with descriptions of Countries, Nations, Incidents, and Adventures, as they appeared to the Author. With 234 Illustrations. By MARK TWAIN. Crown 8vo, cloth extra, 7s. 6d. Uniform with "A Tramp Abroad."

A Tramp Abroad. By MARK TWAIN. With 314 Illustrations. Crown 8vo, cloth extra, 7s. 6d.

"*The fun and tenderness of the conception, of which no living man but Mark Twain is capable, its grace and fantasy and slyness, the wonderful feeling for animals that is manifest in every line, make of all this episode of Jim Baker and his jays a piece of work that is not only delightful as mere reading, but also of a high degree of merit as literature. . . . The book is full of good things, and contains passages and episodes that are equal to the funniest of those that have gone before.*"—ATHENÆUM

Crown 8vo, cloth extra, with Illustrations, 2s. 6d.

Madre Natura v. The Moloch of Fashion.

By LUKE LIMNER. With 32 Illustrations by the Author. FOURTH EDITION, revised and enlarged.

Handsomely printed in facsimile, price 5s.

Magna Charta.

An exact Facsimile of the Original Document in the British Museum, printed on fine plate paper, nearly 3 feet long by 2 feet wide, with the Arms and Seals emblazoned in Gold and Colours.

Post 8vo, cloth limp, 2s. 6d. per volume.

Mayfair Library, The:

The New Republic. By W. H. MALLOCK.

The New Paul and Virginia. By W. H. MALLOCK.

The True History of Joshua Davidson. By E. LYNN LINTON.

Old Stories Re-told. By WALTER THORNBURY.

Thoreau: His Life and Aims. By H. A. PAGE.

By Stream and Sea. By WILLIAM SENIOR.

Jeux d'Esprit. Edited by HENRY S. LEIGH.

Puniana. By the Hon. HUGH ROWLEY.

More Puniana. By the Hon. HUGH ROWLEY.

Puck on Pegasus. By H. CHOLMONDELEY-PENNELL.

The Speeches of Charles Dickens.

Muses of Mayfair. Edited by H. CHOLMONDELEY-PENNELL.

Gastronomy as a Fine Art. By BRILLAT-SAVARIN.

The Philosophy of Handwriting. By DON FELIX DE SALAMANCA.

Curiosities of Criticism. By HENRY J. JENNINGS.

Literary Frivolities, Fancies, Follies, Frolics. By W. T. DOBSON.

Pencil and Palette. By ROBERT KEMPT.

Latter-Day Lyrics. Edited by W. DAVENPORT ADAMS.

Original Plays by W. S. GILBERT. FIRST SERIES. Containing: The Wicked World—Pygmalion and Galatea — Charity — The Princess— The Palace of Truth—Trial by Jury.

Original Plays by W. S. GILBERT. SECOND SERIES. Containing: Broken Hearts — Engaged — Sweethearts — Dan'l Druce — Gretchen— Tom Cobb—The Sorcerer—H.M.S. Pinafore—The Pirates of Penzance.

Carols of Cockayne. By HENRY S. LEIGH.

The Book of Clerical Anecdotes. By JACOB LARWOOD.

The Agony Column of "The Times," from 1800 to 1870. Edited, with an Introduction, by ALICE CLAY.

The Cupboard Papers. By FIN-BEC.

Pastimes and Players. By ROBERT MACGREGOR.

Melancholy Anatomised: A Popular Abridgment of "Burton's Anatomy of Melancholy."

Quips and Quiddities. Selected by W. DAVENPORT ADAMS.

Leaves from a Naturalist's Note-Book. By ANDREW WILSON, F.R.S.E.

The Autocrat of the Breakfast-Table. By OLIVER WENDELL HOLMES. Illustrated by J. GORDON THOMSON.

Balzac's "Comédie Humaine" and its Author. With Translations by H. H. WALKER.

⁎ *Other Volumes are in preparation.*

Small 8vo, cloth limp, with Illustrations, 2s. 6d.

Miller's Physiology for the Young;

Or, The House of Life: Human Physiology, with its Applications to the Preservation of Health. For use in Classes and Popular Reading. With numerous Illustrations. By Mrs. F. FENWICK MILLER.

"*An admirable introduction to a subject which all who value health and enjoy life should have at their fingers' ends.*"—ECHO.

Milton (J. L.), Works by:

The Hygiene of the Skin. A Concise Set of Rules for the Management of the Skin; with Directions for Diet, Wines, Soaps, Baths, &c. By J. L. MILTON, Senior Surgeon to St. John's Hospital. Small 8vo, 1s.; cloth extra, 1s. 6d.

The Bath in Diseases of the Skin. Small 8vo, 1s.; cloth extra, 1s. 6d.

Square 8vo, cloth extra, with numerous Illustrations, 7s. 6d.

North Italian Folk.

By Mrs. COMYNS CARR. Illustrated by RANDOLPH CALDECOTT.

"*A delightful book, of a kind which is far too rare. If anyone wants to really know the North Italian folk, we can honestly advise him to omit the journey, and read Mrs. Carr's pages instead. . . Description with Mrs. Carr is a real gift. . It is rarely that a book is so happily illustrated.*"—CONTEMPORARY REVIEW.

NEW NOVELS.

A NEW NOVEL BY OUIDA.

The Title of which will shortly be announced. 3 vols., crown 8vo.

SOMETHING IN THE CITY.

By GEORGE AUGUSTUS SALA. 3 vols. crown 8vo.

GOD AND THE MAN.

By ROBERT BUCHANAN, Author of "The Shadow of the Sword," &c. 3 vols. crown 8vo. With 11 Illustrations by FRED. BARNARD.

THE COMET OF A SEASON.

By JUSTIN McCARTHY, M.P., Author of "Miss Misanthrope." 3 vols., crown 8vo.

JOSEPH'S COAT.

By DAVID CHRISTIE MURRAY, Author of "A Life's Atonement," &c. With 12 Illustrations by FRED. BARNARD.

PRINCE SARONI'S WIFE, and other Stories.

By JULIAN HAWTHORNE. 3 vols., crown 8vo.

A HEART'S PROBLEM.

By CHARLES GIBBON, Author of "Robin Gray," &c. 2 vols. crown 8vo.

THE BRIDE'S PASS.

By SARAH TYTLER, 2 vols., crown 8vo.

Crown 8vo, cloth extra, with Vignette Portraits, price 6*s*. per Vol.

Old Dramatists, The:

Ben Jonson's Works.
With Notes, Critical and Explanatory, and a Biographical Memoir by WILLIAM GIFFORD. Edited by Colonel CUNNINGHAM. Three Vols. ·

Chapman's Works.
Now First Collected. Complete in Three Vols. Vol. I. contains the Plays complete, including the doubtful ones; Vol. II. the Poems and Minor Translations, with an Introductory Essay

by ALGERNON CHARLES SWINBURNE. Vol. III. the Translations of the Iliad and Odyssey.

Marlowe's Works.
Including his Translations. Edited, with Notes and Introduction, by Col. CUNNINGHAM. One Vol.

Massinger's Plays.
From the Text of WILLIAM GIFFORD. With the addition of the Tragedy of "Believe as you List." Edited by Col. CUNNINGHAM. One Vol.

O'Shaughnessy (Arthur) Works by:

Songs of a Worker. By ARTHUR O'SHAUGHNESSY. Fcap. 8vo, cloth extra, 7*s*. 6*d*.

Music and Moonlight. By ARTHUR O'SHAUGHNESSY. Fcap. 8vo, cloth extra, 7*s*. 6*d*.

Lays of France. By ARTHUR O'SHAUGHNESSY. Crown 8vo, cloth extra, 10*s*. 6*d*.

Crown 8vo, red cloth extra, 5*s*. each.

Ouida's Novels.—Library Edition.

Held in Bondage.	By OUIDA.	**Pascarel.**	By OUIDA.
Strathmore.	By OUIDA.	**Two Wooden Shoes.**	By OUIDA.
Chandos.	By OUIDA.	**Signa.**	By OUIDA.
Under Two Flags.	By OUIDA.	**In a Winter City.**	By OUIDA.
Idalia.	By OUIDA.	**Ariadne.**	By OUIDA.
Cecil Castlemaine.	By OUIDA.	**Friendship.**	By OUIDA.
Tricotrin.	By OUIDA.	**Moths.**	By OUIDA.
Puck.	By OUIDA.	**Pipistrello.**	By OUIDA.
Folle Farine.	By OUIDA.	**A Village Commune.**	By OUIDA.
Dog of Flanders.	By OUIDA.		

*** Also a Cheap Edition of all but the last two, post 8vo, illustrated boards, 2*s*. each.

Post 8vo, cloth limp, 1*s*. 6*d*.

Parliamentary Procedure, A Popular Handbook of. By HENRY W. LUCY.

Large 4to, cloth extra, gilt, beautifully Illustrated, 31*s*. 6*d*.

Pastoral Days;

Or, Memories of a New England Year. By W. HAMILTON GIBSON. With 76 Illustrations in the highest style of Wood Engraving.

"*The volume contains a prose poem, with illustrations in the shape of wood engravings more beautiful than it can well enter into the hearts of most men to conceive.*"—SCOTSMAN.

LIBRARY EDITIONS, mostly Illustrated, crown 8vo, cloth extra, 3*s*. 6*d*. each.

Piccadilly Novels, The.

Popular Stories by the Best Authors.

Maid, Wife, or Widow? By Mrs. ALEXANDER.

Ready-Money Mortiboy. By W. BESANT and JAMES RICE.

My Little Girl. By W. BESANT and JAMES RICE.

The Case of Mr. Lucraft. By W. BESANT and JAMES RICE.

This Son of Vulcan. By W. BESANT and JAMES RICE,

With Harp and Crown. By W. BESANT and JAMES RICE.

The Golden Butterfly. By W. BESANT and JAMES RICE.

By Celia's Arbour. By W. BESANT and JAMES RICE.

The Monks of Thelema. By W. BESANT and JAMES RICE.

'Twas in Trafalgar's Bay. By W. BESANT and JAMES RICE.

The Seamy Side. By WALTER BESANT and JAMES RICE.

Antonina. By WILKIE COLLINS.

Basil. By WILKIE COLLINS.

Hide and Seek. W. COLLINS.

The Dead Secret. W. COLLINS.

Queen of Hearts. W. COLLINS.

My Miscellanies. W. COLLINS.

The Woman in White. By WILKIE COLLINS.

The Moonstone. W. COLLINS.

Man and Wife. W. COLLINS.

Poor Miss Finch. W. COLLINS.

Miss or Mrs.? By W. COLLINS.

The New Magdalen. By WILKIE COLLINS.

The Frozen Deep. W. COLLINS.

The Law and the Lady. By WILKIE COLLINS.

The Two Destinies. By WILKIE COLLINS.

The Haunted Hotel. By WILKIE COLLINS.

The Fallen Leaves. By WILKIE COLLINS.

Jezebel's Daughter. W. COLLINS.

Deceivers Ever. By Mrs. H. LOVETT CAMERON.

Juliet's Guardian. By Mrs. H. LOVETT CAMERON.

Felicia. M. BETHAM-EDWARDS.

Olympia. By R. E. FRANCILLON.

The Capel Girls. By EDWARD GARRETT.

Robin Gray. CHARLES GIBBON.

For Lack of Gold. By CHARLES GIBBON.

In Love and War. By CHARLES GIBBON.

What will the World Say? By CHARLES GIBBON.

For the King. CHARLES GIBBON.

In Honour Bound. By CHARLES GIBBON.

Queen of the Meadow. By CHARLES GIBBON.

In Pastures Green. By CHARLES GIBBON.

Under the Greenwood Tree. By THOMAS HARDY.

Garth. By JULIAN HAWTHORNE.

Ellice Quentin. By JULIAN HAWTHORNE.

Thornicroft's Model. By Mrs. A. W. HUNT.

Fated to be Free. By JEAN INGELOW.

Confidence. HENRY JAMES, Jun.

The Queen of Connaught. By HARRIETT JAY.

The Dark Colleen. By H. JAY.

Number Seventeen. By HENRY KINGSLEY.

Oakshott Castle. H. KINGSLEY.

Patricia Kemball. By E. LYNN LINTON.

The Atonement of Leam Dundas. By E. LYNN LINTON.

The World Well Lost. By E. LYNN LINTON.

Under which Lord? By E. LYNN LINTON.

With a Silken Thread. By E. LYNN LINTON.

The Waterdale Neighbours. By JUSTIN McCARTHY.

PICCADILLY NOVELS—*continued.*

My Enemy's Daughter. By JUSTIN MCCARTHY.

Linley Rochford. By JUSTIN MCCARTHY.

A Fair Saxon. J. MCCARTHY.

Dear Lady Disdain. By JUSTIN MCCARTHY.

Miss Misanthrope. By JUSTIN MCCARTHY.

Donna Quixote. J. MCCARTHY.

Quaker Cousins. By AGNES MACDONELL.

Lost Rose. By KATHARINE S. MACQUOID.

The Evil Eye. By KATHARINE S. MACQUOID.

Open! Sesame! By FLORENCE MARRYAT.

Written in Fire. F. MARRYAT.

Touch and Go. By JEAN MID-DLEMASS.

A Life's Atonement. By D. CHRISTIE MURRAY.

Whiteladies. Mrs. OLIPHANT.

The Best of Husbands. By JAMES PAYN.

Fallen Fortunes. JAMES PAYN.

Halves. By JAMES PAYN.

Walter's Word. JAMES PAYN.

What He Cost Her. J. PAYN.

Less Black than we're Painted. By JAMES PAYN.

By Proxy. By JAMES PAYN.

Under One Roof. JAMES PAYN.

High Spirits. By JAMES PAYN.

Her Mother's Darling. By Mrs. J. H. RIDDELL.

Bound to the Wheel. By JOHN SAUNDERS.

Guy Waterman. J. SAUNDERS.

One Against the World. By JOHN SAUNDERS.

The Lion in the Path. By JOHN SAUNDERS.

The Way We Live Now. By ANTHONY TROLLOPE.

The American Senator. By ANTHONY TROLLOPE.

Diamond Cut Diamond. By T. A. TROLLOPE.

NEW VOLUMES OF "THE PICCADILLY NOVELS."

Put Yourself in his Place. By CHARLES READE.

A Confidential Agent. By JAMES PAYN. With 12 Illustrations.

The Violin-Player. By BERTHA THOMAS.

Queen Cophetua. By R. E. FRANCILLON.

The Leaden Casket. By Mrs. ALFRED HUNT.

Carlyon's Year. By J. PAYN.

The Ten Years' Tenant, and other Stories. By WALTER BESANT and JAMES RICE.

A Child of Nature. By ROBERT BUCHANAN.

Cressida. By BERTHA THOMAS.

From Exile. By JAMES PAYN.

Sebastian Strome. By JULIAN HAWTHORNE.

The Black Robe. By WILKIE COLLINS.

Archie Lovell. By Mrs. ANNIE EDWARDES.

"My Love!" By E. LYNN LINTON.

Lost Sir Massingberd. By JAMES PAYN.

The Chaplain of the Fleet. By WALTER BESANT and JAMES RICE.

Proud Maisie. By BERTHA THOMAS.

The Two Dreamers. By JOHN SAUNDERS.

What She Came through. By SARAH TYTLER.

Crown 8vo, cloth extra, 6s.

Planché.—Songs and Poems, from 1819 to 1879.

By J. R. PLANCHE. Edited, with an Introduction, by his Daughter, Mrs. MACKARNESS.

Post 8vo, illustrated boards, 2*s.* each.

Popular Novels, Cheap Editions of.

[WILKIE COLLINS' NOVELS and BESANT and RICE's NOVELS may also be had in cloth limp at 2*s.* 6*d.* *See, too, the* PICCADILLY NOVELS, *for Library Editions.*]

Confidences. HAMILTON AÏDÉ.

Carr of Carrlyon. H. AÏDÉ.

Maid, Wife, or Widow? By Mrs. ALEXANDER.

Ready-Money Mortiboy. By WALTER BESANT and JAMES RICE.

With Harp and Crown. By WALTER BESANT and JAMES RICE

This Son of Vulcan. By W. BESANT and JAMES RICE.

My Little Girl. By the same.

The Case of Mr. Lucraft. By WALTER BESANT and JAMES RICE.

The Golden Butterfly. By W. BESANT and JAMES RICE.

By Celia's Arbour. By WALTER BESANT and JAMES RICE.

The Monks of Thelema. By WALTER BESANT and JAMES RICE.

'Twas in Trafalgar's Bay. By WALTER BESANT and JAMES RICE.

Seamy Side. BESANT and RICE.

Grantley Grange. By SHELSLEY BEAUCHAMP.

An Heiress of Red Dog. By BRET HARTE.

The Luck of Roaring Camp. By BRET HARTE.

Gabriel Conroy. BRET HARTE.

Surly Tim. By F. E. BURNETT.

Deceivers Ever. By Mrs. L. CAMERON.

Juliet's Guardian. By Mrs. LOVETT CAMERON.

The Cure of Souls. By MACLAREN COBBAN.

The Bar Sinister. By C. ALLSTON COLLINS.

Antonina. By WILKIE COLLINS.

Basil. By WILKIE COLLINS.

Hide and Seek. W. COLLINS.

The Dead Secret. W. COLLINS.

Queen of Hearts. W. COLLINS.

My Miscellanies. W. COLLINS.

Woman in White. W. COLLINS.

The Moonstone. W. COLLINS.

Man and Wife. W. COLLINS.

Poor Miss Finch. W. COLLINS.

Miss or Mrs.? W. COLLINS.

New Magdalen. W. COLLINS.

The Frozen Deep. W. COLLINS.

Law and the Lady. W. COLLINS.

Two Destinies. W. COLLINS.

Haunted Hotel. W. COLLINS.

Fallen Leaves. By W. COLLINS.

Leo. By DUTTON COOK.

A Point of Honour. By Mrs. ANNIE EDWARDES.

Archie Lovell. Mrs A. EDWARDES

Felicia. M. BETHAM-EDWARDS.

Roxy. By EDWARD EGGLESTON.

Polly. By PERCY FITZGERALD.

Bella Donna. P. FITZGERALD.

Never Forgotten. FITZGERALD.

The Second Mrs. Tillotson. By PERCY FITZGERALD.

Seventy-Five Brooke Street. By PERCY FITZGERALD.

Filthy Lucre. By ALBANY DE FONBLANQUE.

Olympia. By R. E. FRANCILLON.

The Capel Girls. By EDWARD GARRETT.

Robin Gray. By CHAS. GIBBON.

For Lack of Gold. C. GIBBON.

What will the World Say? By CHARLES GIBBON.

In Honour Bound. C. GIBBON.

The Dead Heart. By C. GIBBON.

In Love and War. C. GIBBON.

For the King. By C. GIBBON.

Queen of the Meadow. By CHARLES GIBBON.

Dick Temple. By JAMES GREENWOOD.

Every-day Papers. By ANDREW HALLIDAY.

Paul Wynter's Sacrifice. By Lady DUFFUS HARDY.

Under the Greenwood Tree. By THOMAS HARDY.

POPULAR NOVELS—*continued.*

Garth. By JULIAN HAWTHORNE.

Golden Heart. By TOM HOOD.

The Hunchback of Notre Dame. By VICTOR HUGO.

Thornicroft's Model. By Mrs. ALFRED HUNT.

Fated to be Free. By JEAN INGELOW.

Confidence. By HENRY JAMES, Jun.

The Queen of Connaught. By HARRIETT JAY.

The Dark Colleen. By H. JAY.

Number Seventeen. By HENRY KINGSLEY.

Oakshott Castle. H. KINGSLEY.

Patricia Kemball. By E. LYNN LINTON.

Leam Dundas. E. LYNN LINTON.

The World Well Lost. By E. LYNN LINTON.

Under which Lord? By E. LYNN LINTON.

The Waterdale Neighbours. By JUSTIN MCCARTHY.

Dear Lady Disdain. By the same.

My Enemy's Daughter. By JUSTIN MCCARTHY.

A Fair Saxon. J. MCCARTHY.

Linley Rochford. MCCARTHY.

Miss Misanthrope. MCCARTHY.

Donna Quixote. J. MCCARTHY.

The Evil Eye. By KATHARINE S. MACQUOID.

Lost Rose. K. S. MACQUOID.

Open! Sesame! By FLORENCE MARRYAT.

Harvest of Wild Oats. By FLORENCE MARRYAT.

A Little Stepson. F. MARRYAT.

Fighting the Air. F. MARRYAT.

Touch and Go. By JEAN MIDDLEMASS.

Mr. Dorillion. J. MIDDLEMASS.

Whiteladies. By Mrs. OLIPHANT.

Held in Bondage. By OUIDA.

Strathmore. By OUIDA.

Chandos. By OUIDA.

Under Two Flags. By OUIDA.

Idalia. By OUIDA.

Cecil Castlemaine. By OUIDA.

Tricotrin. By OUIDA.

Puck. By OUIDA.

Folle Farine. By OUIDA.

A Dog of Flanders. By OUIDA.

Pascarel. By OUIDA.

Two Little Wooden Shoes. By Signa. By OUIDA. [OUIDA.

In a Winter City. By OUIDA.

Ariadne. By OUIDA.

Friendship. By OUIDA.

Moths. By OUIDA.

Lost Sir Massingberd. J. PAYN.

A Perfect Treasure. J. PAYN.

Bentinck's Tutor. By J. PAYN.

Murphy's Master. By J. PAYN.

A County Family. By J. PAYN.

At Her Mercy. By J. PAYN.

A Woman's Vengeance. J. PAYN.

Cecil's Tryst. By JAMES PAYN.

The Clyffards of Clyffe. J. PAYN.

Family Scapegrace. J. PAYN.

The Foster Brothers. J. PAYN.

Found Dead. By JAMES PAYN.

Gwendoline's Harvest. J. PAYN.

Humorous Stories. J. PAYN.

Like Father, Like Son. J. PAYN.

A Marine Residence. J. PAYN.

Married Beneath Him. J. PAYN.

Mirk Abbey. By JAMES PAYN.

Not Wooed, but Won. J. PAYN.

Two Hundred Pounds Reward. By JAMES PAYN.

Best of Husbands. By J. PAYN.

Walter's Word. By J. PAYN.

Halves. By JAMES PAYN.

Fallen Fortunes. By J. PAYN.

What He Cost Her. J. PAYN.

Less Black than We're Painted. By JAMES PAYN.

By Proxy. By JAMES PAYN.

Under One Roof. By J. PAYN.

High Spirits. By JAS. PAYN.

Paul Ferroll.

Why P. Ferroll Killed his Wife.

The Mystery of Marie Roget. By EDGAR A. POE.

POPULAR NOVELS—*continued.*

Put Yourself in his Place   By CHARLES READE.

Her Mother's Darling. By Mrs. J. H. RIDDELL.

Gaslight and Daylight.   By GEORGE AUGUSTUS SALA.

Bound to the Wheel. By JOHN SAUNDERS.

Guy Waterman. J. SAUNDERS.

One Against the World. By JOHN SAUNDERS.

The Lion in the Path. By JOHN and KATHERINE SAUNDERS.

A Match in the Dark. By A. SKETCHLEY.

Tales for the Marines.   By WALTER THORNBURY.

The Way we Live Now.   By ANTHONY TROLLOPE.

The American Senator. Ditto.

Diamond Cut Diamond. Ditto.

A Pleasure Trip in Europe. By MARK TWAIN.

Tom Sawyer. By MARK TWAIN.

An Idle Excursion. M. TWAIN.

Sabina. By Lady WOOD.

Castaway. By EDMUND YATES.

Forlorn Hope. EDMUND YATES.

Land at Last. EDMUND YATES.

Fcap. 8vo, picture covers, 1s. each.

Jeff Briggs's Love Story. By BRET HARTE.

The Twins of Table Mountain. By BRET HARTE.

Mrs. Gainsborough's Diamonds. By JULIAN HAWTHORNE.

Kathleen Mavourneen. By the Author of "That Lass o' Lowrie's."

Lindsay's Luck. By the Author of "That Lass o' Lowrie's."

Pretty Polly Pemberton. By Author of "That Lass o' Lowrie's."

Trooping with Crows. By Mrs. PIRKIS.

The Professor's Wife. By LEONARD GRAHAM.

Crown 8vo, cloth extra, 6s.

Payn.—Some Private Views.

Being Essays contributed to *The Nineteenth Century* and to *The Times.* By JAMES PAYN, Author of "High Spirits," "By Proxy," "Lost Sir Massingberd," &c.   [*Nearly ready.*

Two Vols. 8vo, cloth extra, with Portraits, 10s. 6d.

Plutarch's Lives of Illustrious Men.

Translated from the Greek, with Notes, Critical and Historical, and a Life of Plutarch, by JOHN and WILLIAM LANGHORNE.

Crown 8vo, cloth extra, with Portrait and Illustrations, 7s. 6d.

Poe's Choice Prose and Poetical Works.

With BAUDELAIRE's "Essay."

Crown 8vo, cloth extra, 7s. 6d.

Primitive Manners and Customs.

By JAMES A. FARRER.

Small 8vo, cloth extra, with 130 Illustrations, 3s. 6d.

Prince of Argolis, The:

A Story of the Old Greek Fairy Time. By J. MOYR SMITH.

Crown 8vo, cloth extra, gilt, 7s. 6d.

Pursuivant of Arms, The;

or, Heraldry founded upon Facts. By J. R. PLANCHÉ, Somerset Herald. With Coloured Frontispiece and 200 Illustrations.

Proctor's (R. A.) Works:

Easy Star Lessons. With Star Maps for Every Night in the Year, Drawings of the Constellations, &c. By RICHARD A. PROCTOR. Crown 8vo, cloth extra, 6s.

Familiar Science Studies. By RICHARD A. PROCTOR. Crown 8vo, cloth extra, 7s. 6d. [*In the press.*

Saturn and its System. By RICHARD A. PROCTOR. New and Revised Edition, demy 8vo, cloth extra, 10s. 6d. [*In preparation.*

Myths and Marvels of Astronomy. By RICH. A. PROCTOR, Author of "Other Worlds than Ours." &c. Crown 8vo, cloth extra, 6s.

Pleasant Ways in Science. By R. A. PROCTOR. Cr. 8vo, cl. ex. 6s.

Rough Ways made Smooth: A Series of Familiar Essays on Scientific Subjects. By R. A. PROCTOR. Crown 8vo, cloth extra, 6s.

Our Place among Infinities: A Series of Essays contrasting our Little Abode in Space and Time with the Infinities Around us. By RICHARD A. PROCTOR. Crown 8vo, cloth extra, 6s.

The Expanse of Heaven: A Series of Essays on the Wonders of the Firmament. By RICHARD A. PROCTOR. Crown 8vo, cloth, 6s.

Wages and Wants of Science Workers. By RICHARD A. PROCTOR. Crown 8vo, 1s. 6d.

Crown 8vo, cloth extra, with Illustrations, 7s. 6d.

Rabelais' Works.

Faithfully Translated from the French, with variorum Notes, and numerous characteristic Illustrations by GUSTAVE DORE.

Crown 8vo, cloth gilt, with numerous Illustrations, and a beautifully executed Chart of the various Spectra, 7s. 6d.

Rambosson's Popular Astronomy.

By J. RAMBOSSON, Laureate of the Institute of France. Translated by C. B. PITMAN. Profusely Illustrated.

Second Edition, Revised, Crown 8vo, 1,200 pages, half-roxburghe, 12s. 6d.

Reader's Handbook (The) of Allusions, Re-

ferences, Plots, and Stories. By the Rev. Dr. Brewer.

Crown 8vo, cloth extra, 6s.

Richardson's (Dr.) A Ministry of Health,

and other Papers. By BENJAMIN WARD RICHARDSON, M.D., &c.

Rimmer (Alfred), Works by:

Our Old Country Towns. With over 50 Illustrations. By ALFRED RIMMER. Square 8vo, cloth extra, gilt, 10s. 6d.

Rambles Round Eton and Harrow. By ALFRED RIMMER. With 50 Illustrations by the Author. Square 8vo, cloth gilt, 10s. 6d.

About England with Dickens. With Illustrations by ALFRED RIMMER and C. A. VANDERHOOF, Sq. 8vo, cloth gilt, 10s. 6d. [*In the press.*

Handsomely printed, price 5s.

Roll of Battle Abbey, The;

or, A List of the Principal Warriors who came over from Normandy with William the Conqueror, and Settled in this Country, A.D. 1066-7. With the principal Arms emblazoned in Gold and Colours.

Two Vols., large 4to, profusely Illustrated, half-morocco, £2 16s.

Rowlandson, the Caricaturist.

A Selection from his Works, with Anecdotal Descriptions of his Famous Caricatures, and a Sketch of his Life, Times, and Contemporaries. With nearly 400 Illustrations, mostly in Facsimile of the Originals. By JOSEPH GREGO, Author of "James Gillray, the Caricaturist; his Life, Works, and Times."

Crown 8vo, cloth extra, profusely Illustrated, 4s. 6d. each.

"Secret Out" Series, The.

The Pyrotechnist's Treasury; or, Complete Art of Making Fireworks. By THOMAS KENTISH. With numerous Illustrations.

The Art of Amusing: A Collection of Graceful Arts, Games, Tricks, Puzzles, and Charades. By FRANK BELLEW. 300 Illustrations.

Hanky-Panky: Very Easy Tricks, Very Difficult Tricks, White Magic, Sleight of Hand. Edited by W. H. CREMER. 200 Illusts.

The Merry Circle: A Book of New Intellectual Games and Amusements. By CLARA BELLEW. Many Illustrations.

Magician's Own Book: Performances with Cups and Balls, Eggs, Hats, Handkerchiefs, &c. All from Actual Experience. Edited by W. H. CREMER. 200 Illustrations.

Magic No Mystery: Tricks with Cards, Dice, Balls, &c., with fully descriptive Directions; the Art of Secret Writing; Training of Performing Animals, &c. Coloured Frontispiece and many Illustrations.

The Secret Out: One Thousand Tricks with Cards, and other Recreations; with Entertaining Experiments in Drawing-room or "White Magic." By W. H. CREMER. 300 Engravings.

Crown 8vo, cloth extra, 6s.

Senior's Travel and Trout in the Antipodes.

An Angler's Sketches in Tasmania and New Zealand. By WILLIAM SENIOR ("Red Spinner"), Author of "By Stream and Sea."

Shakespeare:

Shakespeare, The First Folio. Mr. WILLIAM SHAKESPEARE'S Comedies, Histories, and Tragedies. Published according to the true Originall Copies. London, Printed by ISAAC IAGGARD and ED. BLOUNT, 1623.—A Reproduction of the extremely rare original, in reduced facsimile by a photographic process—ensuring the strictest accuracy in every detail. Small 8vo, half-Roxburghe, 7s. 6d.

Shakespeare, The Lansdowne. Beautifully printed in red and black, in small but very clear type. With engraved facsimile of DROESHOUT's Portrait. Post 8vo, cloth extra, 7s. 6d.

Shakespeare for Children: Tales from Shakespeare. By CHARLES and MARY LAMB. With numerous Illustrations, coloured and plain, by J. MOYR SMITH. Crown 4to, cloth gilt, 10s. 6d.

Shakespeare Music, The Handbook of. Being an Account 350 Pieces of Music, set to Words taken from the Plays and Poems of Shakespeare, the compositions ranging from the Elizabethan Age to the Present Time. By ALFRED ROFFE. 4to, half-Roxburghe, 7s.

Shakespeare, A Study of. By ALGERNON CHARLES SWINBURNE. Crown 8vo, cloth extra, 8s.

Crown 8vo, cloth extra, gilt, with 10 full-page Tinted Illustrations, 7s. 6d.

Sheridan's Complete Works,

with Life and Anecdotes. Including his Dramatic Writings, printed from the Original Editions, his Works in Prose and Poetry, Translations, Speeches, Jokes, Puns, &c. ; with a Collection of Sheridaniana.

Crown 8vo, cloth extra, with 100 Illustrations, 7s. 6d.

Signboards:

Their History. With Anecdotes of Famous Taverns and Remarkable Characters. By JACOB LARWOOD and JOHN CAMDEN HOTTEN.

Crown 8vo, cloth extra, gilt, 6s. 6d.

Slang Dictionary, The:

Etymological, Historical, and Anecdotal. An ENTIRELY NEW EDITION, revised throughout, and considerably Enlarged.

Exquisitely printed in miniature, cloth extra, gilt edges, 2s. 6d.

Smoker's Text-Book, The. By J. HAMER, F.R.S.L.

Crown 8vo, cloth extra, 5s.

Spalding's Elizabethan Demonology:

An Essay in Illustration of the Belief in the Existence of Devils, and the Powers possessed by them. By T. ALFRED SPALDING, LL.B.

Crown 4to, uniform with "Chaucer for Children," with Coloured Illustrations, cloth gilt, 10s. 6d.

Spenser for Children.

By M. H. TOWRY. Illustrations in Colours by WALTER J. MORGAN.

A New Edition, small crown 8vo, cloth extra, 5s.

Staunton.—Laws and Practice of Chess;

Together with an Analysis of the Openings, and a Treatise on End Games. By HOWARD STAUNTON. Edited by ROBERT B. WORMALD.

Crown 8vo, cloth extra, 9s.

Stedman's Victorian Poets:

Critical Essays. By EDMUND CLARENCE STEDMAN.

Post 8vo, cloth extra, 5s.

Stories about Number Nip,

The Spirit of the Giant Mountains. Retold for Children, by WALTER GRAHAME. With Illustrations by J. MOYR SMITH.

Two Vols., crown 8vo, cloth extra, 21s.

Stories from the State Papers.

By ALEX. CHARLES EWALD, F.S.A., Author of "The Life of Prince Charles Stuart," &c. With an Autotype Facsimile.

Two Vols., crown 8vo, with numerous Portraits and Illustrations, 24s.

Strahan.—Twenty Years of a Publisher's

Life. By ALEXANDER STRAHAN. [In the press.

Crown 8vo, cloth extra, with Illustrations, 7s. 6d.

Strutt's Sports and Pastimes of the People

of England; including the Rural and Domestic Recreations, May Games, Mummeries, Shows, Processions, Pageants, and Pompous Spectacles, from the Earliest Period to the Present Time. With 140 Illustrations. Edited by WILLIAM HONE.

Crown 8vo, with a Map of Suburban London, cloth extra, 7s. 6d.

Suburban Homes (The) of London:

A Residential Guide to Favourite London Localities, their Society, Celebrities, and Associations. With Notes on their Rental, Rates, and House Accommodation.

Crown 8vo, cloth extra, with Illustrations, 7s. 6d.

Swift's Choice Works,

In Prose and Verse. With Memoir, Portrait, and Facsimiles of the Maps in the Original Edition of "Gulliver's Travels."

Swinburne's Works:

**The Queen Mother and Rosa-
mond.** Fcap. 8vo, 5s.

Atalanta in Calydon.
A New Edition. Crown 8vo, 6s.

Chastelard.
A Tragedy. Crown 8vo, 7s.

Poems and Ballads.
FIRST SERIES. Fcap. 8vo, 9s. Also in crown 8vo, at same price.

Poems and Ballads.
SECOND SERIES. Fcap. 8vo, 9s. Also in crown 8vo, at same price.

**Notes on "Poems and Bal-
lads."** 8vo, 1s.

William Blake:
A Critical Essay. With Facsimile Paintings. Demy 8vo, 16s.

Songs before Sunrise.
Crown 8vo, 10s. 6d.

Bothwell:
A Tragedy. Crown 8vo, 12s. 6d.

George Chapman:
An Essay. Crown 8vo, 7s.

Songs of Two Nations.
Crown 8vo, 6s.

Essays and Studies.
Crown 8vo, 12s.

Erechtheus:
A Tragedy. Crown 8vo, 6s.

Note of an English Republican
on the Muscovite Crusade. 8vo, 1s.

A Note on Charlotte Brontë.
Crown 8vo, 6s.

A Study of Shakespeare.
Crown 8vo, 8s.

Songs of the Springtides. Cr.
8vo, 6s.

Studies in Song.
Crown 8vo, 7s.

MR. SWINBURNE'S NEW DRAMA.—Crown 8vo, cloth extra, 8s.
Mary Stuart: A Tragedy, in Five Acts. By ALGERNON CHARLES
SWINBURNE. [*In the press.*

Demy 8vo, cloth extra, Illustrated, 21s.

Sword, The Book of the:

Being a History of the Sword, and its Use, in all Times and in all Countries. By Captain RICHARD BURTON. With numerous Illustrations. [*In preparation.*

Medium 8vo, cloth extra, with Illustrations, 7s. 6d.

Syntax's (Dr.) Three Tours,

In Search of the Picturesque, in Search of Consolation, and in Search of a Wife. With the whole of ROWLANDSON'S droll page Illustra-
ions, in Colours, and Life of the Author by J. C. HOTTEN.

Four Vols. small 8vo, cloth boards, 30s.

Taine's History of English Literature.

Translated by HENRY VAN LAUN.

₄ Also a POPULAR EDITION, in Two Vols. crown 8vo, cloth extra, 15s.

Crown 8vo, cloth gilt, profusely Illustrated, 6s.

Tales of Old Thule.

Collected and Illustrated by J. MOYR SMITH.

One Vol. crown 8vo, cloth extra, 7s. 6d.

Taylor's (Tom) Historical Dramas:

"Clancarty," "Jeanne Darc," "'Twixt Axe and Crown," "The Fool's Revenge," "Arkwright's Wife," "Anne Boleyn," "Plot and Passion."

₄ The Plays may also be had separately, at 1s. each.

Crown 8vo, cloth extra, with Coloured Frontispiece and numerous Illustrations, 7s. 6d.

Thackerayana:

Notes and Anecdotes. Illustrated by a profusion of Sketches by WILLIAM MAKEPEACE THACKERAY, depicting Humorous Incidents in his School-life, and Favourite Characters in the books of his everyday reading. With Hundreds of Wood Engravings, facsimiled from Mr. Thackeray's Original Drawings.

Crown 8vo, cloth extra, gilt edges, with Illustrations, 7s. 6d.

Thomson's Seasons and Castle of Indolence.

With a Biographical and Critical Introduction by ALLAN CUNNINGHAM, and over 50 fine Illustrations on Steel and Wood.

Crown 8vo, cloth extra, with numerous Illustrations, 7s. 6d.

Thornbury's (Walter) Haunted London.

A New Edition, Edited by EDWARD WALFORD, M.A., with numerous Illustrations by F. W. FAIRHOLT, F.S.A.

Crown 8vo, cloth extra, with Illustrations, 7s. 6d.

Timbs' Clubs and Club Life in London.

With Anecdotes of its famous Coffee-houses, Hostelries, and Taverns. By JOHN TIMBS, F.S.A. With numerous Illustrations.

Crown 8vo, cloth extra, with Illustrations, 7s. 6d.

Timbs' English Eccentrics and Eccentrici-

ties: Stories of Wealth and Fashion, Delusions, Impostures, and Fanatic Missions, Strange Sights and Sporting Scenes, Eccentric Artists, Theatrical Folks, Men of Letters, &c. By JOHN TIMBS, F.S.A. With nearly 50 Illustrations.

Demy 8vo, cloth extra, 14s.

Torrens' The Marquess Wellesley,

Architect of Empire. An Historic Portrait. *Forming Vol. I. of* PROCONSUL and TRIBUNE: WELLESLEY and O'CONNELL: Historic Portraits. By W. M. TORRENS, M.P. In Two Vols.

Demy 8vo, cloth extra, with Illustrations, 9s.

Tunis : the Land and the People.
By ERNST VON HESSE-WARTEGG. With many fine full-page Illustrations. [In the press.

Crown 8vo, cloth extra, with Coloured Illustrations, 7s. 6d.

Turner's (J. M. W.) Life and Correspondence:
Founded upon Letters and Papers furnished by his Friends and fellow-Academicians. By WALTER THORNBURY. A New Edition, considerably Enlarged. With numerous Illustrations in Colours, facsimiled from Turner's original Drawings.

Two Vols., crown 8vo, cloth extra, with Map and Ground-Plans, 14s.

Walcott's Church Work and Life in English
Minsters ; and the English Student's Monasticon. By the Rev. MACKENZIE E. C. WALCOTT, B.D.

Large crown 8vo, cloth antique, with Illustrations, 7s. 6d.

Walton and Cotton's Complete Angler ;
or, The Contemplative Man's Recreation : being a Discourse of Rivers, Fishponds, Fish and Fishing, written by IZAAK WALTON ; and Instructions how to Angle for a Trout or Grayling in a clear Stream, by CHARLES COTTON. With Original Memoirs and Notes by Sir HARRIS NICOLAS, and 61 Copperplate Illustrations.

The Twenty-second Annual Edition, for 1881, cloth, full gilt, 50s.

Walford's County Families of the United
Kingdom. By EDWARD WALFORD, M. A. Containing Notices of the Descent, Birth, Marriage, Education, &c., of more than 12,000 distinguished Heads of Families, their Heirs Apparent or Presumptive, the Offices they hold or have held, their Town and Country Addresses, Clubs, &c.

Crown 8vo, cloth extra, 3s. 6d. per volume.

Wanderer's Library, The :

Merrie England in the Olden Time. By GEORGE DANIEL. With Illustrations by ROBT. CRUIKSHANK.

The Old Showmen and the Old London Fairs. By THOMAS FROST.

The Wilds of London. By JAMES GREENWOOD.

Tavern Anecdotes and Sayings ; Including the Origin of Signs, and Reminiscences connected with Taverns, Coffee Houses, Clubs, &c. By CHARLES HINDLEY. With Illusts.

Circus Life and Circus Celebrities. By THOMAS FROST.

The Lives of the Conjurers. By THOMAS FROST.

The Life and Adventures of a Cheap Jack. By One of the Fraternity. Edited by CHARLES HINDLEY.

The Story of the London Parks. By JACOB LARWOOD. With Illusts.

Low-Life Deeps. An Account of the Strange Fish to be found there. By JAMES GREENWOOD.

Seven Generations of Executioners : Memoirs of the Sanson Family (1688 to 1847). Edited by HENRY SANSON.

The World Behind the Scenes. By PERCY FITZGERALD.

London Characters. By HENRY MAYHEW. Illustrated.

The Genial Showman : Life and Adventures of Artemus Ward. By E. P. HINGSTON. Frontispiece.

Wanderings in Patagonia ; or, Life among the Ostrich Hunters. By JULIUS BEERBOHM. Illustrated.

Summer Cruising in the South Seas. By CHARLES WARREN STODDARD. Illustrated by WALLIS MACKAY.

Carefully printed on paper to imitate the Original, 22 in. by 14 in., 2*s*.

Warrant to Execute Charles I.

An exact Facsimile of this important Document, with the Fifty-nine Signatures of the Regicides, and corresponding Seals.

Beautifully printed on paper to imitate the Original MS., price 2*s*.

Warrant to Execute Mary Queen of Scots.

An exact Facsimile, including the Signature of Queen Elizabeth, and a Facsimile of the Great Seal.

Crown 8vo, cloth limp, with numerous Illustrations, 4*s*. 6*d*.

Westropp's Handbook of Pottery and Porcelain ;

or, History of those Arts from the Earliest Period. By HODDER M. WESTROPP. With numerous Illustrations, and a List of Marks.

Post 8vo, cloth limp, 2*s*. 6*d*.

What shall my Son be ?

Hints for Parents on the Choice of a Profession or Trade for their Sons. By FRANCIS DAVENANT, M.A.

SEVENTH EDITION.   Square 8vo, 1*s*.

Whistler v. Ruskin: Art and Art Critics.

By J. A. MACNEILL WHISTLER.

A VERY HANDSOME VOLUME.— Large 4to, cloth extra, 31*s*. 6*d*.

White Mountains (The Heart of the):

Their Legend and Scenery. By SAMUEL ADAMS DRAKE. With nearly 100 Illustrations by W. HAMILTON GIBSON, Author of "Pastoral Days." [*Nearly ready.*

Crown 8vo, cloth limp, with Illustrations, 2*s*. 6*d*.

Williams' A Simple Treatise on Heat.

By W. MATTIEU WILLIAMS, F.R.A.S., F.C.S.

Small 8vo, cloth extra, Illustrated, 6*s*.

Wooing (The) of the Water-Witch:

A Northern Oddity. By EVAN DALDORNE. Illust. by J. MOYR SMITH.

Crown 8vo, half-bound, 12*s*. 6*d*.

Words, Facts, and Phrases:

A Dictionary of Curious, Quaint, and Out-of-the-Way Matters. By ELIEZER EDWARDS.

Crown 8vo, cloth extra, with Illustrations, 7*s*. 6*d*.

Wright's Caricature History of the Georges.

(The House of Hanover.) With 400 Pictures, Caricatures, Squibs, Broadsides, Window Pictures, &c. By THOMAS WRIGHT, M.A., F.S.A.

Large post 8vo, cloth extra, gilt, with Illustrations, 7*s*. 6*d*.

Wright's History of Caricature and of the

Grotesque in Art, Literature, Sculpture, and Painting. By THOMAS WRIGHT, F.S.A. Profusely Illustrated by F. W. FAIRHOLT, F.S.A.

J. OGDEN AND CO., PRINTERS, 172, ST. JOHN STREET, E.C.